THE
EMPEROR
MAGE

Books by Tamora Pierce

Alanna: The First Adventure
In the Hand of the Goddess
The Woman Who Rides Like a Man
Lioness Rampant
Wild Magic
Wolf-Speaker
The Emperor Mage

THE EMPEROR MAGE

The Immortals

Tamora Pierce

A Jean Karl Book

Atheneum Books for Young Readers

Atheneum Books for Young Readers
An imprint of Simon & Schuster Children's
Publishing Division
1230 Avenue of the Americas
New York, New York 10020
Text copyright © 1995 by Tamora Pierce

Library of Congress Cataloging-in-Publication Data
Pierce, Tamora.
The Emperor Mage / Tamora Pierce. — 1st ed.
    p.   cm. — (Immortals)
"A Jean Karl book."
Sequel to: Wolf-speaker.
Summary: When she is sent as part of the delegation
from Tortall to negotiate a peace treaty with Carthak,
fifteen-year-old Daine must use her powers to com-
municate with animals for more than healing the
Carthak emperor's dying birds.
ISBN 0-689-31989-4
[1. Fantasy.   2. Human-animal communication—
Fiction.   3. Supernatural—Fiction.]   I. Title.
II. Series: Pierce, Tamora. Immortals.
PZ7.P61464Em   1995   [Fic]—dc20
94-23278   CIP   AC

Book design by Randy Sauchuck

The text of this book is set in Cochin

First edition

Printed in the United States of America

10 9 8 7 6 5 4 3 2

TABLE OF CONTENTS

To those who took a struggling young writer,
cushioned her in her early months in the Big Apple,
and agreed that no idea was too crazy:

Ellen Harris-Brooker
P. J. Snyder
Craig Tenney
and
Robert Wehe

How could I forget?
I couldn't have done it
without you!

THE EMPEROR MAGE

ONE

GUESTS IN CARTHAK

His Royal Highness Kaddar, prince of Siraj, duke of Yamut, count of Amar, first lord of the Imperium, heir apparent to His Most Serene Majesty Emperor Ozorne of Carthak, fanned himself and wished the Tortallans would dock. He had been waiting aboard the imperial gallery since noon, wearing the panoply of his office as the day, hot for autumn, grew hotter. He shot a glare at the nobles and academics on hand to welcome the visitors: they could relax under the awnings. Imperial dignity kept him in this unshaded chair, where a gold surface collected the sun to throw it back into his eyes.

Looking about, the prince saw the captain, leaning on the rail, scowl and make the Sign against evil on his chest. A stinging fly chose that moment to land on Kaddar's arm. He yelped, swatted the fly, got to his feet, and removed the crown. "Enough of this. Bring me something to drink," he ordered the slaves. "Something *cold*."

He went to the captain, trying not to wince as too-long-inactive legs tingled. "What on earth are you staring at?"

"Tired of broiling, Your Highness?" The man spoke without looking away from the commercial harbor outside the breakwater enclosing the imperial docks. He could speak to Kaddar with less formality that most, since he had taught the prince all that young man knew of boats and sailing.

"Very funny. What has you making the Sign?"

The captain handed the prince his spyglass. "See for yourself, Highness."

Kaddar looked through the glass. All around the waterfront, birds made use of every visible perch. On masts, ledges, gutters, and ropes they sat, watching the harbor. He found pelicans, birds of prey — on the highest, loneliest perches — songbirds, the gray-and-brown sparrows that lived in the city. Even ship rails sported a variety of feathered creatures. Eerily, that vast collection was silent. They stared at the harbor without uttering a sound.

"It ain't just birds, Prince," the captain remarked. "Lookit the docks."

Kaddar spied dogs and cats, under apparent truce, on every inch of space available. Not all were scruffy alley mongrels or mangy harbor cats. He saw the flash of bright ribbons, even gold and gem-encrusted collars. Cur or alley cat, noble pet or working rat catcher, they sat without a sound, eyes on the harbor. Looking down, Kaddar found something else: the pilings under the docks swarmed with rats. Everywhere—warehouse, wharf, ship—human movement had stopped. No one cared to disturb that silent, attentive gathering of beasts. Hands shaking, the prince returned the glass and made the Sign against evil on his own chest.

"You know what it is?" asked the captain.

"I've never seen—wait. Could it be—?" Kaddar frowned. "There's a girl, coming with the Tortallans. It's said she has a magic bond with animals, that she can even take on animal shape."

"That's nothin' new," remarked the captain. "There's mages that do it all the time."

"Not like this one, apparently. And she heals animals. They heard my uncle's birds are ill—"

"The *world* knows them birds are ill," muttered the captain. "He can lose a battalion of soldiers in the Yamani Isles and never twitch, but the gods help us if one of his precious birds is off its feed."

Kaddar grimaced. "True. Anyway, as a goodwill gesture, King Jonathan has sent this girl to heal Uncle's birds, if she can. And the university folk want to meet her dragon."

"Dragon! How old *is* this lass anyway?"

"Fifteen. That's why *I'm* out here broiling, instead of my uncle's ministers. He wants me to squire her about when she isn't healing birds or talking to scholars. She'll probably want to visit all the tourist places and gawp at the sights. And Mithros only knows what her table matters are like. She's some commoner from the far north, it's said. I'll be lucky if she knows which fork to use."

"Oh, that won't be a problem," said the

captain, straight-faced. "I understand these northern-ers eat with their hands."

"So nice to have friends aboard," replied the prince tartly.

The captain surveyed the docks through his glass. "A power over animals, *and* a dragon . . . If I was you, Highness, I'd dust off my map of the tourist places and let her eat any way she wants."

At that moment the girl they discussed inched over as far on the bunk as she could, to give the man beside her a bit more room. The dragon in her lap squeaked in protest, but wound her small body into a tighter ball.

The man they were making room for, the mage known as Numair Salmalín, saw their efforts and smiled. "Thank you, Daine. And you, Kitten."

"It's only for a bit," the girl, Daine, said encouragingly.

"If we don't wrap this up soon, *I* will be only a 'bit,'" complained the redheaded woman on Numair's other side. Alanna the Lioness, the King's Champion, was used to larger meeting places.

At last every member of the Tortallan delegation was crammed into the small shipboard cabin. Magical fire, a sign of shields meant to keep anything said in that room from being overheard, filled the corners and framed the door and portholes.

"No one can listen to us, magically or physically?" asked Duke Gareth of Naxen, head of the delegation. A tall, thin, older man, he sat on the room's only chair, hands crossed over his cane.

The mages there nodded. "It's as safe as our power can make it, Your Grace," replied Numair.

Duke Gareth smiled. "Then we are safe indeed." Looking in turn at everyone, from his son, Gareth the Younger, to Lord Martin of Meron, and from Daine to the clerks, he said, "Let me remind all of you one last time: *be very careful* regarding your actions while we are here. Do *nothing* to jeopardize our mission. The emperor is willing to make peace, but that peace is in no manner secure. If negotiations fall through due to an error on our parts, the other Eastern Lands will not support us. We will be on our own, and Carthak will be on *us*.

"We *need* this peace. We cannot match the imperial armies and navy, any more than we can match imperial wealth. In a fight on Tortallan soil, we *might* prevail, but war of any kind would be long and costly, in terms of lives and in terms of our resources."

Alanna frowned. "Do we have to bow and scrape and tug our forelocks then, sir? We don't want to seem weak to these southerners, do we?"

The duke shook his head. "No, but neither should we take risks — particularly not you."

The Champion, whose temper was famous, blushed crimson and held her tongue.

To the others Duke Gareth said, "Go nowhere we are forbidden to go. Do not speak of freedom to the slaves. However we may dislike the practice, it would be unwise to show that dislike publicly. Accept no gifts, boxes, or paper from *anyone* unless they come with the knowledge of the emperor. *Offer* no gifts or pieces of paper to anyone. I understand it is the custom of the palace mages to scatter listening spells through the buildings and grounds. Watch what you say. If a problem arises, let my son, or Lord Martin, or Master Numair know *at once*."

"Kitten will be able to detect listening spells," remarked Numair. "I'm not saying she can't be magicked, but most of the common sorceries won't fool her."

Kitten straightened herself on Daine's lap and chirped. She always knew what was being said around her. A slim creature, she was two feet long from nose to hip, with a twelve-inch tail she used for balance and as an extra limb. Her large eyes were amber, set in a long and slender muzzle. Immature wings that would someday carry her in flight lay flat on her back. Silver claws marked her as an immortal, one of many creatures from the realms of the gods.

Looking at the dragon, the duke smiled. When his eyes moved on to Daine, the smile was replaced with concern. "Daine, be careful. You'll be on your own more than the rest of us, though it's my hope that if you can help his birds, the emperor will let you be. Those birds are his only weakness, I think."

"You understand the rules?" That was Lord Martin. He leaned around the duke to get a better look at Daine. "No childish pranks. Mind your manners, and do as you're told."

Kitten squawked, blue-gold scales bristling at the man's tone.

"Daine understand these things quite well." Numair rested a gentle hand on Kitten's muzzle and slid his thumb under her chin, so she was unable to voice whistles of outrage. "I trust her judgment, and have done so on far more dangerous missions than this."

"We would not have brought her if we believed otherwise," said Duke Gareth. "Remember, Master Numair, you, too, must be careful. The emperor was extraordinarily gracious to grant a pardon to you, and to allow you to meet with scholars at the palace. Don't forget the conditions of that pardon. If he catches you in wrongdoing, he will be able to arrest, try, even execute you, and we will be helpless to stop him."

Numair smiled crookedly, long lashes veiling his brown eyes. "Believe me, Your Grace, I don't plan to give Ozorne any excuse to rescind my pardon. I was in his dungeons once and see no reason to repeat the experience."

The duke nodded. "Now, my friends—it is time we prepared to dock. I hope that Mithros will bless our company with the light of wisdom, and that the Goddess will grant us patience."

"So mote it be," murmured the others.

Daine waited for those closest to the door to file out, fiddling with the heavy silver claw that hung on a chain at her neck. Once the way outside was clear, she ran to the tiny room below decks that had been granted to her. Kitten stayed topside, fascinated by the docking preparations.

In her cabin, Daine shed her ordinary clothes, changing to garments suitable for meeting the emperor's welcoming party. They wouldn't see the emperor himself until that night—the palace lay three hours' sail upriver—but it was still important to make a good impression on those sent to welcome them.

First came the gray silk shirt with bloused sleeves. Carefully she tucked her claw underneath, then slid into blue linen breeches. She checked the mirror to fasten silver buttons that closed the embroidered neck band high on her throat. Over all this splendor (as she privately thought of it) went a blue linen dress tunic. It was hard to believe that back home the leaves were turning color. Here it was warm still, warm enough that the palace seamstresses had kept to summer cloth while making her clothes for the journey.

A few rapid brush strokes put her curls in order, and a pale blue ribbon kept them out of her face. Carefully she put sapphire drops, Numair's Midwinter gift, in her earlobes and sat on the bunk to pull on her highly polished boots.

From a hole in the corner emerged the ship's boss rat. He balanced on his hindquarters there, his nose twitching. So you're off? he asked. Good. Now my boat will get back to normal.

"Don't celebrate yet," she advised. "I come back soon."

What a disappointment, he retorted. When do I get to see the last of you for good?

Silver light filled the cabin; a heavy, musky smell drifted in the air. When the light, if not the smell, faded, a badger sat on the bunk where Kitten slept. *—Begone, pest—* he ordered.

The rat was brave in the way of his kind, but the smell of *this* friend of Daine's sent the rodent into his hole. He had not known Daine was on visiting terms with the badger god.

Daine smiled at the first owner of her silver claw. "You look well. How long's it been?"

The badger was not in the least interested in polite conversation. *— Why are you here?—* he demanded harshly. *—What possessed you to leave your home sett? You are a creature of pine and chestnut forests, and cold lakes. This hot, swampy land is no country for you! Why are you here?—*

Daine made a face. "I'll tell you, if you'll stop growling at me." She sat on the bunk opposite him, and explained what the Tortallans in general, and she in particular, were doing this far south.

The badger listened, growling softly to himself. *—Peace? I thought you humans were convinced Emperor Ozorne was the one who tore holes in the barriers between the human realms and the realms of the gods, to loose a plague of immortals on you.—*

Daine shrugged. "*He* says it wasn't him or his mages who did that. Renegades at the imperial university stole the unlocking spells. They were caught and tried last spring, and executed."

The badger snorted.

"Well, no one can prove if it's the truth or not. And the king says we need peace with Carthak more than we need to get revenge."

—No one needs to talk peace or any other thing here. This is the worst possible place you can be now. You have no idea . . . . Turn around and go home. Convince your friends to leave.—

"I can't, and *we* can't!" she protested. "Weren't you listening? The emperor knows I'm coming to look at his birds. If I go home now, when he expects me— think of the insult to him! And it's not the birds' fault they live here, is it?"

With no room for him to pace, he was forced to settle for shifting his bulk from one side to the other as he muttered to himself. *—I must talk them out of it, that's* *all. When they know—even they will have to understand the situation. It's not like a mortal girl has the freedom they do, after all.—*

"Who will understand?" Daine asked, intensely curious. In all the time she had known him, she had never seen him so uncertain, or so jittery. Like all badgers, he had rages, and would knock her top over teakettle if she vexed him; but that was very different from the way he acted now. "And what's going on here? Can't you tell me?"

—It's the Great Gods, the ones two-leggers worship— the badger replied. *—They have lost patience with the emperor, perhaps with this entire realm. Things could get very—chancy—here soon. You are sure you cannot make your friends turn back?—*

Daine shook her head.

—No, of course not. You said it was impossible, and you never mislead me.— Suddenly he cocked his head upward, as if listening to something, or someone. He growled, hackles rising, and snapped at the air. Then—slowly—he relaxed, and nodded. *—As you wish.—*

"As who wishes?" asked Daine.

He looked at her, an odd light in his eyes. *—Come here, Daine.—*

"What?" she asked, even as she obeyed.

—I have a gift for you. Something to help you if all goes ill.—

His words made her edgy. "Badger, I can't misbehave while I'm here. There's too much at stake. You ought to talk to Duke Gareth of Naxen. You know every time you teach me a lesson or give me a gift or anything, there's always an uncommon lot of ruction, and I've been told not to cause *any!*"

—Enough! Kneel!—

She had thought to refuse, but her knees bent, and she was face to face with him. Opening his jaws, the great animal breathed on her. His breath came out visible, a swirling fog that glowed bright silver. It wrapped around Daine's head, filling her nose, mouth, and eyes, trickling under her shirt, flowing down her arms. She gasped, and the mist ran deep into her throat and lungs. She could feel it throughout her body, expanding to fill her skin.

When her eyes cleared, he was gone.

Stunned and trembling, Daine got to her feet. What was all *that* about?

The door opened and Kitten entered. "You just missed the badger," Daine informed her.

Kitten, who had met the animal god before, whistled her disappointment.

"I'm sorry. He was being *very* strange, and he left in a hurry." Worried both about what he had said, and about what he didn't say, she picked up Kitten and steadied her on one hip, then walked out on deck. When they reached the ship's rail, the animals awaiting her on the docks burst into an ear-piercing welcome. Dogs howled; birds cried out in their many languages. Only the cats welcomed her quietly, purring as hard as they could. The girl listened with a smile. She was so lucky, to have friends wherever she went!

Thank you for meeting me, she called silently, her magic carrying the words to her listeners. It is very kind, and I liked it so much! I hope I'll have a chance to get to know some of you while I'm here. For now, though, please stop calling, and go home. We're making the two-leggers nervous!

They knew she was right. Birds took flight by groups, careful not to bump into one another; dogs and cats left the docks. Only the rats stayed, their attitude of decided *un*welcome a steady itch in her mind.

Piffle to you, she told them, and went to join Numair at the rail. He was dressed simply, but well, for their arrival. His soft, wavy black hair was tied in a short horsetail, accenting a long nose and full, sensitive mouth. A black silk robe that buttoned high on the throat billowed around his powerful frame. Long, wide sleeves covered his arms to the wrists; the hem stopped short of the toes of his boots. That robe was donned by only a handful of mages, the most powerful in the world. Not even the famed Emperor Mage was allowed to wear it. Numair always played it down. He said the learning needed to win the black robe was not worth much in the real world, but Daine knew better. Once, when Numair was pressed by an enemy sorcerer, she saw him turn the other man into a tree.

"Are you all right?" she asked, squinting up at him. The effort strained her neck: he was a foot taller than her five feet five inches. His dark eyes were emotionless as he watched the dock. Only his big hands, white-knuckled as they gripped the rail, showed tension. She had wanted to talk about the badger's visit, but she could see that this was not a good time. "Is something wrong?"

"No, magelet," he said, using his private name for her. "And I am as well as may be expected. I can't say which prospect makes me more apprehensive— that of meeting old enemies, or old friends." His voice was unusually somber.

"Old enemies, surely?" She understood his

concern. Carthak's great university had been his home for eleven years. Shortly before his twenty-first birthday he had fled, accused of treason against his best friend—the emperor. Now, almost thirty, he was, in a way, coming home.

"I don't know," was his quiet reply. "I was very different then. And you know what the wise men say— 'Only birds can return to old nests.'" He shook his head, and smiled down at her, white teeth flashing against his swarthy face. "Mithros bless. *You* look very pretty."

Kitten chortled while Daine blushed. "You think so really?" she asked, feeling shy. "I know I don't hold a candle to Alanna, or the queen—"

He held up a hand. "That isn't strictly accurate. The Lioness is one of my dearest friends, but she is *not* an exemplar of female beauty. Years and experience have given her charm, and her eyes are extraordinary, but she is not beautiful. Queen Thayet is astoundingly attractive, it's true, but you have your own—something." He scrutinized her as she giggled. "You should wear blue more often. It brings out matching shades in your eyes."

"I heard that about *my* looks," Lady Alanna said, joining them them. "I'll get you later." Like Daine, she wore a tunic and breeches. Hers were violet silk trimmed with gold braid, over a white silk shirt. At her waist hung her sword. She grinned at Daine. "You do look good."

"Thanks," Daine said, blushing once more. "So do you."

The others, clad in daytime finery, joined them now that the ship was about to dock. Under their conversation, Daine tugged Numair's sleeve. "I need to talk to you as soon as you can manage," she whispered as the sailors made the ship fast. "It's really, really important."

He nodded, but his eyes were on the ships around them. She couldn't be sure he'd even heard.

Across the harbor a gong crashed three times. The Carthakis on the docks knelt and touched their heads to the ground as slow, regular drumbeats sounded. A path had opened from their ship across the busy harbor to what appeared to be a canal lock. Down that path came a high-prowed boat rowed by shaved-headed slaves. Its gilded surfaces threw off painful flashes as it swept along.

Daine peered at the man seated on a thronelike chair on the deck. He wore a crown like a cap, one covered with diamonds, that glittered fiercely. "Who is *that*?"

Gareth the Younger said, "Probably a lesser prince, one of the imperial court."

"This prince isn't a lesser one." Numair's stage whisper carried to those behind him. "See the lapis lazuli rod in his left hand? That is an attribute of the heir — what's his name?"

"His nephew Kaddar," one of the others said. "Age sixteen. Studies at the university."

The Tortallans got into the ship's boat and were rowed to the galley, where a heavy ladder was dropped to them. Daine waited for the senior members of her party to board, then followed. Kitten lost patience with her slow progress up the ladder and scrambled up past her, beating her onto the deck. Their order, as they gathered before the prince, was roughly that of importance, with Duke Gareth, Lord Martin, and Lady Alanna in front, Numair and the other officials behind them. Gareth the Younger, Daine, Kitten, and the Tortallan clerks kept to the back.

Someone called orders. A drummer sounded a beat. Sunburned and tanned backs on Daine's left stretched forward. The left bank of oars dipped; the boat began to turn.

Standing by the prince was a herald. He wore a gold robe cut like those Daine had already seen on other Carthakis, a knee-length tunic with short sleeves. Thumping his staff of office on the deck, he cried, "His Imperial Highness, Kaddar Gazanoi Iliniat, Head of House Khazoi, Prince of Siraj—"

Daine lost track of the rest. She was interested in the boat: once it had turned, both sets of oars rose and fell on drumbeats, and the vessel raced across the harbor. On either side of the deck the rowers sat at their benches. Each time they stretched forward or pulled back, she heard a clatter under the drum's thud and the men's grunts of effort. It took her a moment to realize that it was the noise of the chain that linked their ankle cuffs.

Her skin prickled. She made herself look away and listen to the herald. "—His Most Serene and Imperial Majesty, Ozorne Muhassin Tasikhe, Emperor of Carthak—"

Kitten went to the end of a bench, chirping and peering at the man seated there. The girl went after her. "I'm sorry," she told the man, who watched the dragon from the corner of his eye. "She doesn't know not to interrupt when folk are working—" The slave looked up at her, startled.

"Eyes to your oar!" snarled a voice nearby. A lash snaked out to flick the man on the cheek. The slave hardly blinked, though the whip had come dangerously close to his eye. Daine bit the inside of her cheek and went back to her place, hoisting Kitten onto her hip.

Someone passed a handkerchief to her as the herald began to name their company to the prince. She quickly wiped her eyes. By the time she was under control, Gareth the Younger and the dean of mages at the Tortallan royal university were bowing to the prince, who greeted them both with distant courtesy. They bowed again, and stepped to the side so that Daine and Kitten were revealed.

Awed, the girl saw that the odd shape of the prince's eyes came from dark lines drawn on both lids and extended to his temples. He was a light-skinned black, with thin lips and long, thick eyelashes, dressed in a calf-length tunic of crimson silk. His jewels shimmered in the sun. He boasted three gold rings in his left ear, a gold bangle shaped like a many-flamed sun, and a ruby drop in the right. Another ruby served him as a nose button. He wore a collar-like necklace of gold inlaid with mother-of-pearl strips. Rings decorated fingers and thumbs; bracelets hung on both wrists. A flash drew her eyes to his feet, where she found rings on toes bared by his sandals. It occurred to her that she might not possess as much jewelry in her entire lifetime as the prince wore right now.

"Veralidaine Sarrasri," the herald proclaimed. "The dragon Skysong."

"I greet you in the name of my august kinsman, the Emperor Mage of Carthak," the prince said formally. Then he leaned forward, eyes sparkling with interest. "It's a true dragon?" His voice was light and fast. "Not a basilisk, which we've seen, but maybe a young basilisk—"

Kitten walked to the raised chair and rose, balancing on her hindquarters as she gazed at the young man. "She's a true dragon, Your Highness," replied Daine. She saw intelligence in his eyes, paint or no. "Basilisks have pebbled skin, almost like beading. Kit—her name's Skysong, but mostly folk call her Kitten—she has scales. Her ma was the same."

The prince frowned. "A mother? We were told there is only one dragon in the mortal realms."

"There is. Her ma was killed by—" She almost said "Carthaki raiders," but stopped herself. As she had been told over and over, no one could *prove* they were Carthaki. "Pirates," she went on. "She gave birth to Kitten a week before she died, and I've been raising Kit ever since."

"Is it hard? What does she eat? Does she hunt live prey, or—"

The herald coughed. "Your Highness, the ambassadors have yet to greet the delegation."

The prince looked like any of Daine's Rider friends caught in a misstep. He made a noise that sounded like a sigh and eased back in his chair, holding the blue stone rod and gold fan crossed on his chest once more. "It is my hope that, should you have idle hours during your stay with us, you will permit me to show you some of Carthak's wonders."

Duke Gareth had told her such as offer would be made by a Carthaki noble, so Daine had an answer ready. She bowed. "I'd be honored, Your Highness," she said, while thinking, He sounds *so* thrilled.

"May I present you of Tortall to your colleagues and fellow ambassadors," intoned the herald, more as a command than a request. He led their group to the spot where men, some dressed like the prince, some in robes cut in the same fashion as Numair's, waited under a canopy. Most of their names escaped Daine, at the rear of the Tortallan delegation. She would have to deal with almost none of these dignitaries, and saw no reason to memorize alien names and titles.

One, a mage, did make an impression. He was a different fish among so many black-, brown-, and olive-skinned southerners—a tall northerner, tan and weathered from sun and wind, with earnest blue eyes and silver streaks in his flyaway blond hair. He stood with lesser mages and nobles, wearing a scarlet robe with earth-brown cuffs and hem. He wore his robe unfastened, over a northern-style shirt and breeches made of undyed cotton. When the herald gave his name—Lindhall Reed—he and Numair embraced. Daine smiled. Ever since she had met Numair two years ago, she had heard much of his old teaching master.

"Arram," Lindhall said, using Numair's birth name, "welcome, if that is the proper word."

Numair's eyes were overbright. "I'm surprised you remembered our arrival," he replied, voice scratchy. "I thought I'd have to root you out of your workroom."

"No, no." Reed's voice was quiet, cultured, and fast, as if he fought to breathe. "I have a good assistant, better than you were. She keeps track of everything. Unfortunately, she's about to go live with the merfolk and study their culture. I hear they're moving in all along the Tortallan coast. I'd thought they'd live in rookeries, like sea lions, but their nature appears to be more tribal. And you are Arram's student," he said without a break, looking at Daine. She jumped at the change of topic. "He wrote me so much about you. He says you *know* how bats avoid objects and catch prey. When I was a student I incurred censure when I hypothesized that they do it with manipulation of sound, and Arram said you proved that to be true."

Daine smiled up at this man, who was nearly as tall as Numair. "Well, yes. They squeak at things. Their ears move separately, to gather in what they hear, and each sound has a meaning—"

"I don't like to interrupt," Numair said apologetically, "but Lindhall, I have questions that require answers. Forgive me, both of you."

Lindhall looked wistfully at Daine. After friendship with Numair, she recognized someone who would rather talk about learning than anything else. "Duty calls," the older mage commented. "And I know we shall have other chances to confer, since you are here for the emperor's birds, and I help him to care for them. Very well, Arram, I am yours, for the time being. Unless—" His face brightened. "I know you've always had encounters with whales. It is true, their songs are communication, not merely noise? Or communication in the sense of birdcalls, proclaiming territory, and so forth? I—"

"*Lindhall*," Numair said firmly, and dragged his old friend away.

I didn't even get to ask him what's wrong with the emperor's birds, Daine thought, and sighed.

"Daine," called Alanna, "can you spare Kitten? Duke Etiakret and Master Chioké would like a closer look at her, if she doesn't mind."

Kitten whistled an inquiry to Daine, who smiled. "Go on. They want to admire you." Kitten, always open to admiration, galloped off.

Trying not to look at the slave rowers, Daine went to the prow of the boat, where she could see the riverbank. During the introductions, they had left the port city of Thak's Gate behind, following canals that led finally into the River Zekoi. As the oars tugged the barge south, the city on Daine's side of the boat gave up its claims to the riverbank.

An army replaced it. From here she saw barracks in long rows, taking up hundreds of acres. Companies of soldiers stood side by side on the riverbank, each soldier with a bright, rectangular shield on one arm, a spear in the opposite hand. Looking at them, she swallowed hard. She was no stranger to military camps. Since her arrival in Tortall she had visited home bases for the army and the Queen's Riders alike, but none of them were as big as this.

As the imperial vessel passed the first company of soldiers, Daine heard a shouted order. As one man, the soldiers banged their spears three times on their shields, then thrust the spears into the air with a roar. The second company followed suit, then the third, then the fourth. It seemed to go on forever, drowning out all conversation and making Daine's ears ring. *Duke Gareth is right,* she thought, feeling ill. *Even if we could* beat *so many, what would be left afterward?*

The gods are up to something, she remembered abruptly. Something that might put a crimp in the style of this army. If only I could find out what's going to happen!

"That is just the Army of the North." The prince joined her at the rail as they sailed past the last soldiers. "My uncle has three other armies of identical size, all in combat readiness."

It was hard to read his face, but he sounded as if he wasn't proud of the imperial forces. "What's over here?" she asked, turning. They now had a good view of the far bank also. This side of the Zekoi was untamed. Reeds grew head high; a web of streams emptied into the river. The loglike shapes on the far bank were not dead wood, she realized, but animals.

"Crocodiles." The prince had seen what she looked at. "Do you have them in the north?"

"No," she replied, calling with her magic. They stirred, drunk with the sun. "They're giant lizards, aren't they? I have a book that tells of them." She called again, and felt a soft reply.

"*Giant*, water-swimming, *vicious* lizards," replied the prince.

Daine counted to three, then said politely, "There's few animals that're 'vicious' by nature, if you'll forgive my saying so. Usually there's a good reason for them acting nasty—like you're stepping in their nests, or you're stealing their food."

Food, agreed a low voice in her mind. Hungry, commented another. A third voice added, Waiting for food.

"Like all females, you are sentimental about animals," the prince replied, his tone superior. "If you had a croc after you in the water, you wouldn't be so quick to stand up for them."

"They came after *you* personally?" She couldn't see this painted fellow doing anything that might wrinkle his clothes.

"Well, no, but everyone says they do."

Someday I must read this scholar Everyone, she thought as she bit her tongue to keep from giving a rude answer. He seems to have written so much — all of it wrong.

She called to the crocodiles again. I'm Daine, she told the great creatures. I come from the north.

You are odd, replied the one who had spoken last. You smell of frozen water and too many trees. Do not scold that two-legger. If he enters our water, we will eat him gladly.

A private boat, brightly painted, floated by. A man in a low-backed chair read under a canopy; a slave chased a boy who ran with something that struggled in his arms. Cornering the child at the rail, the slave tried to make him release his prize. The child leaned away. Suddenly he screeched. His arms flew open, and his captive tumbled into the water.

"If you can't hold on to pets, you don't deserve to have any," scolded the slave. The child screamed as she dragged him away without another look at the animal in the river. The crocodiles did not share her disinterest. They slid into the water from their riverbank.

"No, don't!" Daine cried to them aloud, forgetting her companion. "Let it be!"

Hungry, said a voice. Food is food.

It will die anyway, replied the one who spoke most. Look at it.

The crocodile was right. The tiny creature,

whatever it was, couldn't swim. It fought to stay up, but the current dragged on its fur and limbs.

Stripping off her boots, Daine jumped over the rail and into the river. Swimming against the current, she struck out for the drowning animal. *Please stop,* she told the crocodiles silently. *It isn't more than a mouthful!* One last pump of her arms, and she had reached the sufferer.

I hope you do not interfere in too many meals, remarked the talkative crocodile as the reptiles swam off. *We do not have enough food as it is.*

I'll try not to, Daine promised. Treading water, she pumped liquid from the pet's lungs. He gasped. "Shh," she said. "It's all right. I've got you." He was a monkey, tiny enough to sit on her palm, with huge gray-green eyes. Around his neck was a jeweled collar. "No wonder you couldn't swim." She unbuckled the thing and let it fall. "That was probably too heavy dry, let alone wet."

Black, sparkling fire yanked them from the river and pulled them through the air. Daine soothed the frantic monkey until Numair's magic deposited them on the deck of the imperial barge.

The Carthakis, from prince to slaves, gaped at her and her new friend. Kitten began to scold as Daine blushed. Muddy water formed a pool on the polished deck; her hair dripped. Her linen and silk were ruined. Someone—a female—giggled. A man snorted. Daine glanced at Duke Gareth and saw that he had covered his face with one hand as his son's broad shoulders quivered with suppressed laughter. More than anything at the moment, she wished she had the power simply to vanish.

✤✤✤

They went from their quarters to the women guests' baths soon after their arrival, to Daine's relief. Not only was she able to wash, but maids brought a basin and extra mild soap so that she could bathe her new friend. They even gave her towels for him. She dried him quickly there, then returned with him and Kitten to her room to do a more thorough job.

She used the work to get acquainted with this odd creature. Lindhall had called him a pygmy marmoset. Imported from the Copper Isles, he'd been the pet of the child he called the Monsterboy, the one who had let him fall into the river. His fur was strange—a mix of yellow, brown, gray, and olive green, which looked as if it might turn its wearer invisible in a proper forest. The marmoset gave his name, but it was in whistles and clucks, impossible for her to pronounce. She asked if he would mind if she called him Zekoi, or Zek, after the river she had taken him from. He seemed quite taken with that, even trying to pronounce it on his own.

Finished with Zek's grooming, Daine got to her feet. "I need to change," she told the marmoset when he clung to her. "Hold on to Kitten." Zek eyed the dragon with misgiving. Kitten chirped, and offered her forepaw. He clutched it and watched Daine's every movement.

Drawing on a shift, the girl surveyed her room. It was simple, elegant, and costly. Walls, floor, and ceiling were polished marble. Carved cedar window screens gave off their famous scent. The bed was delicately carved, the sheets fine cotton. Over it lay a silk comforter in autumn colors. The clean, sweet-scented privy lay off a small dressing room. That chamber, a few feet from the bed, was furnished with a table and matching chair, a long mirror, and a number of tiny jars, which held various cosmetics, salves, and perfumes.

There was but one feature she disliked—a tiger-skin rug. Its jaws were open in a snarl; yellow glass eyes glared at the world. "I have to ask them to move this," she told her audience. "I can't sleep with it here." Kneeling, Daine touched it sadly. She had seen tigers in the king's menagerie. They were magnificent cats, and she preferred the ones whose skin was still attached.

Her palms felt hot, itchy. Suddenly they pulsed. White fire spilled from her hands onto the tiger. Slowly, the eyelids fell, and rose again. The jaw relaxed; the great mouth closed.

She thrust herself away so quickly that she fell over. "Did you *see* that?" she demanded of Kitten and Zek. "What *was* it?" Both stared at her, plainly as bewildered as she was.

Although she waited, the skin did not move again. Using a long-handled brush, she shoved it under her bed, poking it repeatedly to keep any part from sticking out. At last it was securely tucked away, and she could dress.

TWO

IMPERIAL WELCOME

∾♋♋♋♋♋

Some hours later, Daine looked round the antechamber to the throne room with awe. Kitten did the same. The marmoset Zek, who had refused to stay behind, observed everything from his hiding place under her hair, at the back of her neck.

There was much to stare at. The room was filled with nobles and mages dressed in their finest. Shaved-headed slaves were everywhere, offering food, drinks, flower garlands, and feathered or jeweled fans. Huge screens had been pushed back to reveal a broad terrace and gardens. Light came from large globes hung by chains from the ceiling. As the sky darkened, the globes shone brighter.

"How do the lamps keep burning?" Daine asked.

"Magic." The speaker was Harailt of Aili, dean of magical studies at the royal university in Tortall. He was a stocky, round-faced man with an endless supply of jokes. Stuck in this outer room, waiting to bow to the emperor, Daine had been grateful for each and every jest. "Numair, why didn't you tell us about this light spell?" Harailt asked. "To have strong, steady illumination—"

Numair looked up. "They didn't have it when I was here," he said absently. "They did something with glass balls, but they faded after a short time. These aren't glass."

"The globes are filled with crystals," Lindhall Reed explained. "Remind me and I'll have one of the craft mages explain it for you." Seeing the door to the emperor's audience chamber open, he added, "You'll be all right, Arra— I'm sorry—Numair?"

The younger mage smiled. "I have to be, don't I?" As a page beckoned their group forward, he took a deep breath. "Here we go, into the presence of the one and only Emperor Mage. Huzza."

The Tortallans entered the imperial audience chamber, Daine, Zek, and Kitten at the back of the company with the clerks. The admiring looks of that group of young men told Daine that not only had she been wise to wear this twilight-blue silk gown, but that she had done well to accept the royal gift of a wardrobe for this trip. "You go as a representative of the Crown, just like the ambassadors," Queen Thayet had said, hazel eyes smiling. "My lord and I insist. Trust me: there is nothing like a good appearance to give a woman confidence." The queen had been right. It was hard to feel insignificant in a gown that whispered as she moved and winked with silver embroidery.

Introduced by a herald, Duke Gareth gave his speech to the emperor, announcing their desire to meet Carthak halfway and their hopes for a lasting peace. He then presented gifts from the king and queen to the emperor. As he spoke, Daine studied the ruler of Carthak, who sat on a tall throne before them, flanked by his ministers and nobles.

She had never heard of him until two-and-a-half years ago, when she had come from Galla to Tortall after her mother's death. Now she knew him all too well. Most Tortallans believed it was this emperor who had managed to break the walls between mortal and divine realms on frequent occasions, turning loose the creatures known as immortals to prey upon Carthak's enemies. Daine herself, working with Numair a year ago, had found evidence that Ozorne was helping to plan a rebellion against the rulers of Tortall. When the monarchs of the other Eastern Lands, those countries north of the Inland Sea, had learned of Emperor Ozorne's plot against one of them, they had united. The threat of the entire northern continent going to war against the southern one had caused Emperor Ozorne to back down, and to open peace talks with Tortall.

Her first sight of the infamous Emperor Mage filled her with awe. She had thought the prince was fine, but he was a barnyard rooster to his uncles' peacock. Gold frosted Ozorne's hair; gold beads hung from a wealth of thin braids. Gold paint shimmered on lips, brows, even his eyelashes. Gold rings marched up the curve of each ear; a diamond hung from his left earlobe. His neck was ringed with six rows of deep-blue stones that sparked with many-colored fires: black opals, expensive stones prized because they could hold magical power. Beneath them he wore the calf-length, short-sleeved robe of his people in heavy gold brocade. Looped at his right hip and passing over his left shoulder was a crimson drape. The long end of the cloth was linked to the emperor's left wrist by a gold bracelet. Each finger sported a ring. His sandals were gilded. Like the prince, he wore toe rings, and added to them ankle bracelets.

She'd heard of Carthak's wealth and power, but it was one matter to hear such things, another to see one man decked out like an idol in gold and gems.

Duke Gareth had finished. Now the line of Tortallans started forward as Duke Gareth gave their names, each bowing to the emperor as they were presented. Watching them, Daine felt a rush of pride. Carthak might be proud and great, but Tortall had sent wise and famous people to work out a peace settlement. Alanna the Lioness was a legend in the Eastern *and* Southern Lands, one the Carthakis couldn't match; and as far as Daine was concerned, Numair was the fish their hosts had allowed to get away.

At last her name and Kitten's were called. Taking a deep breath, Daine walked up to the first step of the dais on which the throne stood, and curtsied, spreading her blue skirts at her sides. The queen had worked on the movement with her for hours, and she was glad to do her teacher proud. Kitten walked up the steps, halting only when she reached the emperor's feet.

"Greetings, dragon child. This *is* a pleasure."
He reached down. Kitten sniffed his fingers, and
sneezed. Grasping his hand with her forepaws, she
examined the gems on his rings with interest. "And
you are her keeper?" inquired the emperor. "The one
who is also a healer of animals?"

She didn't like that word, *keeper*, but she nodded. Lord Martin cleared his throat, and she realized
she was supposed to answer the ruler of Carthak. "I
take care of her, Your Imperial Majesty. And I have
wild magic with animals of all kinds."

"How was she taken, your dragon? A trap, or
a pit? A net?"

Daine swallowed. Traps or snares for Kitten?
"I don't think you understand our relationship, Your
Imperial Majesty. I'm not a keeper; I didn't take her.
Kit's—Kitten's—ma died to protect my friends and
me. She left Kitten to my care."

"Indeed?" He looked at her with curious
amber eyes. "It is true, then. You are able to commune
with the immortals."

"The ones like animals, sire. The griffins, and
winged horses. Dragons. The ones that are part
human, no." She made a face. "They can communicate
without my help."

Kitten, bored with the conversation, voiced a
whistle-croak. The gems on the emperor's fingers
blazed with light.

"Amazing!" he cried, delighted. "Has she
always been able to do that?"

"No, sir. She learned a year ago, from a basilisk.
She learns things fast."

"Then she is blessed, as we are blessed to look

upon her." He nodded a dismissal, and Daine stepped back to join the others.

Introductions over, the emperor said, "To you, representatives of our royal cousins Jonathan and Thayet we say, welcome to Carthak. We pray that peace will reign between our lands and know that with such a distinguished company to smooth the way, peace is all but assured. And now, there is food outside, and drink, music, and good company. In your time among us, we have arranged for entertainment that we hope will arouse wonder and interest in our empire. Enjoy all these things, please. If you desire anything, only voice it to our servants. Within reason it shall be granted you."

Dismissed from the imperial presence, the Tortallans bowed as they backed up, until they were outside again. Once they had left the area closest to the door of the audience chamber, a gong sounded and a grinding noise filled the air. Everyone, guests and servants, froze in place. Slowly the walls that cut the audience chamber off from the antechamber sank into the floor. Now the emperor's dais commanded a view of the combined rooms. Everyone bowed or curtsied deeply to the golden man on the golden throne. He waved a hand; talk and movement picked up where they'd left off. A slave knelt beside the throne, offering a bowl of fruit. The emperor selected a fig, and nibbled it.

Daine felt like a puppet whose strings had been cut. Luckily niches in the walls held couches, with brightly colored pillows to cushion those who wished to sit. She nearly fell into the closest one. Zek squeaked and left his place of concealment to climb into her lap. Duke Gareth and Numair sat beside her, and the remaining Tortallans gathered around.

"Are you all right?" Numair asked softly, cupping her cheek with one large hand. "I had forgotten how intimidating he can be when he has all his imperialness on."

The girl looked at the gilded figure on the dais. "I noticed. Are *you* all right? Did he say anything to you?"

He smiled. "No. If I'm lucky, he'll ignore me for the rest of our stay. That's how he always managed such things when we were boys, anyway. If someone bested him at anything, he just pretended that person didn't exist. He got to be very good at it."

Duke Gareth remarked, "It went quite well. You did us credit, Daine."

The girl blushed and smiled at him. "Thank you, Your Grace."

Gareth the Younger and Harailt, who had quietly left them, returned with servants bearing trays of cups. "Fruit juices," the mage said as his companions helped themselves.

"So far, so good." Lindhall had come with the servants. "Numair, did he speak to you?"

"He didn't even look at me. He spoke the most with Daine."

"But what about his birds?" the girl asked, confused. "I came all this way to see them, and he didn't mention them at all."

"Rulers don't act as other men," Duke Gareth told her. "All requirements of protocol must be met before personal considerations may intrude. You must be patient until he sends for you."

"But more of them might get sick then," she muttered. Numair looked at her and put a finger to his lips. Daine sighed, but obeyed the command to be quiet.

"*Arram*," said a female voice. Everyone looked around. A blue-eyed blonde in an open mage's robe of cream-colored silk approached, hands out. Her pretty face was artfully colored with the contents of pots like those that were on Daine's dressing-room table. Under the robe was a northern-style dress of rose-petal pink, cut to accent a narrow waist and a richly curved figure. Daine, thinking of her own modest curves, sighed with envy.

Numair rose, a stunned look on his face. Alanna slid into the place he'd just left.

"Varice?"

"The same old Varice Kingsford," the newcomer replied, smiling. "I'm surprised you remember me."

Numair kissed first one of her offered hands, then the other, and continued to hold both. "How could I forget you, my dear? You're lovelier than I remember. You must tell me *everything* I've missed. What changes are in the palace, and at the university? Are you married; may I kill your husband—" Laughing, Varice drew Numair through the crowd, leading him to a niche across the room, where they sat down.

"Is that who I think it is?" Alanna directed the question to Lindhall, who had come to lean against the wall beside the Lioness and Daine.

"She was his lover before he fled the country," the older mage replied. "Apparently there were no hard feelings."

Daine frowned. "Why didn't she go with him?"

"He didn't ask, and evidently she didn't offer," said Lindhall. "But she never married, either, and she's had a few serious proposals."

One by one, Ozorne's ministers came to speak with various Tortallans and to introduce them to Carthakis. Mages came for Harailt. Lord Martin and both Gareths were led away by the minister who'd stood closest to the emperor in the audience chamber. Even Alanna, who was uncomfortable in social situations, was deep in talk with a general in the crimson kilt and gold-washed armor of the Imperial Guard, better known as the Red Legion.

Lindhall beckoned to a slave with a tray of fruit. "Your small friend will like grapes," he told Daine, pointing to Zek. "You may also." He put a bowl of grapes and plums beside her. Zek devoured the grapes, while Kitten selected a plum.

"What does *she* do here? Lady Varice?" Daine asked.

"She is Ozorne's official hostess," Lindhall replied, his voice neutral. "Her magic allows her to specialize in things such as entertainment and cookery." He frowned. "I hope Arram—Numair—realizes that Varice is now completely devoted to imperial interests."

Daine looked up at him and realized that here was someone who genuinely cared about her lanky friend. "You've missed him, haven't you, sir?"

Lindhall smiled. "I never had another student whose interests so closely matched my own, and when he was no longer my student, we became friends. It's good to see him now, though I am apprehensive. The emperor never forgives. I doubt that he would imperil the peace talks to settle his score with Numair, but I cannot feel easy in my mind about his reasons for issuing that pardon."

Daine looked down, fighting the urge to tell this man of her own worries and the badger's ominous warning. She knew it was a bad idea, however nice Lindhall seemed, but she needed to tell someone. If only she could get Numair or Alanna someplace where they couldn't be overheard! She *didn't* want to tell Duke Gareth or any of the others. They didn't know her like Alanna and Numair did, nor did they know about the badger.

"Master Lindhall, could we have a word?" someone called.

Lindhall sighed. "You'll be all right here?" he asked Daine.

"Yes, thank you," she replied, smiling. "I'm not going to budge."

Lindhall looked at the crowds before them. "Probably that's just as well. I promise, when we get the chance, I would like to have a good, long chat about wildlife."

"Master Lindhall, the emperor's birds—"

The mage smiled, pale eyes sympathetic. "The emperor will explain, in his own time. That is how things are done here."

She watched him thread his way through the crowd, and shuddered at the thought of meeting so many strangers. Zek gravely offered her a grape; she accepted, with thanks. Looking around, she wished her pony, Cloud, were here. It had made sense to leave her at home, but now Daine longed for Cloud's horse sense and tart opinions. She felt lost among so many adults and such magnificent surroundings. The rulers of Tortall didn't have the kind of wealth, or a surplus of mages, to create rooms like this for their palace.

Suddenly Kitten began to trill, producing sounds that rose and fell like music. At intervals she uttered a *chk!* sound. Each time she did so, the girls could see a man-sized distortion in the air to her left, where Kitten stared intently.

"She sees you," the girl told the distorted spot. "It's the first thing student mages at the royal university try—the invisibility trick. It doesn't work with her. You do it well, the best I've ever seen, but if you don't show yourself now, she'll bite. She *really* dislikes invisibility spells."

The air rippled: there stood the Emperor Mage. "I trust she won't bite me," he said in a mild voice. "I would hate to bleed on this robe."

Daine's jaw dropped; she turned to look at the throne. He sat there, too, a figure identical to the one beside her. "Simulacrum," he explained. "A living puppet. I'm uncomfortable at state occasions. They really don't want *me* in attendance, just something to awe the empire's guests. I mastered the art of magical copies so that I might be able to move around. May I sit down?"

"It's your couch," she replied. For a moment she had spoken to him as she might have to King Jonathan or Queen Thayet, monarchs who insisted on informality. Belatedly remembering her instructions on proper behavior with the emperor, she said, "I'm sorry, Your Imperial Majesty. I should bow, or stand, but I'd upset Zek and the fruit and all."

"Then let us not upset Zek," said Ozorne, looking at the marmoset in Daine's lap. "He is the creature you dived so impetuously into the river to save?" The girl blushed and nodded. A smile tugged the emperor's lips. "It was a kind deed. We need more of them."

Embarrassed, Daine changed the subject. "About the copies of you—can't the mages tell it's only sorcery?"

Ozorne snapped his fingers, and a shimmering curtain of light enveloped the dais, hiding the other emperor from sight. "No. I *am* very good at them. Practice, you see—plenty of state occasions that require the emperor's image, not the man. I tried to teach your master, the former Arram Draper, how to make them, but he was never as adept as I am."

She ignored the jibe about Numair. "Can it do magic, or look like it has magic? The sim—"

"Simulacrum." He put his chin on his hand, amber eyes thoughtful. "No. The fabric of the copy won't hold the chain of spells that would give it the seeming of my magical Gift."

Numair can do it, she thought. If the emperor hasn't heard it, though, *I'm* not going to tell him. "Why did you pardon Numair and let him come back, if you're still angry with him?"

He smiled. "My dear girl—no, you don't care for that, do you? he asked, correctly interpreting the look on her face. "Then I shall call you Veralidaine."

"Daine, please, Your Imperial Majesty."

"Daine? What is the point of so beautiful a name if it's not used? Veralidaine. At the risk of destroying your illusions, I must tell you I have little control over what is done in this kingdom." He offered his hand to Kitten. The dragon shook her head, and crouched to examine his toe rings.

"I don't mean to be rude, but of course you do. It's your kingdom, isn't it?"

"Indeed, but—does my royal cousin Jonathan have complete freedom to order what he likes? I assume he has councils and nobles and law to answer to, does he not? I believe Sir Gareth the Younger is the head of his private council, to which Master Numair and Lady Alanna also belong. Duke Gareth leads the Council of Lords, which numbers also Lord Martin of Meron, and Harailt of Aili is head of his Council of Mages. Such men are the real power in any realm, Veralidaine."

"But they're just advisors. The king can do as he wants, surely."

The emperor shook his head. "Alienating one's nobles is a sure way to put a nation into chaos. There are always those who think they can do a ruler's job better. They need little encouragement."

Daine thought of Yolane of Dunlath, who had planned rebellion in Tortall with *this* ruler's encouragement, and bit her tongue. Her orders from the king and queen had been specific. She was not to mention the emperor's attempts to weaken Tortall, no matter how much she might want to.

Zek, unconcerned by the emperor's nearness or his scent, a mix of amber and cinnamon, picked his way through the bowl of fruit. When his stomach bulged with his discoveries there, he offered Daine the next grape he found.

"No, thank you," she said. "Perhaps His Imperial Majesty would like it." Zek held the grape up for Ozorne.

He accepted it gravely. "Thank you, Master Zek."

Watching him eat the grape, Daine said hesitantly, "I—heard your birds are sick. It's why I came, but—are they better? Do you not need me to look at them?"

Ozorne's face brightened. "No, but I thought—after your journey, and all this—when do you wish to see them? I can arrange it for the morning tomorrow, if you don't mind."

"Um—if they're sick, I'd *like* to see them now. If you can have a servant show me the way—"

"Servants don't go near my birds, except to prepare their food. Are you certain? It seems too much to ask, to have you look at them the night you arrive."

She grinned. "Keeping me here when you have sick animals is asking too much."

He got to his feet, and she followed. "Do you mind if I veil us?" he asked. "Otherwise we will be followed; my ministers will want me to stay. . . ."

Daine looked around. "I really should tell the others." The problem was that she could spot no one else from her company. While she had been in conversation with the emperor, the crowd had moved away from them to watch dancers in the garden. All she could see were richly dressed backs.

Ozorne raised a hand, and a slave appeared at his elbow. "Inform Duke Gareth of the Tortallan guests that Mistress Veralidaine has gone to look at our birds. And send the mage Lindhall Reed to us in the aviary."

The slave bowed deeply, and the emperor offered Daine his arm. She didn't see how she could refuse without being rude, and surely the slave would obey the order to tell Duke Gareth where she was. Carefully she rested her palm on Ozorne's forearm, as she had seen court ladies do at home. The emperor gestured, and a copy of him split away from them to walk back to his throne. The shining barrier that hid the raised seat vanished when the copy reached the dais, and the illusion blended with the copy on the throne. Daine watched it, fascinated, as Ozorne led her through a small door at the back of the antechamber and into a narrow hall. Kitten followed, while Zek settled himself comfortably on Daine's shoulder.

Globes like those in the room they had just left were placed at intervals along the hall. Passing the first, Ozorne gestured. It lifted free of the clawed iron foot that held it up and followed them, lighting their way through a maze of corridors and empty public rooms.

"I've tried everything," he explained. Since the humans they passed bowed to them, Daine realized he must have dropped the invisibility spell once they'd left the reception. "The new quarters were finished this spring, and after we moved them in they seemed fine. Then some of my birds took sick. I noticed a palsy in their heads. They became listless; their appetites fell off. Within two weeks of the first signs, the victims die. I know a great deal of bird medicine, and Lindhall Reed has made a study of it, which is why I asked him to join us. Indeed, there he is now."

Lindhall awaited them in front of a pair of broad white doors on which green flowering vines had been painted. He bowed low to the emperor and smiled at Daine, then turned and opened both doors, thrusting them wide. He clapped twice. Light-globes in the hall that lay before them came to life, to reveal a wonder. On the walls, birds had been inlaid with gold strips. Tiny gems served them as eyes, while craftsmen had used pieces of bright, colorful stone for their plumage. Kitten trilled her appreciation.

"Oh, *glory*," breathed Daine. "Your Imperial Majesty, this is—*wondrous*."

"It is well enough," the emperor said cooly, surveying the inlays. "We thought it pretty when we designed it, but no image can take the place of a living bird."

She couldn't disagree, but the walls still had to be the finest thing to come from human hands.

At the end of the hall stood another pair of doors, these made of long glass panels. They were frosted, and set in a network of metal pieces enameled a bright, emerald green and shaped like vines.

"I am a *fool*." Ozorne was upset. "They will be asleep. We can have light-globes—they are used to that; I often read here at night, but to disturb their rest, even to care for sick ones . . ."

"You must leave that to me," Daine told him. "I won't frighten them, and I won't let the ones who are well interrupt their rest. It's more important to start work now."

"Master Lindhall, will you remain and get whatever Veralidaine needs?" inquired the emperor. When Daine looked at him curiously, he tried to smile. "To see them ill, and to be helpless—do you think less of me? I cannot watch."

She smiled. "I don't think less of you, sire. I know what it's like to be helpless when a creature you love is ill and you can't do anything."

Lindhall sketched a rune in the air with a glowing finger. When the design was complete, the glass doors opened. He bowed deeply to the emperor, holding the posture, until Daine realized that both of them were waiting for her to do the same. Again she'd forgotten that she was not dealing with King Jonathan! She curtsied, wobbling a bit, as Zek squeaked and hung on to her curls. Kitten sat up on her hindquarters and bowed, too.

Emperor Ozorne nodded and left, vanishing in plain view as he passed the white doors.

Lindhall went into the aviary first, using finger-snaps to wake two small light-globes near the entrance. They illuminated the area around the door, revealing a marble bench and walks that led between banks of large, thick-leafed plants. Daine looked up and saw the shadows of trees overhead. In the darkness she could hear the murmur of fountains and brooks, and the brush of damp greenery. In her mind, she could hear the whispers of sleeping and waking birds, both well and ill.

Lindhall closed the doors behind them.

"You don't have to stay," she said quietly. The number of birds in this chamber was surprising, and the thread of ill health weaving through her senses made her feel slightly ill herself. She was starting to regret the last grape she'd eaten. "It'll be fair boring."

"I believe I will stay in any event," he said, breathy voice kind. "Partly because I should like to see you at work, but also partly because I know Numair will feel better if I am with you."

Daine nodded. "Would you mind holding Zek, then?" she asked. To the marmoset she explained, "I'm going to need that shoulder."

Resigned, the tiny animal climbed down her outstretched arm and onto Lindall's immense palm. Zek was beginning to realize that his new friend had her own ways of doing things. Lindhall sat on the bench, stroking Zek's many-colored fur with one finger, while Kitten leaped up beside him and settled down to wait. "Daine, may I give you a word of warning?"

Looking around, the girl saw the immense bole of a tree nearby. "About what, sir?" She settled into a fold between two large roots, resting her back against the tree.

"The emperor." Lindall's pale eyes were troubled. "He shows his best side in regard to his birds, and to animals in general. He possesses—other sides."

She smiled at him. "I'll keep it in mind." She didn't think she had needed the extra warning—not after two years of finding imperial claws hooked into all parts of Tortall. Closing her eyes, she called her patients to her.

The ones in the best condition came first, heads bobbing on weakened necks. Some barely had the strength to fly, a result both of the disease and of the appetite loss that went with it. Daine looked deep inside herself until she found the pool of her magic. She drew it up not in threads, but in ropes, sending fibers of it into each of the birds resting on her shoulders and legs.

If they had a disease, it was like none she had ever seen. To her inner eyes, it shadowed the dab of copper fire that was each bird's wild magic, leaving a film that grew until it blotted out the animal's fire, and its life. She burned the shadows away in every bird that could reach her, then rose to find those that couldn't. She ached all over, particularly in her joints. She ignored it and felt her way into the shrubbery that concealed the rest of her patients from her. Many were on the ground, too weak to move. Three had died since the last time the place was cleaned. She stubbornly went after each flickering life light she could sense.

Some had made it to aboveground nests. The thought of climbing the large trees of this indoor enclosure was daunting, but she found a stair that followed the walls in an upward spiral. Using it, she searched out the rest of her patients. At last she had seen to all of them. Lindhall must have heard her coming down the stair: he, Kitten, and Zek met her at the bottom.

"How did it go?" the man asked.

"They're healed—for now, at least. Oh, dear." Now that she was in somewhat better light, she could properly see that her hands, arms, and dress were coated with heavy, white droppings. Before coming down, she'd scraped the worst off with leaves and twigs, but her splendid gown was ruined. Even one of Kitten's magical sounds wouldn't save the cloth.

"Perhaps I should continue to hold Zek," Lindhall said tactfully. "Would you like me to show you to your room?" She brightened, looking up at him, and he laughed. "My dear, I've lost more garments to animal droppings than I can count. Clothing is not worth a candle when placed against what you have done here. Come. We'll go through the gardens, where no one will see you."

Kitten, following them down the hall with the

bird inlays on the walls, whistle-croaked. The stone birds lit up. Lindhall grinned with pleasure as lapis, jade, and citrine shimmered in their natural colors. Once that had faded, they went out into the gardens.

"What was wrong with the birds?" he asked, navigating the tangled paths.

"It's not a disease. Could they have eaten moldy seed or anything like that? I think they were poisoned somehow."

"It's possible, though the slaves are vigilant with the food that goes to those birds. They have to be. Do you think the poisoning was deliberate?" They passed a large, many-tiered fountain lit from within by glowing stones.

"I don't know. If they get sick again, I can check their food and things like that. Should I mention poisoning to the emperor?"

"Please don't. He would kill the slaves. It wouldn't matter to him if the poisoning were deliberate or not—only that it happened. He might torture them first, to see if it *was* deliberate, but it wouldn't do much good. All his personal slaves are mutes."

Daine shivered as they entered another wing of the palace. Now she knew their surroundings: the guest quarters, near the wing set aside for the Tortallan delegation. A slave dozing in the central area onto which the rooms opened jumped to his feet and held the door to Daine's room, trying not to stare at her.

"She will be going out to bathe in a few moments," Lindhall said. The slave nodded without looking up. "Daine, will you be all right? Shall I have Lady Alanna look in on you?"

She smiled up at him. "I'm just tired, and I need to wash, that's all. Thank you, Master Lindhall. Numair said you are *very* kind, and he was right."

To her amusement, the lanky mage blushed. "Well, good night, then."

About to enter her room, she said, "Oh, wait — if it's possible, can the birds be left alone all day tomorrow? They can be fed as long as food's left *quietly*." She had seen food trays and water bowls somewhere in the aviary. "If there's a way to keep it dark in the aviary for half of the day, I'd use it."

He looked interested. "Of course — I can manage it, actually. Glass walls conduct magic well, and it's no great matter to make them dark. You want the birds to sleep? Even the healthy ones?"

"It won't harm them, and the extra rest will get the sick ones over their reaction to the healing. Birds are funny." She yawned. "When they're up and alert, their bodies use energy faster than any other animals. The magic sticks better if they can sleep for a while after I'm done."

"I shall take care of it. Try not to fall asleep in your bath. Good night, Veralidaine — and welcome to Carthak." He closed the door for her.

"I like him," the girl told Zek and Kitten drowsily.

So do I, replied the marmoset as Kitten also nodded agreement.

Slowly, half asleep already, Daine began to gather her bathing things.

She woke early, with no ill effects from the previous night's work. By the time she dressed and left her room, a large breakfast had been laid out in the area common to the bedchambers occupied by the Tortallans. The others were emerging from their rooms to eat there.

"It went quite well last night," Duke Gareth said once they were settled. "Some of the imperial ministers are more forthcoming than others, but that is to be expected. I am *particularly* happy with the reports I've had of *you*, Daine."

Startled, the girl looked up, her teeth halfway into a bite of melon. Blushing crimson, she put the forkful onto her plate again. "*Me*, Your Grace?"

"Emperor Ozorne heard from Master Lindhall that you cured his birds in one session," explained Harailt of Aili. "The emperor is *very* pleased—says he has to think of a proper way to express his thanks."

"It's like that with some men in high places," commented Gareth the Younger, buttering a roll. "Things that would impress *us* have no effect on them, but a kindness done to creatures they love, they never forget." He looked at Daine, brown eyes uncomfortably keen. "I hope you'll continue to stay on his good side. The ministers' definition of concessions they will and won't make changed to our benefit after the emperor thanked us for bringing you."

Daine frowned as she passed a roll to Kitten. That didn't sound much like the way Ozorne had described himself—as a ruler whose lords told *him* what to do.

"Which reminds me," Numair said, feeding Zek as the marmoset sat on his lap. "We're scheduled to have a tour of the imperial menagerie after breakfast."

Daine gulped. "A menagerie?" King Jonathan had possessed rare, caged animals when she first came to Tortall. Even going near it had been a torment until the king began to change it, making it into enclosures that resembled the captives' original homes.

"Ozorne would never ill-treat his animals," said Numair, seeing the discomfort in her eyes.

"Don't slight him by staying behind," added Gareth the Younger.

Alanna hugged Daine around the shoulders. "She wouldn't think of it, Gary. Leave her be."

Daine smiled at her friend, and slipped the rest of her melon to Kitten. Somehow she wasn't hungry anymore.

They had just gotten up from the table when their guides arrived, Prince Kaddar and Varice Kingsford. Daine scowled as the lady, dressed in clinging green silk with a transparent white veil over her hair, kissed Numair's cheek, smiling flirtatiously at him. "I shall walk with His Grace," the lady told Numair, "but stay close, please. You know so much more about animals than I do."

Duke Gareth bowed over Varice's hand. "Numair's loss is my gain, Lady Varice."

Prince Kaddar bowed to Alanna. "May I offer you my escort, Lioness?"

Alanna grinned, resting her hands on her sword belt. "On such a beautiful day you shouldn't be stuck with an old lady like me," she said wickedly. "I don't believe Daine has an escort."

Kaddar smiled and turned to Daine. "Then I am free to offer my arm to you, lady."

My friend, Daine thought, glaring at the

Lioness. To Kaddar she gave a lukewarm smile. "I'm no lady, Your Highness—just Daine."

The amenities over, the group was led by Varice and the prince down a maze of paths that led past a formal garden and partway around the shore of an ornamental lake. Daine closed off the links her magic formed to the animal world around her. She could no more hear Zek's thoughts and feelings than she would hear the zoo captives, but the marmoset understood when she explained why she was closing herself off. I don't like cages either, he said balefully, chittering in anger. They put my mate and our little ones and me in a cage, and then we were sold.

At last they walked through wrought-iron gates topped by the imperial seal: a crossed sword and wand, topped by a crown, wrapped in a jagged circle.

THREE

ᕼALL OF BONES

"My uncle loves animals," the prince said dryly as the girl stared at the scene before her. "He tries to give them room, and the foods they prefer, and companionship. The ones that don't thrive in captivity he sends back to their homes."

She should have realized that the man who showed such devotion to his birds might pay similar attention to other creatures. While the animals here were contained, they had far more space in which to move than she had seen in the royal menagerie when she had first arrived in Tortall.

Lions basked in the sun, living at the bottom of a well too deep for escape. A lively brook flowed through the enclosure, and desert trees grew on one side, offering shade from the midday sun. Chimpanzees raced around an immense cage equipped with a large, many-branched and leafless "tree" for their enjoyment. On an island in the middle of a deep pond, strange, reddish-faced monkeys Kaddar identified as macaques climbed over and around heaped rocks.

Giraffes gazed at her solemnly over a tall iron fence. Daine couldn't help herself: she went to them, hands out, letting the wards on her power fall slightly. Startled, the giraffes dropped their heads low on their impossibly long necks to lip her fingers and say hello while Zek warned them to behave themselves.

"It's all right," the girl told him, smiling as a young giraffe snuffled her tunic. "They're grazers. They won't hurt you."

We don't have *anything* like that where *I* come from, the marmoset replied with offended dignity. We have *proper* animals there.

Kaddar, who'd been taken aside by a keeper, rejoined her. "Has your king anything this good?"

Daine bristled at the smugness in his voice. The hot reply on her lips was cut off by Harailt. "Actually, we're trying something a bit uncommon." He gave Daine a half wink. "We *royal* university mages are working with builders on a new kind of menagerie, a bit like this one, but much broader in scope. We duplicate the lands each animal comes from—plants, weather, and all; you see where the mages come in. When it's done, within the confines of the royal menagerie, a guest will visit small pieces of Carthak, and the Copper Isles, and Scanra."

Kaddar's eyes lit with enthusiasm. As he pelted Harailt with questions, Daine wandered down the curving path with Zek and Kitten, out of sight of the others. Here she discovered a pit in which giant, long-nosed pigs drowsed in a deep pond. Their noses, shorter than an elephant's but nearly as flexible, pointed toward Daine as she passed. Opposite them, a colony of mongooses watched her from behind wire mesh that enclosed a high and far-reaching mound of burrows. Beyond them the path took an abrupt left turn.

This last enclosure lay below ground level, inside a glassy wall four yards down from the girl's feet. The area was less well kept than the others. A small pond lay near the wall, but much of the water in it had evaporated. The grass was brown-edged and lay in patches on bare, dusty-looking ground. The remains of shattered bones lay everywhere. In back, lying out of the sun in a shallow cave, were three shaggy, spotted brown bodies.

She opened a wider crack in her magic's defenses, reaching for these strangers. "Please come out," she called aloud. A twitch of movement: three rounded pairs of ears came to bear on her.

You smell of cold places, one voice, commanding and female, said. You smell of frozen rain and pine trees. You smell of far away. Me and my boys never had a whiff of someone like you.

Blinking huge eyes in the sunlight, the speaker came to the foot of the wall. She was followed by two smaller males.

Daine wished she could meet the god who had molded these creatures. There was a god with *imagination*. The source of the shattered bones had to be those powerful jaws, equipped with strong teeth. The least of these creatures weighed more than she did. On their fours they were tallest and heaviest at the shoulder, their spotted fur covering slablike muscle. Their hindquarters were low and short, but strong. Small tails sported jaunty tufts at the end.

"They're *beautiful*," she breathed.

"Spotted hyenas," Numair said at her elbow. "From the grass plains of Ekallatum, far to the south. Night hunters, for the most part—see the eyes? They have the strongest bite of any mortal predator—it crushes even the bones of water buffalo. Hyena packs are matriarchal—"

"Matri-what?" she asked. Kitten voiced an inquiring whistle of her own.

Numair smiled. "Their society is ruled by females. Each pack is led by sisters."

"Sensible of them," Daine said, grinning up at him.

"Excuse me." It was Varice. She bore down on them with a brittle-looking smile. "I'm sorry. These animals aren't to be shown to visitors. I don't know why the emperor keeps them, when he doesn't even like them. . . . Numair, Daine, please come back. There's another part of the menagerie you haven't seen." Linking her arm through Numair's, she led him away from the hyenas.

Come back sometime, offered the female hyena. Me and my boys are always around.

"I'll do my best," Daine promised. "C'mon, Kit."

When she caught up to the rest of the group, the prince led them through a second barred gate. "This is my uncle's other collection," he announced.

"Each and every one was captured and brought here for causing trouble for humans."

Kitten screeched. Daine hushed her, but felt like screeching herself. The cages in this wide courtyard, none of them as pleasant as those for the mortal animals, held immortals. Brass plates on each cage identified killer unicorns, griffins, the flesh-eating winged horses called hurroks, and giant, lizardlike hunters known as Coldfangs. Here, too, she saw unlikely combinations of human and animal: giant, human-headed spiders called spidrens and centaurs of both the peaceful and blood-hungry kinds, the former with hooves and hands, the latter with talons.

To her surprise, one cage held a man and a woman with steel-feathered wings and claws instead of arms and legs—Stormwings. The male had a pale, intense face, aquiline nose, and fixed, hungry eyes. The female's nose was hawklike, her dark eyes imperious. She had been beautiful in her youth, it was plain, and now, older, she was haughty and commanding.

Daine looked at Kaddar. "I thought your uncle was allied with the Stormwings!"

"He is," replied Ozorne's nephew. "The price of the pact with the Stormwing King Jokhun was that Queen Barzha and her mate Hebakh be kept here. Believe me, she would have caused as much havoc in Carthak as Stormwings have in the north, if my uncle had not made the alliance."

Daine was trembling. "What do you feed them?" she asked, shaking off someone's restraining hand. "Do you bring folk in and scare them, so they can live on that? And these cages are too small. The griffin can barely open its wings." Kitten muttered unpleasant things in dragon.

"They don't need food, and they don't require more room," said Varice impatiently. "You know these monsters don't fall ill and die. Unless you kill one, they live forever. Would you rather let them raid villages and destroy crops?"

"We mean no criticism of the way the emperor chooses to run his domain," said Duke Gareth. His eyes locked on Daine with a message she couldn't ignore. She looked at her shoes, biting her lip before more rash words spilled out. "Daine speaks only because her bond with all creatures gives her a dislike of cages. Your Highness, my lady, I regret to say I am not as young as I was. Might we find someplace shaded, and sit for a moment? Your sun is fierce, even this early."

Their group streamed out through the gates. Daine alone hesitated, staring at these captives. She had no reason to like spidrens, Stormwings, hurroks, Coldfangs, and their kind. Too much of her time in Tortall had gone to fighting immortals like these. Stormwings in particular had caused her, personally, a great many problems. She ought to be glad these were locked away from doing more harm—oughtn't she?

At midmorning she returned to her rooms, to find an old servant woman there, straightening things. "Don't mind me," she said, her grin revealing a handful of teeth. "You sit down. I won't be but another minute." She flicked a duster over one of the carved screens.

Awkward and unsure of what to say, Daine sat

on a chair. She guessed this was a slave, though she was much older than the other palace slaves that she had seen. The woman's dress was undyed cotton, looped over one bony shoulder and hanging just to skinny knees. She wore straw sandals. Her only ornament, if it could be called that, was a tattooed bracelet of snaky lines that twined around each other.

Putting aside her duster, the old woman took the pillow from the bed and plumped it. "You're from up north, aren't you?" she asked. "Up Tortall way?"

Kitten trotted over and tugged the woman's dress, chattering loudly.

"Not now, dearie," the slave told her, apparently comfortable with a dragon in the room. "I have things to do."

"Over here, Kit," summoned Daine.

The slave laid her hand on Kitten's muzzle. "Enough," she said, black eyes dancing wickedly in a seamed face. The dragon was instantly silent. Turning back to the bed, the woman grappled with the slippery comforter.

Daine barely noticed Kitten's abrupt silence. Her upbringing got the better of her, and she stood, placing Zek on her seat. Ma had not raised her to sit idle, not when housework was to be done. She also had not been raised to let an elder work without aid. "Here, grandmother—let me help. Kit, move." The dragon ducked under the chair. Together the girl and the old woman bared the sheets on the bed and began to neaten them.

"Yes, I'm from Tortall," Daine said. "From Galla, before that."

"Your first trip to Carthak? What do you make

of us Southerners, eh? D'you like it here?"

It occurred to Daine that the woman might be a spy, there to get information from her. "It's all right," she said hesitantly. "It's very different from home, of course."

"It's in trouble, you know—the Empire." The gnarled old hands were busy, tugging and straightening. "Famine in the south, five years running—did they tell you? Locusts—folk out of work—wells drying up. It's as if the gods have turned their faces from the emperor."

"It—it's not my place to say," Daine stammered.

"You ought to look around a bit. *Really* look. Long as you're here. The priests don't like the omens, you know. They whisper that a cold wind's blowing from the Divine Realms. Might be next time you visit Carthak, it won't be here. Hard to argue with gods, when they're done being nice to mortals." Briskly she patted the coverlet into place.

Daine blinked at the woman. Her words sounded too much like what the badger had said. And weren't slaves supposed to be quiet and timid? None of the others had talked to her like this one did: all they'd said was "Yes, Nobility," "No, Nobility," and "Right away, Nobility."

"Do *you* think the gods are vexed with Carthak?" she asked digging her hands into her pockets.

The slave ran her duster over the writing desk. "Ask them to show you the temples," she advised, apparently not hearing Daine's question. "The shrines. They used to be the glory of the Empire. Now they think mages and armies are imperial glory. They think—the emperor thinks—he doesn't *need* the gods." Wickedly she reached with the duster and flicked the end of Kitten's nose as the dragon peered out from under the chair.

Kitten sneezed, then squealed with outrage as her scales turned angry red. Her voice rose as she hooted and chattered with fury. Daine begged her to be quiet, but there was no silencing the dragon this time. The girl knelt and clamped her hands on her muzzle. "Stop that this instant!" she ordered. "Look at Zek— you're hurting his poor ears, and you're hurting mine!"

Kitten glanced at Zek. The marmoset sat gravely on the back of the chair, paws over his ears. Slowly turning a sullen gray, the dragon whistled what sounded like an apology.

"She wants discipline," remarked the old lady, sounding breathless. "Her own folk would never allow her to speak out of turn."

Concentrating on Kitten and Zek, Daine had taken her eyes off her visitor. When she turned to ask the servant what she had meant, she discovered that the old woman had dragged the tiger-skin rug from under the bed and was attempting to stand with it bundled into her arms.

Daine's reaction was automatic. "Here, grandmother—I'll take that," she said, holding out her hands. "Just tell me where it goes—"

The woman dumped the bundle into Daine's grip, and white light flared. Kitten shrieked as the skin began to writhe. The girl dropped it, horrified. Her head swam, and she toppled over, landing on her hands and knees next to the fur.

As she gasped for air, the skin rippled. The great forepaw, by her toes, flexed. Long, razor claws shot out, then resheathed themselves. By her nose a hind paw stretched, then braced itself on the floor. The rump, no longer flat on the stone, wriggled. Slowly, as if a body filled the empty hide, the cat got to its feet, hindquarters first, then forepaws. The tail lashed.

Daine scooted away from it. "Grandmother, you'd best get out of here!" she cried.

The door opened. A slave peered in, seeing first Zek and Kitten by the chair, then Daine. The door hid the rug from her view. The slave knelt and bowed her head, putting her right fist on her left shoulder. "You called this unworthy one, Nobility?"

"No," said Daine. "I mean, yes, I mean—"

The slave touched the floor with her forehead. Daine lunged to her feet. "Please don't do that," she pleaded, not sure if she spoke to the slave or the tiger. "I don't—I can't—I'm not a Nobility, all right?"

"Forgive this one's faults, Nobility. What do you need? This unworthy one is here to serve."

She took a breath and got herself in hand. "Please get up. And—where's the old woman?"

"Old woman, Nobility?" asked the slave. "There is no old woman here."

Baffled, Daine looked around. The old servant was gone, feather duster and all. "She was just here a moment ago—you must have passed her." She grabbed the door, holding it so that the kneeling slave would have no glimpse of the tiger behind it. "She was cleaning in here."

The slave looked up. "The care of your room is this unworthy one's task, Nobility," she said, clearly frightened. "It was done some time ago, shortly after the Nobilities from the north went with the prince and Lady Varice."

Daine thought fast. The old slave must have fled in that moment when the light blazed. No doubt she'd been frightened out of her wits; Daine knew her own knees were decidedly weak. She had to calm down, because now she was scaring this poor girl as well. "It's all right," she said, attempting a smile. "I—I must have been napping, and had a—a dream or something. I—"

She looked behind the door. The tiger skin lay on the marble tiles, all four paws tucked underneath, tail curled around its chest. The head rested on the floor, eyes closed. If she hadn't known better, she would have sworn the thing looked smug—except, of course, that dead animal skins couldn't manage that kind of expression.

"Would you do me a favor?" She closed the door so that the slave could see the tiger skin. "This— rug. It's very—upsetting, to have it here. Will you take it away? *Far* away?"

From the look on her face as she rose, the slave was used to odd requests. "Yes, Nobility." The rug offered her no more resistance than a blanket might have done. With a last bow, she left.

Trembling, Daine said, "Thank you," and started to close the door.

"Daine?" Alanna was in the central room outside, dressed for the opening of the peace negotiations. "You'd best hurry, or we'll be late for the banquet."

Daine winced and shut the door. Between talking to the old slave, having the rug come to life on her, and handling the young slave, she had forgotten she had to clean up and change again. "I don't know how much more excitement I can take," she told Zek and Kitten as she stripped off her tunic and shirt. "To think the king thought I might get bored while I was here!"

The opening banquet started at noon, a feast of the light, cool foods preferred in warmer lands for daytime. From the talk around Daine, such meals were Varice Kingsford's special pride. It was the kind of thing that had foreigners from all over the Eastern and Southern lands singing the praises of the emperor's table. The girl surveyed the bewildering variety of choices and let Zek help her choose. The marmoset was an expert on plant foods, at least.

Varice was everywhere, seeing to the comfort of the Tortallan delegation and the foreign ambassadors to Carthak who had been invited to observe the talks on behalf of their rulers. With so many lords to attend to, she didn't appear to notice that Numair barely touched his food.

Daine noticed, and felt sorry for her tall friend. Varice had filled his plate herself, heaping it with delicacies like eel pastry, elephant-ear soup, and snake medallions in a black bean and wine sauce. It was the worst thing she could have done. Numair's body did not always travel well, particularly not after a sea or river voyage. Usually he spent several days in a new place eating mild, simple foods—the only things he could keep down. He nodded and gave polite thanks when she stopped to ask how he did, but Daine could see a tinge of green around his lips.

Luckily the dogs and cats who served as palace mouse and rat catchers were everywhere, even here in the banquet hall. Daine silently asked two dogs for help. When a paw on the mage's knee caused Numair to look down, he saw them at his feet, willing to be fed. The look he gave Daine was filled with gratitude. She didn't see the costly food leave his plate, but she didn't expect to: Numair's hobby was sleight of hand. The dogs she heard clearly. They were delighted with their feast.

At last the emperor led them to the room where the talks would be held. Tables and chairs had been placed in a loose square, and unshuttered windows allowed breezes and garden scents to pass through. The Tortallans, the foreign ambassadors, and the Carthaki ministers were given seats, their places marked with nameplates of gold inlaid with silver. Jugs of water, juice, and herbal teas were at all the tables. Carthaki scribes sat cross-legged against one wall, ready to take notes, while the Tortallan scribes had their own table, directly behind Duke Gareth's seat. Those who would not take part, such as Lindhall Reed and lesser nobles and officials, sat in chairs behind the delegations. Daine sat at the end of her table, uncomfortable even there. Kitten had a stool to perch on, beside the girl; Zek hid in his usual place under Daine's hair.

Ozorne rose to speak, dressed in a blindingly white robe and green shoulder wrap. His hair, ungilded today, proved to be reddish brown, though it was still in many fine braids, each tipped with a gold filigree bead. Black paint lined his amber eyes back to his temples. He glittered with gems.

"We bid you welcome, representatives of our eminent cousin, King Jonathan of Tortall, and of his queen, Thayet the Peerless, and of our fellow monarchs and neighbors." His voice filled the room. "This day has been too long in coming. At last we are met in a spirit of mutual aid and support for our lands, so long at odds. Villains conspired to bring us to the brink of war, but wisdom and vigilance have kept us from stepping over. All our hearts desire only peace.

"Without our knowledge and consent, evil men contrived four years ago to steal arcane learning secretly held for centuries. With this ill-gained knowledge, they reversed what the writers of those spells had dedicated their lives to achieve, the banning from our human, mortal existence those creatures loosely called immortals, the semidivine beings who may live forever unless accident or force brings their life spans to a halt.

"To our sorrow, our person and our university were blamed for this dreadful misuse of power. Our cousins of Tortall, sore beset by immortals and by those who prey on a land open to attack, felt we were to blame, and who could contest it? Loving freedom and commerce, we kept too little watch on our library, on our shipwrights, on those who hired men and paid them in Carthaki gold. To our shame and sorrow, our lack of awareness caused our Tortallan cousins to think we condoned the behavior of pirates, bandits, and rogues. Let us now set the matter straight. Let us strive together for peace between our peoples, and put aside all past misunderstandings.

"May the gods bless our endeavors, and may they foster the peace for which we all long." Clasping his hands together, he touched them to his forehead in a kind of salute, and sat down.

Duke Gareth rose to make his reply, reading from a letter written to Ozorne and his ministers by King Jonathan. Daine hid a yawn under one hand. She might have found the letter more interesting if she had not heard discussions about its contents on the voyage to Carthak. Instead her mind kept skipping away from Duke Gareth's voice, returning to the tigerskin rug, or to the badger's visit, over and over. She had mentioned the need to talk to Numair and Alanna on their way to the noon banquet, but she knew it might be some time before they could get the chance to safely hear what she had to say. As the emperor's guests, most of their time away from the talks would be taken up with entertainments and activities. Both had promised to do what they could, and Daine had to be content with that.

If only I *knew* what the gods had in mind, or *when* it was going to happen, she thought as the foreign ambassadors read messages from their own rulers. I don't know what Numair or Alanna can do with "Something bad is going to happen." I don't even know what *I* would do with it!

Once the ambassadors were done, each of Ozorne's delegates had a speech to make, followed by a speech from each Tortallan official. Daine's yawns began to come thick and fast.

Suddenly a clerk tapped her on the shoulder and passed her a note from Duke Gareth.

There is no reason for you to remain for all this —
your presence in Carthak has nothing to do with being

bored to death. Why don't you go? No one will mind. Just
remember to be changed and ready for the supper banquet
this evening, and go nowhere that is not permitted.

When she stuffed the note into her pocket, Zek woke from his after-lunch nap. We're done now? he asked, hopeful.

That was enough to decide her. Maybe *they* aren't done, but I am, she told the marmoset. Leaning around Alanna, she caught the duke's eye and nodded. He smiled at her, and Alanna gave her shoulder a pat.

"Kit," the girl whispered, "I'm leaving. Come on."

The dragon shook her head. She appeared fascinated by the speakers. Daine tugged her paw; Kitten shook her head again. With a shrug, the girl left her, and quietly made her way out of the room. Looking back as she let the door close, she saw her dragon climb into the vacated chair.

Outside, she found herself in a long breezeway that opened on both sides to gardens. She sat on a marble bench with a sigh of relief, and lifted Zek down into her lap. "Amazing how much two-leggers can talk, isn't it?" she asked him.

"Given that the alternative to speech this time is war, I imagine talk is a little better." Lindhall had followed her. He sat on the end of the bench and offered a hand to Zek. Curious, the marmoset went to inspect his fingers. "I would like to show you something of interest—something you would not see at home. Unless you had planned to return to the deliberations of the mighty?"

"Goddess, no!" she exclaimed with a shudder, and picked up Zek.

As they set off through the palace, Lindhall said, "I wanted to ask—is it true marmosets form monogamous groups in the wild? No one's ever been able to actually observe them in their native wilderness. There are other tales, of course, such as the one that claims they vanish in plain sight and reappear in another part of the forest, which is clearly false—isn't it?"

Daine, politely waiting for him to finish, realized that he had. "Zek says they don't vanish. They freeze. The way their fur is colored, they seem part of the tree. Or they zip around to the far side of the trunk and keep it between them and whoever is watching. And yes, they have just one marriage. Zek used to live with his wife and their three children before they were trapped."

Lindhall shook his head. "Wild things should remain in the wild. Down this corridor."

They now entered the heart of the palace, where throne rooms, reception halls, and waiting rooms were located. Lindhall stopped before a large double door that bore a brass nameplate: The Hall of Bones. The handles on each flap were very large bones of some kind. Daine and Zek touched one with curious fingers.

"What do you know of fossils?" the mage asked.

"They're creatures and plants that lived so long ago no mortals remember them. There are some in the royal museum—shells, batlike creatures, fishes and such. Numair says there are others, skeletons of huge beasts called dinosaurs, but no one has found any in the Eastern Lands yet."

"Quite true," replied Lindhall. He spoke a word in a language she didn't know, and both door flaps swung inward. Daine squeaked; Zek darted under her hair. Peering at them from the shadows was a *very* large skull. Three horns sprang from the bony face: a short one, near the end of its nose, and two longer ones that pointed forward over the eyes.

"Oh, you beautiful thing," the girl whispered, and went up to it, hardly believing what she saw. She only came as high as one of the large eye sockets. "What is it?" With trembling fingers she touched the beaklike plate of bone that seemed to be the creature's upper lip.

Lindhall clapped. Overhead, throughout that immense hall, light-globes began to glow. "One of the horn-faced lizards. We call them lizards because they resemble lizards more than other creatures, but they didn't *act* like our modern reptiles do." Daine blinked up at Lindhall, who smiled. "This one is a great three-horn. All the horn-faced lizards had some type of facial protrusions. The three-horns and one-horns also had a simple or ornate bone frill behind the skull. This fellow was the largest of his family—the others varied from eighteen to twenty feet in length."

She saw a massive, curved fan of bone behind the long horns. "Neck armor?" she asked. The hand with which she touched the skull itched.

"Apparently."

"And they weren't lizards?"

"No. The appearance was reptilian, but most were quite agile, and less vulnerable to changes in temperature than modern lizards are. They seem to have behaved more like birds than lizards. We know so much thanks to those seers who are able to look back in time. The real world has little use for them, but in a university they are in great demand."

"Nobility—" A slave had appeared in the doorway. Lindhall went to speak to him.

Slowly enough that at first Daine thought she imagined it, the skull turned to train a single eye socket on her. The girl stared at it, appalled. She had missed that flare of white light in the flicker of the overhead globes. "Hold still," she hissed, flapping her hands at it. "Quit moving!"

The head cocked slightly to one side, as if to ask why she made such an odd request. Carefully the dinosaur raised a bony foot and wriggled its three toes.

"Daine, are you all right here?" asked Lindhall. "There's something I must tend to."

"I'll be fine," she replied, not taking her eyes from the skeleton. She watched it for some time after the mage left, but the bones' period of movement was over.

That was fun, Zek remarked. Why were you angry with it? Touch some more of them.

Dead should *stay* dead, she replied silently and firmly. I will not touch *any* of them. To emphasize her point, she thrust her hands into her pockets, where they could start no more trouble, and looked around.

To the right of the three-horn, where the large hall connected with a smaller one, she discovered a far different dinosaur. Ten inches tall, it stood beside a nest of eggs, some whole, some broken.

"A mountain-runner lizard. We don't know what killed him, but at least we kept him with his nest." Lindhall had returned. "There's an adult of his kind standing guard." Daine looked where he pointed, and found a somewhat larger skeleton, eight feet long, peering at her. They were clearly the same animal, and there did seem to be a protective air about the big one. It stood in front of a doorway that led to a chamber full of smaller dinosaurs.

"They almost look as if they could move, don't they?" the mage asked.

Daine winced. "How did you fit the bones together?" she asked. "Did you find them like this?"

"The process is fascinating," replied Lindhall. "It was developed by the School of Bardic Arts and the School of Magecraft. If you understand magical theory, you know that things once bound to one another retain the occult tie, even when separated. Knowing that, the bards and mages create special musical pipes. Played correctly, they call the bones together to form the original owner."

Daine nodded; she had seen Numair do the same thing with skeletons at home. Together she and Lindhall roamed the collection. Behind the three-horn she had briefly awakened, she discovered another, smaller three-horn, whose neck frill was larger and flatter and whose brow horns curved up, rather than pointed straight ahead. A brass plaque set into the base of his stand identified him as a bull three-horn, listing his height, weight, and the place he was found. Following this line of skeleton stands, which ran down the center of this branch of the hall, she discovered other horn-faced lizards, whose neck frills grew more and more ornate: a spiked three-horn whose frill was topped by large, curved spines; the thick-nosed horn-face with extra bone plates instead of a nose horn; and the so-called well-horned three-horn, who boasted down-turned spikes on his frill. None of them were less than eighteen feet in length, from nose to tail tip.

"Don't you wish you could have seen them when they were alive?" the girl asked Zek.

The marmoset, as fascinated as she was, shuddered. Daine translated his answer aloud for Lindhall: "Only if they were grass eaters. Even so, I should prefer to see them from the top of a very tall tree." The mage laughed at that.

They saw bony-headed skeletons like giant, long-legged crocodiles, covered with back and head spikes and wearing solid bone clubs on their tail tips. All were more than ten feet long and belonged to a family called armored lizards. They gave way to cousins, plated lizards, each with leaf-shaped plates and spikes running along their backs. These, too, were giants, ranging from thirteen to thirty feet in length. Each one's tail was laden with a collection of spikes that looked like a mace.

"There's so much learning here," she remarked softly. "The king's trying to build a university to equal yours, but it'll take years. And when it comes to things like this . . ."

"Once Carthak was famous largely for its treasures." Lindhall's voice was equally soft. "It was a citadel of learning, arts, and culture. It still has those things in abundance, but now the army and the navy garner the attention of the world and of the emperor."

When she glanced to her left, her jaw dropped. The skeleton before her, labeled Great Snake-neck, was ninety feet long. Its tiny head, at the end of an extremely long neck, stared down at her from nearly twenty-five feet in the air. With small teeth only at the front of a light jaw, and eyes that faced to the sides like the three-horns, she knew it was a plant eater—"A very *large* plant eater," she told Zek quietly. The marmoset, who had climbed on top of her head for a better look, agreed. Behind this one, she saw other snake-necks, though none so large.

Near the snake-neck was another, frightening skeleton, for all he was only two-thirds as long as his neighbor. His eye sockets faced forward, and his heavy jaws bore a collection of sharp and jagged teeth, marks of a meat eater. He had cousins, too, Daine saw.

They found a cluster of duck-billed skeletons and, behind them, dinosaurs who sported odd, bony crests on their skulls. One reminded her of a basilisk, only the skeleton had a long, freestanding head knob, like a large bone feather on its owner's head.

"Now *there's* a hat," she remarked. Zek sniffed with disdain.

She had viewed nearly ten crested skeletons when she found a second hall in the rear of the collection. Curious, she ventured inside, Lindhall behind her. Here stood a double row of elephants. The four closest ones were strange-looking, with hides covered in shaggy fur and tusks curved up in an incomplete circle. The next four elephants had four tusks; two sharp ones on top, two smaller ones on the bottom.

"Mammoths," Lindhall told her. "The world used to be much colder, as I'm sure Numair has taught you. In those days, elephants needed fur."

"I don't understand. Were these alive once?

How are they here, in their skins? Are they in a magical sleep?"

"They were brought from ice fields in the distant south," explained the mage. "They froze to death, and the ice preserved them until we could work the spells to keep them as they are. I use *we* in a general sense, since they were found a century to two centuries ago."

Daine stared at the great animals. "You have such wonders here. I almost wish I could stay longer and see them all."

"I noticed you said *almost*. I can't say that I blame you, though I wish that were not the case. I have a feeling we could learn as much from you as you might learn from us."

Daine laughed at that. "I doubt it, Master Lindhall. I'm just a girl with wild magic, when all's said and done. When I leave in six days, Carthak won't even remember I was here."

Lindhall smiled. "But *I* will remember, and so will the emperor's birds."

"I couldn't ask for more," she said with a grin.

Nightfall saw her in a lilac muslin dress and the long, sleeveless surcoat that had just come into fashion in the north. Hers was gold silk, as frail as a butterfly's wing, with a beaded hem to make it hang properly. The outfit made her nervous. She was sure that at any moment she would step on the hem and rip it out.

She and the adults were in a reception room with floors tiled in squares of night-blue lapis lazuli and white marble. The talks were over for the day. While the guests sipped fruit juices and nibbled delicacies, Daine waited for Numair to finish a conversation with the ambassador from Galla. At last that gentleman bowed to him, and wandered off.

Turning, Numair smiled. "You're becoming a young lady." He brushed a curl from her cheek. "If I'm not careful, you'll be grown and married to a deserving fellow before I realize it."

She ignored this as being too silly for comment. "When can we talk?" she demanded. "You've got to find a way, somehow. It may be fair important."

"'It *may be*'?"

"I don't know. I'm not sure." She thought for a moment and decided she had to take a chance and give him some clue as to what she wanted. "I spoke to the badger yesterday."

That startled him. "Where?"

"Aboard ship. In my cabin. He was"—she groped for a phrase—"not himself."

Long brows drew together. "*Not*—" The doors swung open. "Very well—I'll try to develop some opportunity," he said quickly. "They've scheduled these meetings so tightly we barely have time to scratch, let alone talk."

The group of people surged forward, taking them with it. In the banquet hall the emperor waited beside a long, low railing made of gold. Behind it large, open windows gave a view of the sky and a small lake. Ozorne was as splendid as on the night before, although his theme now was silver, from the beads on his hair to the paint on his eyelids His long underrobe was silver cloth. Over it he wore a black velvet drape like a cloak that covered his back to the knees and left one shoulder bare. Strings of flashing opals linked the free end of the drape to his wrist. He blazed with gems at fingers and toes. Silver armlets like giant snakes wound about his wrists.

Now, through the windows, two Stormwings dropped in to perch on the gold bar. One was an older male with a pinkish-gray face, tight lips, and small brown eyes. He wore a black iron crown on thinning dark hair. The younger male was green-eyed and lean-faced. He wore bones braided into his long blond hair. While Ozorne and the crowned male spoke privately, the younger one shifted from foot to foot, clearly not pleased to be there.

Numair frowned. "Daine, isn't that—from Dunlath?"

"None other," she said. The last time she had seen the green-eyed Stormwing, he had been in her bow sight. "How nice for us all. We can have a reunion."

FOUR

STRANGE
CONVERSATIONS

❧❈❦

Ozorne beckoned everyone forward. "Honored
guests, we present King Jokhun Foulreek, our ally
from the Stone Tree nation of Stormwings, and his
vassal, Lord Rikash Moonsword. They will join us."
He didn't seem to care whether or not his guests
wished to meet Stormwings. Coolly he presented each
of them to the immortals by name. Duke Gareth, bowing to them in greeting, caught a faceful of Stormwing
odor and coughed.

Daine watched the immortals as the introductions unfolded. Jokhun stared at those being presented,
not bothering to speak to them. The only time he
showed emotion was when he saw Kitten: he frowned,
and murmured to his companion. Rikash glanced over.

Seeing Kitten, he found Daine and scowled.

"His face will freeze like that if he isn't careful," muttered Daine, shifting Zek from the crook of her arm to her shoulder. In Dunlath a year ago, Rikash had acted for Ozorne in the plot to overthrow King Jonathan, and had lost to Daine and Numair.

They were the last of the group to be presented to the immortals. Jokhun paid them no more attention than he might a fly on the wall, but Rikash bated. "We've met," he said coldly.

"*Moonsword?*" She had never known his last name. "That's very pretty."

The Stormwing grimaced. "My ancestors were a sentimental lot. I know you, too, mage," he told Numair. "I remember the onion bomb you threw at me."

Ozorne smiled. "Lord Rikash, did you not say the wild animals of Dunlath behaved oddly?"

"I certainly did," the Stormwing replied.

"You have Daine to thank," said the emperor. "She is bonded to animals through wild magic."

The look on Rikash's face was one of mixed rage, chagrin, and laughter. King Jokhun turned watery eyes on Daine. "Some day we must meet less formally—when you are not protected by your host." There was an annoying hint of a whine in the king's nasal voice. "We will discuss a number of Stormwing deaths that are laid to your account."

"Anytime," Daine told him, smiling as sweetly as she could.

Numair bowed and nudged her to do the same. Once they were away from the emperor and the immortals, he murmured, "This visit gets better all the time, doesn't it?"

Daine nodded. She wasn't sure how she felt about seeing Rikash again. He was a Stormwing, a race of immortals she hated, but personally he hadn't seemed to be such a bad sort.

"*There* you are." Varice, in a red satin gown that fitted like her skin, took charge of them. Numair she guided to the very end of the head table, far to Ozorne's right. The only seat next to his was the one she would occupy herself. Daine, feeling cross, realized immediately that the woman had arranged things so that she would have Numair to herself.

With Numair seated, Varice led Daine to the opposite end of the main board, where Prince Kaddar waited. Daine curtsied slightly, pleased by the elegant sigh of her skirts, and once more silently thanked the queen for her wardrobe. She never could have faced these elegant people in the clothes she normally dressed up in—a blue wool gown for winter, and a pink cotton for summer. Even in *these* garments, she couldn't hope to match the prince. He was as finely dressed as he had been on the ship, in a calf-length robe of fine wool tinted a delicate aquamarine, and a shoulder drape of white silk shot through with gold threads. He glittered with jewels; against his dark face, his eyes could easily have been black gems, for all the emotion they showed as he bowed her to her seat.

"You'll be fine with His Highness," Varice told Daine, and left them there.

Kitten, unnoticed by Varice, sat up on her hindquarters and chirped, drawing a smile from the prince. "I don't know if your food will be very good for her," he admitted.

"She eats anything," Daine replied. "Trust me."

Kaddar lifted a hand, and a male slave appeared by his elbow. An exchange of whispers resulted in a stool being produced for Kitten. Discovering that she could see over the table if she sat on it, she cheeped and whistled softly.

"She's thanking you," explained the girl. "And so do I. It was a nice thing for you to do."

A smile tugged at Kaddar's mouth. "I read that dragons are curious about everything."

Daine nodded. "They understand as much as two-leggers. More, because they know the speech of animals as well as human tongues. I can't speak dragon, but if she wants me to understand her, she makes her meaning clear."

Ozorne clapped his hands. Slaves began to move in streams, bringing dishes to the diners so that they could select what they wanted. Female slaves, wearing loincloths and nothing else, went from guest to guest, filling wine goblets.

For Daine and Kaddar, the dragon was clearly a safe topic of conversation. Her wariness of him began to fade when she found he asked intelligent questions, and listened to her answers. The moment he felt his friend relax, Zek popped out of the sleeve where he'd been hiding and climbed onto Daine's shoulder. For a moment the prince struggled with well-bred dismay, then suddenly grinned, for the first time looking like a young man not much older than she was.

"Anyone else?" he asked. "A sparrow in your pocket? A snake as your belt?"

Daine blushed and looked down. "No one else. Zek just doesn't like to be parted from me. I think he's so relieved to be in my care that he doesn't want to let me out of his sight."

"Understandably," replied Kaddar, stretching a hand out to the marmoset. Zek observed his fingers with the same grave air as he did everything, then climbed on. With that, the ice was broken between prince and guest. They talked about a number of subjects, comparing stories of their lives. The only awkward moment came when a slave arrived with the meat course: antelope steaks.

Daine swallowed hard. She had managed skewers of roast duck and peppers, smoked salmon and herring, and tarts filled with cheese and ham. She had even tried snails in garlic butter. At the risk of giving offense, she could *not* eat this. Worse, she knew Kaddar was bound by social custom to eat only the things she did. "I'm sorry," she whispered. "I can't."

Kaddar frowned. "Please? They're my favorite."

Her cheeks were hot. "Look—don't mind me. You go ahead."

"It would be churlish of me to eat something that causes *you* distress." Kaddar sighed, and shook his head at the slave, who removed the offending dish. "At least tell me why."

Daine rubbed her face tiredly. "What do you know about me? About what I can do?"

"Well, you heal animals, and talk to them inside your head, and they do your bidding."

"You won't like that," Daine told Zek, who was investigating a small dish of hot peppers. To Kaddar she said, " I *ask* them to do things, most of the time. I don't like to order them around. Would *your* friends like it if you always told them what to do?"

Thin lips twitched. "Point taken. So you ask them to do things and you talk to them and heal."

"I can also *be* them. I learned how to shape-shift a year ago. My first mistake was when I thought I'd try deer shape, one day last winter. See, I didn't know the royal huntsmen would be out, looking for some game—"

"I think I can see where this is going." He watched her with interest, leaning his cheek on one hand. "So you can't eat deer—"

"Last spring we were rounding up killer unicorns, and bandits cornered me. I'd gotten separated from Numair and panicked. I changed into a wild goose." Remembering, she sighed.

"Big mistake?" There was sympathy in his voice.

"They got me with a barbed arrow. I escaped, but almost lost the arm. Anyway, ever since I could take on a creature's mind or shape, I can't eat game of any kind. I eat fish, and domestic meat, like beef and chicken, but then, I never wanted to be a fish, and I close out the thoughts of barnyard animals. I'm sorry. I used to hunt and eat game with the best of them, but not anymore."

The prince looked thoughtful. "So there are drawbacks to your power."

"There's drawbacks to *any* power, Your Highness."

Musicians had entered the room as they talked. Now, in the cleared space before the main board, acrobats started a whirling, athletic dance. Kaddar was feeding bits of smoked eel to Kitten, leaving the girl free to admire the performance. When it was over, she remarked that she'd never thought two-leggers had that much bend in them, which made her companion laugh.

The acrobats were replaced by a number of unusually small black men and women and their animal companions. One old man held the leashes for a pair of tall, rangy, spotted cats. Twin girls carried an assortment of monkeys, while dogs of varying sizes and colors followed the entire company. The minute they saw Daine, all of the animals broke from their handlers to go to her. Quickly the girl stood and walked around to the front of the table, knowing that they would knock the table over to say hello if she didn't. Zek squeaked in fear and burrowed under Kaddar's drape as one of the cats rose on his hind legs to plant his forepaws on the girl's shoulders.

Daine petted her new friend. "Hello—you're a beauty, aren't you?" Silently she asked, How do they treat you, these trainers of yours? Do they hurt you to teach you things? In Tortall she'd found that many animal trainers used pain to make lessons stick.

The animals gathered around were quick to reassure her. Our two-leggers are wise, the cheetah male who had laid his paws on her shoulders said. They speak almost as clearly as other beast-People do. They never hurt us.

Daine saw why as the trainers, none of them taller than her earlobe, came to her behind their animals. Flashes of copper fire—wild magic—sparked in their eyes and around their hands as they chattered in a language that combined clicks and whistles with wordlike sounds. One woman coaxed the cheetah back from Daine, but the monkeys and dogs crowded into his place.

"They are Banjiku tribesmen, from Zallara in the south." Emperor Ozorne had left his dais and come over to the group. "They are saying that they think you are a god."

Someone laughed. Daine turned red. "Please excuse me, but I'm no such thing."

"You are god," said the oldest man in heavily accented Common. "I am Tano, the cat-man. The cats come to me, also to my wife. We have cat-children." Daine realized his face was tattooed with feline whiskers and ears. "Cholombi is dog-man." The man thus named raised his hands to show dog-pad tattoos on his palms. "Twins are monkey-girls." The young women with monkeylike tattoos bowed and grinned at Daine. "See? We all one-kind beast. If you are not god, then you god-child. Yes? Which god?"

Her blush worsened, and Daine knelt to bury her face in the female cheetah's fur. The cat chirped.

"I don't know who my da is." She wouldn't have minded telling these nice humans in private, but doing so in front of the emperor hurt. "My ma died before she could tell me."

The Banjiku chattered briefly.

"They think it's too bad you don't know your father." Numair had also come over. "They wish they knew his name. They would sacrifice to him and ask him to visit their daughters as he did your mother."

Daine was about to protest that she was *not* the child of a god when she remembered visions she'd had since her mother's death, of her ma doing everyday tasks in a forest cottage. All included a horned man with hints of green in his darkly tanned skin. Could it be . . .?

Ozorne watched Daine and Numair, face

unreadable as he waved a jeweled fan idly. "The Banjiku skill with animals is legendary," he remarked. "It was through their legends that your teacher came to believe in the existence of wild magic. It seems he was right—in this case, at least. And now, if they would be so kind as to do the work for which they have been summoned?"

The Banjiku bowed to Daine, and moved into place for their performance. She returned to her seat and watched the entire thing without seeing it. Surely it wasn't possible that her da, unknown for all these years, was a god! And yet—Ma had always told her that she'd been conceived in the forest on Beltane, and that her father was a stranger.

Applause brought her back to her surroundings. The Banjiku and their animals had performed beautifully and were leaving the room. Daine nodded when the cat man winked at her. They would see each other again.

The banquet over, the emperor's guests returned to the reception area. Musicians played in a corner while slaves offered pastries and drinks to everyone. Daine was talking about the habits of griffins with Numair and Lindhall when a slave approached, pushing a wheeled cart. Perched on its surface was Rikash. Jokhun had left during the banquet, but evidently his vassal had other plans.

"Go away," he ordered the slave, then nodded to Numair and Daine.

Zek, on Daine's shoulder, craned forward to stare at the immortal, holding a tiny paw over his nose.

Rikash grimaced at him. "Still consorting with tree rats, I see."

Daine smiled. Rikash's last encounter with her

had involved a squirrel named Flicker. "Now you know what disease the Dunlath animals had."

"Was that you, shape-changed?" he asked.

The girl shook her head. "Not then. I had just learned how to put myself within an animal's mind. Flicker and that eagle were helping me."

"Shape-shifting goes with that skill," the Stormwing lord pointed out. "I would have thought you would know that by now."

Numair grinned. "She does."

"How delightful for us all," the immortal said, voice extremely dry. "I must remember to give Tortall a wide berth."

Idly he scratched the brass that sheathed the top of the cart under his feet, drawing squeals from it with his steel claws. Daine gritted her teeth; Numair winced.

Lindhall bowed. "If you will excuse me?" He patted the humans on the shoulders and left.

"We were having a nice talk before you came," Daine informed Rikash.

"I am devastated to have ruined your fun." Looking down, he asked in a very different voice, "Do you hear from Maura of Dunlath?"

"She writes Daine often," said Numair.

"She misses you," Daine told the Stormwing. "She says her guardian is nice, but he doesn't have your sense of humor. You *could* visit her, you know. She'd like that."

Rikash pried up a bit of the metal he stood on. "I must remain here with King Jokhun, for now," he replied. "I believe my stay will not endure for much longer, and then I may be free to pursue my own life.

If that is the case, I would like to see Maura again."

"Oh?" Numair asked. "It sounds as if you anticipate a momentous event. What is it?"

Rikash looked at him sharply, then grinned. "Finish your business here quickly, mage. Carthak's unhealthy. It will get worse before it gets better." To Daine he said, "Frankly, I'm surprised to find either of you at this court. It is wise to make a peace with the man who tried to overthrow your king?"

"It's very wise, if the greatest army and navy are on your enemy's side," Numair said dryly.

Daine toyed with the silver claw at her throat. "It's no different from what you did, is it?"

Rikash stamped the pulled-up brass into place. "What is that supposed to mean?"

"Don't play innocent." It was such a relief to be able to speak her mind to *someone*. Rikash, at least, would never complain of her lack of diplomacy. "We've *seen* the menagerie, *Lord* Rikash. They have one of your queens and her consort there."

Kitten whistled confirmation, and silenced when the Stormwing glared at her.

"You are wrong," he said flatly. "There are no queens missing from the other flocks, and I have no queen in mine. The old one was slain in combat by King Jokhun, after our custom."

"Then maybe the prince was mistaken," said Numair with a shrug. "He seemed convinced that Barzha was a queen."

Rikash's steel feathers ruffled, then settled into place with a series of muted clicks. "*What* did you say her name was?"

"Barzha," Daine replied as she scratched

Kitten behind an ear. "Her consort was named Hebakh. The prince said their being in a cage here was the price of the alliance with King Jokhun."

Rikash's frown deepened. Suddenly he leaped from the cart, wings pumping. Guests scattered as he flew through the window into the night. In his wake, nobles and slaves alike struggled to repair their dignities.

"I wonder where he was going," murmured Numair. "Is it possible he did not know of Ozorne's special menagerie? And what was that about the health of Carthak?"

Daine chewed her lower lip. She had a feeling Rikash meant the same thing the badger had.

I don't like all this, Zek told her. Back home, we know the feeling of a coming storm, and we hide. This feels like a really bad storm in the air, but it doesn't smell like water.

What does it smell like? Daine asked silently as Numair went to find Lindhall.

Zek thought for a moment or two, tiny nostrils flaring as he took deep breaths of the air. *Fire*, he said at last. A storm of fire.

Soon after that, Daine found the emperor at her elbow. "Veralidaine, good evening. The birds have been left all day, as you ordered," he said, offering Kitten one of his rings to play with. "Can they be visited tomorrow?"

Daine nodded. Off and on during the day she had called to the aviary with her magic, touching the minds of the occupants to see how they did. "They'll be up with the sun if they can see it. I should warn you, they'll be fair hungry. Figure they'll need at least double, prob'ly triple rations."

The emperor smiled. Daine realized that his watchful air vanished only when he talked about his birds. "They shall have them," he promised. "You may ask any price of me, any reward."

"I got the only reward I want—knowing they're better. I'm not always lucky enough to save animals when they're sick. Sometimes they die, no matter what I do for them. It happens often enough that I never get tired of making them well again."

Kitten offered the ring back to Ozorne with an inquiring whistle. Smiling, he replaced it on his finger, then vanished. Kitten squawked her irritation.

Daine sighed, feeling as if she'd been clamped in a vise for hours. She yawned and stretched. "Let's get some air, Kit."

With a cheerful whistle, the dragon led the way onto the terrace. Prince Kaddar found them there, watching the moon rise.

"This is beautiful," Daine said, waving at the formal garden lying off the terrace. It was laid out in patterns, with hedges and flowers forming precise, graceful curves and spirals. "We don't have anything that's this fine."

"Your king spends his money on very different things," replied the prince, watching the silver-gilded pattern. Before she could ask what he meant, he said, "I have to go, but I wanted to ask, would you like a guided tour in the morning? I could meet you when your friends leave for the talks. Your Duke Gareth said it was all right, when my uncle asked him."

Daine inspected his face. "Are you sure you don't mind? I would be at loose ends, it's true, but I can always amuse myself."

He grinned, teeth flashing wickedly. "I would like something to do, frankly. We're between quarters at the imperial university, and there's little going on for me until classes start."

"Then I accept with pleasure," she replied, seeing no resentment in him.

"I'll come for you tomorrow, when the talks open," he promised, bowing over her hand. He left her there, and once more the girl, marmoset, and dragon had the terrace to themselves.

Taking advantage of her solitude, Daine went down and around the side of the steps, where the raised wall of the terrace met the ground. Out of sight in this niche, she slid off her surcoat, folding it neatly and giving it to Kitten to hold. Zek she placed in an opening of the marble banister, where he would be safe. Unencumbered, she let the garden bats come to say hello, as they had clamored to do since she had walked into the open. They arrived a dozen at a time, to cling to her hair, dress, hands, and shoulders, talking in their high, clear voices. She loved bats, but had learned years ago that few humans agreed. It was always better to sit and gossip with them in private.

She didn't keep them long. There were still pounds of insects for them to catch, and she ought to return to the silk-and-perfume air inside. She sighed as, one by one, the bats left her, and wished them good hunting. More than anything, she would have liked to shape-change and go with them, but she had the feeling that Alanna and Numair would frown if she did. That was funny in itself, because Alanna liked elegant parties far less than Daine did.

"And I'm getting fair tired of them myself," she

murmured to Zek. "Kit, would you do the neaten-up trick?"

The dragon drew herself up. Suddenly her eyes glowed silver; she made a soft, cooing sound. Curl by curl, Daine's hair, mussed by the small mammals that had clung to it, straightened to lie neatly under its lilac velvet ribbon. Small threads in her gown, pulled free by claws, plunged back into their proper weave once more. Little spots, the kinds left by creatures who never had to worry about clothes, vanished. Creases flattened; pockets of musty odor evaporated. It never would have worked on a dress saturated with bird droppings, but it was perfect for little messes. Daine had discovered this bit of dragon magic months ago, when Kitten fixed her appearance after she'd been called from riding to hear a noble's complaint about winged horses.

"Thanks!" The girl accepted the surcoat from the dragon and donned it. "Why did you do it so quiet? You—"

The dragon held a claw to her muzzle, signaling Daine to hush, and pointed to the terrace behind them. Confused, Daine peered through the openings in the rail. In the shadows where terrace met building, hidden from the view of those inside, was the old slave woman. Perched on the rail in front of her, talking softly and fiercely, was Rikash.

Daine frowned. She wasn't sure which was odder: the conversation itself, or the parties to it. Why would Rikash talk to a slave, *any* slave? He was hopping in fury, waving his wings as he tried to make a point; the slave shook her head. A slave, refusing an order from *anyone*?

Something else troubled Daine. She was sure this was the slave she had seen that morning, but now the woman's shaved head was covered by stubbly hair. Her rough gown hung from both shoulders, not just one, and her sandals were leather, not straw. They laced all the way up to those bony knees.

Suddenly the old woman produced a gleaming silver cup. Showing it to Rikash, she rattled it, producing the unmistakable sound of dice.

Daine collected Zek and marched up the short flight of steps, Kitten beside her. Rikash would get the poor old thing into trouble, and the gods alone knew what might happen to her if one of her masters saw this.

"Seven," the slave remarked. She and Rikash stared at the flat surface of the rail beside the upended dice cup. "You win. For now." She turned, and winked at the approaching Daine. "Push this bad boy off the rail, there's a dear," she said. "He's going to beat a poor old lady out of her life's savings."

Grabbing the dice cup, she placed a hand on the rail and nimbly vaulted over. When Daine ran to stare down at her probable landing site, sure the woman had broken an ankle at least, she was nowhere to be seen.

"Who was that?" demanded the girl of Rikash. "What were you doing with her?"

The immortal's eyes danced. "You saw her? Who was she?"

"The poor old slave they made clean my rooms this morning!"

The Stormwing guffawed. "Oh, indeed?" he said when he had calmed down. "Well, if you want to believe that, go right ahead. You'll learn."

"There's something you're not telling me."

"No, it's *her*. Ask *her* what she's not telling you. And be careful. She's tricky."

Something glittered on the rail where the dice cup had been. It was a metal feather. "Are you molting?" asked Daine. "*Do* you molt? You don't *look* like you lost a feather."

"Never mind that," he snapped. The girl shrugged and turned to go. "No—wait. Please."

She moved to stand upwind of him. "Well?" she asked, when he didn't seem inclined to speak again. "Anything?" He remained silent, frowning in thought. "You left in a hurry before."

"I would apologize for my rudeness, if I had manners. Happily, I don't. You ought to try *our* shape sometime. People expect you to be crude. I'm told it's liberating for most humans."

She snorted. "You won't catch *me* that way. Numair warned me what happens when humans take on the shapes of immortals—we can't change back."

"Wanted to try dragon's shape, did you?"

She stuck her tongue out at him, and he smiled.

"I wasn't lying—about the Stormwings in the menagerie." She fiddled with the feather on the rail, careful not to touch the edges. If it was one of his, it would cut better than a knife.

"I know. I saw them—Barzha and Hebakh. They told me how they came to be there."

"I'm sorry."

"I am angry, not sorry. Jokhun lied when he took over our flock. He said he killed Barzha and Hebakh in combat, and their bodies dropped into one of your oceans." Rikash had begun to rock from foot to foot; his green eyes sparkled angrily as his feathers bristled. "We believed him because we were tired of battles. . . . Stormwings—tired of battles! We betrayed her, just as he did. And to find *this* smiling, lying mortal in league with him—"

Humans came onto the terrace. Globes sailed overhead to light the darkness. Ozorne was in the forefront, with Alanna on his arm and Duke Gareth on his other side. Seeing them, he came over.

"Follow my lead," Rikash muttered softly. "Please."

She looked at him, puzzled, but nodded. She didn't think he would get her into trouble, enemy or no. She did have to admit their talks here weren't hostile—more like the exchanges between friends who enjoyed a good argument. That was enough to make her head spin.

"Veralidaine and Lord Rikash," said the emperor, smiling mischievously. "Now here is an odd pairing. We had heard this young lady hates Stormwings."

The immortal shrugged. "We value a good enemy, Imperial Majesty. If I may be permitted to say so, opponents come in many guises. It is well to get to know them all."

The emperor nodded. Alanna frowned, looking from him to Rikash to Daine. The girl shrugged to let her friend know that she hadn't the least idea of what the Stormwing meant.

"Forgive me for my departure earlier, but I had thought of a gift to make to you, as a personal token of my appreciation for our association. It would be my very great pleasure if you would accept it." Rikash nodded toward the feather. "Give it to him, if you please."

Daine carefully picked up the feather and offered it to Ozorne, who smiled and took it, holding it with care. "Is some *particular* virtue attached to this gift?" he asked.

"Indeed," replied the Stormwing. "Any such token from an immortal has—qualities." Daine touched her throat, brushing the chain for the badger's claw.

"Heed me," Rikash went on. "If ever you are in peril of life and throne—and it must be peril that drives you, not curiosity—take this feather and thrust it into your flesh. When it mixes with your blood, you will fly from your enemies as if winged with steel, and escape beyond the Black God's reach for all time."

Ozorne replied evenly. "Neither our life nor our throne is in peril, Lord Rikash, nor do we believe they will ever be. Our hold on our empire is firm indeed."

"But the wheel turns," Rikash answered. "What is up may come down; what is brought low may rise. The gods are not fickle—but they have been known to change their minds. One day you will know the value of Stormwing esteem." He bowed to the emperor, then looked at Daine. "I never know what to make of you," he said dryly. "I suppose I never will."

He took off, and vanished into the dark. Daine watched for the last sweep of his wings. You aren't alone, she thought.

The sun was not even above the horizon when she woke the next morning. It would be an hour or more before Numair and the others began to stir, and Kitten and Zek were still deep in slumber. With no mind to go back to sleep and no books to read, she decided to visit the emperor's birds. Leaving the dragon and marmoset, she asked the mousers and rat catchers for a path to the aviary. The one they gave her took her through gardens to a door in a glass wall. It was open, with no magical lock to undo. She slipped inside and closed the door softly behind her.

The first to come meet her were small, green birds with red faces and tails, called parrot finches. They eyed her from a branch several yards away before dropping to her shoulders. The next arrivals were unlike any bird she'd ever seen, finches who looked as if they had rolled on an artist's paint board, sporting red, yellow-orange, or black faces, aqua collars and tails, emerald wings, yellow bellies, and purple breasts. Twittering, they hopped on nearby twigs and on her fingers, eyes bright in their vivid faces. What had she done to herself, to be dressed as a dirt-walker? they asked.

I was born this way, she told them silently, hearing quiet male voices from the direction of the door into the palace. I'm a two-legger *and* People.

The finches were not sure they approved.

Red-crested cardinals arrived. With them came tanagers whose plumage shimmered green and gold or green and blue. None of the birds could remember much of their first encounter with Daine; they had been too sick. Now they inspected her eagerly.

Greetings over, a tanager pair invited Daine to come see their nest. Finding the stair nearby, she accepted the invitation, ascending as quietly as she could.

Most of the birds stayed with her, though some left to get food. Chattering, being rude to their companions, they explained that the Man fed and talked to them. He came at all hours, but he didn't wake them if it was dark, and he always brought their favorite treats in his pockets.

Daine shook her head. The more she saw or heard of the emperor, the more confused she felt.

At the topmost level of the aviary, she found a very small colony of leafbirds, some with blue-violet stripes breaking their bodies into halves, the top green and the bottom orange-gold, some with orange heads and red edges to their wings. Here, too, were royal bluebirds, who appeared drab until they turned in the light to reveal wings and tails of a blue so intense it seemed to glow.

She was beginning to see why humans from the western islands to the eastern kingdoms of the Roof of the World came to see the emperor's aviary. These birds were like feathered jewels. She also noted the care they received, which impressed her more than all the emperor's wealth.

Checking the sun's position, she saw there was plenty of time before she needed to return for breakfast. I'm going to change, she told her new friends. Don't worry—I won't hurt anyone.

Removing her boots, she crouched on the platform and closed her eyes, remaking herself as a starling. Her body shrank swiftly, clothes falling away. She sprouted bronze-and-black speckled feathers, and grew a yellow beak. Her legs became stilts, her feet three long toes. Done, she ruffled her feathers and cackled, then took to the air.

The leafbirds joined her. The parrot finches came behind, twittering in their eagerness to show her the nooks and crannies they had discovered. The birds had nests tucked everywhere in this huge room. Not only had they made use of the trees and bushes that were natural choices, but they had built in the joints of the enameled green metal strips that supported the panes of glass forming the ceiling and most of the walls. Only one wall was stone. This the birds followed down, headed for the Man and his treats. While the food and water dishes throughout the aviary were kept full, the Man always had something extra good.

She was so wrapped up in the flock that she nearly followed them to beg a treat from Ozorne. Only when she saw him and a newly arrived companion did she back up hurriedly, almost colliding with the finches. The emperor would know that a starling did not belong with his exotic treasures. She perched, concealing herself in a clump of leaves. Ozorne's companion was Numair.

Once out of view, she changed the shape of her head and ears, becoming more like an owl than a starling. Now she could hear the men clearly.

"—checked the baths, and the gardens, and she is nowhere to be found. If she is here and you are concealing her from me—"

"Be assured, Draper, she is *not* here. We had hoped she would be, to see how our birds have improved."

"If they have, then you have no further need of her. We *all* prefer that you leave her in peace."

"*We* are inclined to give her grace and favor."

Ozorne's tone was haughty. "She has served us well, and we wish to reward her."

"She requires no rewards of your providing, *Your Imperial Majesty*." Never before had the girl heard Numair sound this harsh. "She is well enough as she is."

"Such heat over a girl child, and one without family or connections to recommend her. Why concern yourself in her affairs? You will forget she exists the moment some rare tome of magic comes into your hands, or some arcane toy. That has always been your way. You take up with someone, make them feel you are their sworn friend, then turn on them the moment you have what you wanted from them."

"How like you to see it in those terms," retorted Numair. "She is my *student*. You will never understand that. You never could sustain so profound a tie. Once you gained your throne, you decided you no longer required mere *human* bonds."

Stop it, Numair! Daine thought, watching the emperor's eyes flicker with some odd emotion. Can't you see he *wants* to upset you?

"Human bonds," Ozorne said quietly, studying gilded nails. "I am certain you and your lovely *student* have a most profound bond. Must you share a bed with her animals as well as with her?"

Numair's hand lashed, and slammed against the suddenly visible sheet of emerald fire that appeared around the emperor. Lights flared where he struck; he yanked the hand back, rubbing it. "If you interfere with her, if you harm her in any way, it will be a breach of the peace accords." His breath came hard under the words. "All of the Eastern Lands will unite to destroy you." He stalked out of the aviary, dark cheeks burning crimson.

Daine was breathless. What had *possessed* him to hit Ozorne? The suggestion that Numair was interested in her for sexual reasons had been made before; he'd laughed it off. If *anyone* took offense over such things, it was Daine herself, and only because the speaker did not understand Numair was too honorable ever to take advantage of her.

The emperor remained oddly still for several long moments after Numair's exit. Wondering if he were in a trance, she changed once more, until she looked at him with an eagle's eyes. Now she saw fine-pearled sweat on Ozorne's face. The pupils of his eyes had opened all the way up, in defiance of the light that streamed through the glass walls. His breathing came deep and soft; his mouth trembled slightly.

Slowly he lifted his right hand and held it palm up. Emerald light in four different streamers spiraled from the air before him, forming a small and fiery cyclone in his open palm. Bit by bit it solidified into a human shape. It was Numair dressed in rags, hair tumbling around his face.

When the image was complete, Ozorne, left hand palm-down, began to crush it. The image shrieked, its tiny voice a perfect copy of Numair's own. It screamed and screamed as Ozorne bore down. The emperor was smiling.

Daine fled to her clothes. She heard the image's cries as she became human, dressed, and left the aviary as silently as she could. Racing back to the guest wing, even with her hands over her ears, she thought the screams followed her.

❀ ❀ ❀

Numair said nothing when she came late to breakfast, picking at his food as she told the others she'd paid a predawn visit to the aviary and gotten lost coming back. If anyone noticed that she barely ate, or that she trembled so hard that she spilled her juice, they made no comment. Afterward, as they were preparing to go, Numair said, "Daine, you asked to speak to me alone. Let's go to my room."

Alanna heard. "Then I go, too."

"It isn't needful—it's just a magic thing," explained the girl. She'd prefer to confront him about what she'd seen with no witnesses.

"If you visit a man's room, you need a chaperon." The lady knight shook her head. "Really, Numair, you know Carthakis. They think an unveiled woman is no better than she ought to be. Until we leave here, you can't talk with her unless she is chaperoned or you can manage it in public."

"A fine thing, when I can't talk to my student alone," said Numair, red-faced. "Let's go, then."

Inside his room, Daine smelled perfume in the air, a mixed-flower scent she recognized. "Did *Varice* have a chaperon?" she muttered to Alanna.

The woman kicked her lightly. "Perhaps she didn't *want* one for what she was here to do."

Daine scowled. A midwife's daughter, she knew very well that men enjoyed going to bed with women they weren't necessarily married to. Lately, the knowledge that Numair had such affairs had begun to irk her. She didn't want to mention that to him; she was afraid he'd laugh.

Once inside, the door closed, Numair spoke a

word. Black fire bloomed in every corner, covering the windows and door. "It's safe now." He sat on the bed next to Alanna. "Talk."

Daine told them what the badger had said, and reminded Numair of Rikash's words. "It's hardly new," the mage said once she was done. "Seers throughout the Eastern and Southern Lands have been giving warnings of some disaster that looms over Carthak. Without better information, we have no reason to break off the talks and return home. Have you such information?"

Daine shook her head.

"Next time, tell the badger he must be more specific, if the warning is to be of any use."

"What about that breath thing the badger did?" Alanna inquired. "Do you know what it is?"

"Oh, I know," said Daine grimly. "And I don't like it—not one bit."

A dead animal was on display in this room as well as in hers: not a tiger, but a stuffed king vulture, fully two-and-a-half feet long. It was posed on a tall pedestal in the corner, the purples, reds, oranges, and yellows of its head were as bright as if the huge bird were still alive. Daine went over and removed the handkerchief someone had put over its skull. Looking at it, she saw that the fine cambric bore a delicately embroidered initial, *V.*

Scowling, she thrust it into her pocket and looked at the adults. *"Here's* what the badger did." She rubbed her palms on her breeches, then grasped the vulture with both hands. Light blazed around her fingers, blinding her. She blinked rapidly, trying to clear her vision, but the first hint that she had succeeded came when a wing brushed her ear. When the spots were gone, she found the vulture leaning forward, his many-colored face inches from hers.

Daine smiled. "Hello," she told him. "I need to sit." Her knees quivered; she went to the bed. Once sitting, she put her head between her knees to hold off a faint.

FIVE

PALACE TOUR

⟨⟨⟨⟨⟩⟩⟩⟩

"Daine?" Alanna came over to check her pulse.

"I'm fine. Just dizzy." She closed her eyes and took a few deep breaths, then sat up. From some pocket Numair had produced his vial of wakeflower, a scent guaranteed to revive the dead. Just the threat of having to smell it cleared her mind.

The vulture flapped awkwardly across the room, clutching the wooden screen over the window. He pecked at the openings in the wood. Six feet in wingspan, he made the room *much* smaller.

"Is your weakness part of this new working?" asked Numair.

"I don't know. The times it happened before— the tiger rug in my room, and a three-horn skeleton in the Hall of Bones—it was just a flash. They didn't move about for long."

"I need to sit," Alanna said, and did. "The— what did you say?—tiger, and the three-horn. Did you bring them to life on purpose?"

"No. It was an accident." The vulture hopped onto the bed and leaned against Daine.

"That may explain why you're weak. This time you *tried* to do it." The Champion looked at Numair. "Do you agree?"

The mage tugged his long nose. Daine braced herself. That tug always came before a flood of learning. "To reason without information is fruitless. To acquire more information, Daine must conduct further experiments." Numair rubbed his temples. "What precisely did the badger say?"

She repeated it as closely as she could remember.

"The tiger and three-horn—what happened?" He paced as she explained, the vulture watching him with interest. "You are sure neither the slave in your room nor Lindhall saw anything?"

"No. I don't think they could have covered up if they saw."

Alanna laughed shakily. "Nor could I!"

Daine tickled the bird's foot, and he nibbled her hair. "I can't talk with him. It's like he's got no mind. But he must, mustn't he? He *looks* like he can think."

"The timing is inconvenient," Numair said, toying with his black-opal pendant. "We can't investigate properly while we are here. I will say this much— what you have done sounds like no wild magic I have ever heard. Only the gods can bring the dead back even to a seeming of life."

"I'm no god," protested Daine. "What if the badger passed some of his godness on to me?"

The mage shook his head. "There is nothing in the writings about animal gods to indicate they are able to do such a transfer. Not only that, but normally their power affects only those of their own species. The badger's magic should apply to badgers alone, as the wolf god applies only to wolves, and so on. Only the great gods have power that translates across species: Mithros, the Goddess, the Black God, the Graveyard Hag, the Master of Dream Gainel—"

"Don't name them all," Alanna said, too patiently.

Numair smiled. "No—of course not. In the meantime, Daine, I think it would be best if you said nothing of this and, in particular, *did* nothing with it until we got home."

"I'll *try*. It keeps getting away from me, though."

"What about him?" asked the Champion, pointing to the vulture. "We can't just let him run around in here. He's losing feathers, for one thing."

It was true: the bird's movements had shaken a number of small feathers from their moorings.

Daine asked, "What do *you* want to do, wing-brother?"

The vulture hopped from the bed, landing on the deep windowsill. Keeping his balance with the help of his wings, he pecked at the cedar screen.

"You want out?"

"Taking him out now is tough," Alanna

remarked. "People will ask questions. I assume you want this kept quiet."

"As quiet as possible," Numair said. "You don't know Ozorne. If he found out she could do this . . . You don't ever want him to find out."

Daine said nothing. After what she had seen that morning, she planned to give Ozorne as wide a berth as possible. Something about the way he'd made the image scream without letup had chilled her to the bone. To the vulture she said, "If I take you to my rooms, will you stay there and pretend to be stuffed if the servants come in? When it's dark, we'll go outside."

The vulture nodded.

Numair reached into his belt pouch and produced a round stone. "This cat's-eye agate will make you two invisible once the spell is activated. When you're in your room, put it in your pocket. Out of the light, the charm will end. Don't bump into anyone, or they will see you, spell or no."

"Come on," Daine told the vulture. "You'd best walk. You're too big to carry."

The bird hopped to the floor, wings half opened for balance. Numair made a sign over the cat's-eye, then gave it to Daine. Without looking at her tall friend, she said quietly, "Numair—you shouldn't have tried to hit him. I don't think he liked it."

Quickly, before he could answer, she left, the vulture hopping beside her.

Kitten dropped a pawful of ribbons and screeched when Daine walked into her room. Zek, absorbed in the paint pots on the dressing table, didn't see Daine and her companion until the girl put the invisibility stone away. The vulture looked at him, and Zek chattered unhappily.

"He's all right," Daine assured the marmoset. "He's dead. He won't hurt you."

Did you do the thing to him you did with the tiger and the big skeleton? Zek asked.

"Yes. Seemingly, if I do it a-purpose, it lasts longer." The vulture hopped onto her desk and folded his wings. "Tonight I'll take you out and put you where you won't be found," she told him. "And you two leave all this alone," she scolded Zek and Kitten, seeing the mess on the dressing table. "Pick those things up, Kit." Replacing tops on the jars, she noticed her hair in the mirror.

"Goddess!" Sitting, she grabbed the brush and attacked her curls. "It looks like birds nested in it." Someone tapped on her door. "Come in."

Alanna entered, smiling when she saw Daine in front of the mirror. Then, looking at each corner of the suite of rooms, she flicked her fingers, sending balls of purple fire into them. Once they reached their destinations, they stretched, lengthened, and turned into sheets of purple light that covered the door and windows. Coming to Daine, she took a ribbon from Kitten and began to thread it through the girl's hair.

Daine looked at her in the mirror. "Why'd you ward the room? Are we talking secrets now?"

"Who did Numair try to hit?"

Daine related what she had seen. When she was done, Alanna cursed under her breath. "You're right to be upset. I can't believe he was so foolish!"

"He gets fair protective of me, sometimes."

"He also as much as *told* the emperor you're his weak spot."

Daine nodded.

"I don't *think* Ozorne would endanger these talks, but—there is life after them to be considered. When we go home, it will be hard to stop Ozorne's spies from trying to hurt either of you. Men! Why they can't just keep *quiet* about things—" Outside a gong sounded the call to the talks. Alanna sighed. "I have to go. Be *careful* in what you say to the prince. Remember he *is* the emperor's heir."

"I'm hardly likely to forget, as much jewelry as he wears," Daine said dryly.

Alanna grinned. "Be polite. And if you see Numair about to do anything else stupid, try to stop him."

Kitten chattered agreement. Daine nodded. "Believe me, I will."

Alanna clapped her on the shoulder and left.

The girl looked at the vulture. "Are you still awake?" Its great wings spread, and folded again. "All right. Remember what I said."

The bird's feathers ruffled, then went smooth, as another hand rapped on the door. "Excuse me— Lady Daine? It's Prince Kaddar."

"And here we go," she told Kitten and Zek, lifting the marmoset onto her shoulder. Kitten raced ahead and opened the door.

Kaddar blinked when he saw her companions. "Won't they be happier inside?"

"No, they would not, thank you. Kitten's a smart creature. If you don't give her new things to do and see, she finds them."

"Like a puppy and my new slippers?" he inquired.

"Like a bear cub in your wardrobe, only bear cubs don't have magic. *She* does. She can whistle locks off doors—among other things."

"Very well. You would know best, of course. Since we're touring the palace, is there any area in particular that you would like to see?"

She took a breath. "Actually, I'd like to look at chapels and temples and such. Have you any here?" Until that moment she had forgotten the old slave woman had suggested it. I'd like to have a nice long talk with her, next time I see her, she thought grimly.

Kaddar frowned. "Well—yes, but—they're nothing special. You probably have finer ones at home. Except for the temple of Mithros in Carthak City—it's very beautiful."

"If it's all the same, I'd like to see your temples here, please." His reluctance hardened her resolve. She smiled up at him. "I'm making a study of them, you see."

It was the right argument to employ with a young man who attended the imperial university. "Very well, though I still think you'll be disappointed. It's also a bit of a walk."

When he offered his arm, Daine put Zek there instead of hanging on to it as he seemed to expect. He laughed, and let Zek climb to his shoulder, then set off through the gardens.

Daine walked beside him, looking at him side-long. He looked different from the times she'd seen him before. He still wore his ruby drop and ruby nose button, but had switched his other earrings to small hoops. He wore only a single, heavy silver bracelet and no rings; boots; a white shirt; and loose, maroon breeches. An open collar revealed a muscular chest, and his dark hands were large and strong-looking.

"Are you related to the emperor on your mother's side, or your father's?" she asked, curious.

Kaddar, grinning as Zek inspected the gold rings in his left ear, asked, "What?" She repeated the question. "My mother, Princess Fazia, is my uncle's sister. My father was a prince of the Chelogu province in Zallara, far to the south. As you can see"—his teeth flashed in a broad grin—"my father was *much* darker than my mother."

"Forgive me for asking, but you said he *was*?"

"Five years ago he was killed, putting down a rebellion in Siraj— What in Mithros's name is going on here?"

They had turned onto a broad walk lined with trees. Coming toward them was a squad of five soldiers, marching in order, armed with spears and small, round shields. Instead of armor they wore gilded breastplates over knee-length scarlet tunics. The emblem on shields and breastplates alike was part of the imperial seal of Carthak, a crown wrapped in a jagged circle.

"What's the matter?" she asked.

"They're members of the Red Legion—soldiers—and they're here. The army isn't allowed on palace grounds—*ever*. Will you excuse me for a moment? I must speak with these men."

Daine took Zek back from him. "Go ahead."

He left briskly, seeming to grow an inch or two in authority as he advanced on the solders. They bowed deeply in unison, right hands placed on their hearts. When he spoke to them, Daine could see he addressed them as a prince, not as a teenager, and their leader spoke to him with respect. She wondered if she ought to improve her hearing to eavesdrop, and decided against it. Instead she looked around, wondering where she was.

To her left, on the far side of a bed of late roses, she saw an arch that led to an enclosed garden. At its center was a fountain, a tower of ornamental sculpture rising from a wide, deep bowl. On its rim sat the old slave woman. At least, Daine was fairly sure of the sitter's identity, but her appearance had changed again. The black stubble on her head was now at least an inch long. Parts of it were even longer, and gray. Her gown reached to her calves; the leather sandals of last night had been changed for worn slippers with holes through which the lady's bunions protruded. A knobby walking stick leaned against the rim beside her.

More startling than the change in her appearance was her company, a mass of black and brown rats. She was feeding them—at her feet, in her lap, and from her hands. Frowning, Daine headed for the fountain. Whatever was going on here, she wanted to know what it was—no more hints!

Kitten squawked a demand, and the old woman looked up. One of her wicked black eyes was gone; a mass of old scar tissue filled the socket. The other eye danced at the sight of Daine as its owner grinned and waved. The rats turned to stare at girl, dragon, and marmoset.

Daine stepped up her pace, only to find that no matter how fast she walked, the woman and courtyard moved away, keeping the same distance from her as they had been when she first saw them. Kitten stretched her long neck out and trilled, the sound harsh in Daine's ears. Undoubtedly it was a spell of some kind, but it had no effect on the gap between Daine and her quarry.

When the girl halted to catch her breath, the receding courtyard picked up speed, getting smaller and smaller as it moved away. At last it vanished.

That was interesting, commented Zek. Can *you* do that?

"No." Vexed, Daine put her hands on her hips. "Something *funny* is going on here."

Kitten nodded agreement, her eyes half silver, her scales pink with irritation.

"Daine, what in the name of Bright Mithros are you *doing?*" Kaddar, panting, ran up to them. "Didn't you hear me call? You were supposed to stay where I left you!"

Her legs and feet suddenly felt odd, the muscles loose and trembling, as if she'd run, or walked hard, for a long time. She slumped onto a nearby bench and rubbed her aching calves. "But I just turned aside to look in the courtyard—"

"*What* courtyard?"

"It was right off that walk where you left me." She looked around, and gaped. The trees, the walk, the five soldiers—all had vanished. Instead they were at the top of a long, dusty street, with no courtyards or fountains in sight. Buildings, each with a statue over the door, lined the avenue. At its far end loomed a big temple-like structure with a golden dome. "Where are we?"

"The Sacred District." Kaddar yanked out a handkerchief and wiped his sweaty face, patting carefully to avoid smearing the paint that lined his eyes. "And you couldn't have seen it from where we were, because it's a quarter mile away from there. You've been here before, haven't you?"

She stared up at him. "Are you crazy? I've never been to Carthak in my life." The additional thought—that she was starting to wish she hadn't come now—she kept to herself.

"Nonsense. You walked as if you were born here. And you didn't stop for me! Don't you *realize* you can't run around here without an escort?"

Daine blotted her own face on her sleeve. The direct sun was brutal without trees to shield them. "I *didn't* walk here. I saw the old slave woman by the fountain, and I was *trying* to reach her. Do *you* know who she is? An old woman, about my height? I thought she was a slave. Yesterday she straightened my room—"

Kaddar's eyebrows snapped together. "Why would I care about *any* slave, young or old?"

Daine felt as if she'd been punched. She fiddled with the cuffs on her shirt and collected herself. At last she said quietly, "Because I thought you were a decent human being."

Kaddar scowled and walked away for a few paces, rubbing the back of his neck.

All right, Daine told herself, it's plain the old woman isn't a slave. A slave wouldn't feed rats, or dice with Rikash. And I'm sorry he's in a pet, but I *did* think maybe he cared more about other people than some of them that live here.

None of the furred ones care about no-furs—what you call slaves, said Zek. That is, they care when they hit the slaves, and that's all. The slaves work and try not to make the furred ones notice them. When furred ones—

Owners, Daine told him silently, to keep the prince from hearing. Two-leggers with fur—with hair—who order slaves to do work are the owners of the slaves.

Like the Monsterboy owned me? asked the marmoset.

The girl petted him gently. It's much the same.

Kaddar had mastered himself. "I'm sorry if I was rude," he said as he returned, his voice cold and clipped. "You must understand, I'm responsible for you. If any harm came to you, my uncle would be—displeased. And your old woman cannot be a slave. When palace slaves reach a certain age, they are given tasks better suited to them, in the weaving rooms or warehouses or nurseries. The slaves in the guest quarters, and the imperial and nobles' quarters, are young. Now, if you please, you asked to see our chapels."

Kitten made an extremely rude noise. For a moment Daine thought the prince would lose his temper again. He fought the urge, and smiled at last. "She knows what that sound means?"

"She knows the meaning of every sound she makes." Daine tried on a smile of her own as she got to her feet. After hearing that the old weren't allowed to work where they would be seen by anyone important, she knew it wasn't a good smile, but Kaddar accepted it.

He guided her into the first of a series of small

chapels. This was dedicated to a god of the inner desert, far to the south, and a statue made of red sandstone was placed over the altar.

While statues and altars changed from building to building, certain things were the same everywhere. Dust lay in corners and under what few benches or offering tables remained. Daine saw none of the things she expected to see: incense, flowers, candles, lamps. The air in these houses of worship was stale and unmoving. The dust in the shrine dedicated to the Threefold Goddess was so thick that Daine couldn't make out the details of the wall mosaics.

There were exceptions to the lack of offerings. The Trickster, god of thieves and players, presided over an altar where lay scattered playing cards and a few wilted bouquets of weeds. Several someones had left shells or bits of coral for the Wave Walker, but the gilt on the sea goddess's statue was peeling. Hidden behind the altar of Shakith, goddess of seers, were a score of candle stubs and a battered lamp. For Gainel, the Master of Dream, Kitten found two lavender-stuffed packets, too small to be called pillows, concealed under a bench.

"Are these less-known temples?" Daine asked. "Are there others—more popular ones?"

Kaddar's smile was crooked. "These are the only palace temples. The ones in the city are not in such bad shape as these."

Only Mithros's temple, the one with the golden dome, had serving priests—a three-man staff, explained Kaddar, with two boys as acolytes. All of them came running to greet their guests by dropping to their knees and touching their heads to the ground, a gesture that made Daine uncomfortable. Priests of any god should only bow to other humans, not genuflect as the Carthakis expected their slaves to do.

This temple was in better condition. Brightly polished sun disks caught outdoor light and reflected it into the sanctuary, but streaks of soot above wall brackets told her that light after sunset came not from lamps or candles, but inexpensive torches. She smelled incense burning, and freshly cut flowers lay on the large altar, but the priests were underfed.

Once they'd looked around, Kaddar led her toward the back of the temple, past the altar. "Where are we going?" she asked. "Aren't we returning the way we came?"

"There's one more," explained the prince. "Mithros is the best known, and the king of the gods, but our empire had its own, personal goddess. Uncle built her a temple behind Mithros's house, so he could make offerings to her once he was finished with his duties as the Sun Lord's high priest."

Passing through a small door, they entered a long, open gallery. At its end was a door inlaid with a pattern of black-and-scarlet dice. Statues of hyenas sat on either side of the portal. A group of three rats sat over it.

Daine looked at those carvings for so long that Kaddar had to reach back and pull her through the entrance. Inside, the air held a faint odor of perfumes, but the silver candlesticks and chalices on the altar were tarnished, and the floor was unswept.

Behind the altar was the image of the temple's goddess, the most unusual statue Daine had ever seen. For one thing, hyenas and rats crouched at her feet like pets. One hyena held a dice box in its jaws, while two rats offered a die each to their mistress.

Except for the Threefold Goddess in her third aspect of the Hag, or Crone, goddesses tended to be young or mature women. This one did not show wisdom or grace as statues of the aged Goddess did. This Hag was bent, leaning on a gnarled stick, grinning so widely that the onlooker could see that she had only a few teeth left. Her eyebrows were bushy; one of them was cut in two by the strip of an eye patch.

Daine and Kitten stared at it, gape-mouthed, while Zek chittered his shock.

"What is it?" asked Kaddar, bewildered. "Daine? What's the matter?"

"It's — I think it is. I can't say for sure, with her hood up, and being stone, not colored like a — "

"What *are* you talking about?" Kaddar demanded.

"Her. It's — " She was about to say "the slave" when her throat closed off, and she half swallowed her tongue. She choked, then coughed until her eyes ran.

"Are you all right?" The prince thumped her between the shoulder blades. "Would you like water, or something else to drink?"

Daine shook her head. "I'm fine," she gasped. "I was just going to say, that statue — "

Coughs erupted, tearing at her throat. Both her nose and eyes ran this time. Whenever she thought she was better, each time she tried to explain about the resemblance between the slave and the Graveyard Hag, she began to hack as if she had lung disease. The explosions didn't let up until Kaddar took her outside, into a garden. She sat on a bench and took deep breaths through her nose, while the prince went to find water for her.

I know what this is, Daine thought furiously, clenching her teeth to stop the explosions. She thinks she can silence me this way. What I'm going to say to her the next time we meet . . .

Who are you talking to? asked Zek, confused.

Her. That—*Hag* these southerners worship. I'm coughing because she doesn't want me telling Kaddar she's been about!

Then don't say anything, if she doesn't like it, Zek said. Our gods, Chrrik and Preet, don't like us talking about them to outsiders.

Daine blew her nose. Chrrik and Preet?

Chrrik is the first male of the pygmy marmosets, explained Zek. Preet is his mate. They are very private gods.

Daine ran a finger down the marmoset's vari-colored fur. That I can believe, she told him. But from all Numair has said this is *not* a private goddess, and she cannot play with me! I don't know why she's here and showing herself to me, but she can either let me speak out or leave me alone!

She doesn't only show herself to you, Zek pointed out. She was talking to the Big Stinker—Rikash—and to the rats.

Kitten, following the conversation, nodded vigorously. The girl scowled. They were right. Moreover, Rikash had acted like the old lady was someone important.

"And he didn't tell me who she was," she remarked aloud, her voice a croak. "Maybe he couldn't. But why stop me from talking about her?"

"What did you say?" Kaddar had returned. With him came a young slave bearing a tray, a pitcher, and two cups. "I thought grape juice might help." At his nod, the boy put the tray on a nearby bench and poured juice for both of them. Once he presented the cups to Daine and Kaddar, the prince ordered, "Leave us, but don't forget to return and clean this up."

"Thank you," Daine told the boy with a smile. He bowed deeply and retreated, still bowing.

"Perhaps your body reacted to the incense or flowers in the temples," Kaddar remarked when Daine emptied her cup. "My life is a misery with sneezes and coughing at haying time, and my mother cannot be near roses without her eyes watering."

Daine knew her problem had a very different cause, but she appreciated his concern. "I feel better now, thank you," she told him, thinking that seemingly she'd go *on* feeling better if she didn't tell anyone their Hag was out and about!

"No doubt you're wondering about the temples." He didn't meet her eyes, but fiddled instead with his ruby-drop earring.

"Perhaps folk here keep shrines in their homes?"

Kaddar shook his head. "I wish I could explain. There *is* no good—never mind."

"What's the matter?" Daine asked. "Is something bothering you?"

Kaddar shook his head and put a finger to his lips. The girl frowned, not understanding. With a sigh, he reached up and tugged his ears. Pale green magical fire sparkled around his fingers.

Magic? Ears? Daine thought, then remembered Duke Gareth's warnings. "There's no listening spells on *us*, Your Highness. Kitten wouldn't allow it."

Kaddar frowned. "What is that supposed to mean?"

"Kit?"

The dragon voiced an ear-splitting whistle. Light flared, from the rubies at Kaddar's nose and ear, from the etched and heavy silver ring on his left wrist.

"So the only magic is on the things that glowed—is that so, Kit?" asked Daine. The dragon nodded. "Your jewels are magicked," the girl told Kaddar.

He covered his bracelet and the ruby drops with his hands. "Not by Uncle or his mages."

"What are they for?"

He looked at her, tugging the drop. "Kitten really knows if there's magic near?"

Daine nodded. "If she feels it, she uses a sound to make it appear. Unless it's invisibility or illusions—those she sees normally. She caught your uncle, our first night here, sneaking around the reception while he was invisible."

Kaddar took his hand from the bracelet. "Do you want to stay here?" he asked Kitten. "You'd have whatever you desire. Do you know how valuable she is, Daine? A creature that can tell when a spell is in place? Our nobles would give you her weight in diamonds."

"She's not for sale," replied Daine. "She's her own self, and goes where *she* wants."

Kaddar sighed. "Oh, well. Did you know rubies are protective stones?" Daine nodded. "Mine ward me from the sendings of lesser mages, though they may not work against a powerful one. The bracelet works on drugs and poison in my food. Even if I eat them, the magic turns them harmless. That one was so costly my mother won't tell what she paid the Shusini mage who made it. I think she sold family heirlooms to pay for it, but I don't like to ask, because it's saved me five times."

Daine shuddered. "What of the temples?" she asked, putting the subject of Kaddar's close calls out of her mind for now. "You were going to say why they're so neglected."

"My uncle decreed that, since the gods are eternal and he is not, the people should not spend their money on offerings, but on taxes. Anyone caught making an offering to a god is fined the cost of the item. The priests, all but one or two, and those the oldest, have been put to work for the empire as clerks and overseers. City temples fare somewhat better than the ones here, but even they don't look their best anymore. On the other hand, the treasury is full. That's all my uncle cares about—more gold for weapons, and the armies, and mages." He seemed relieved to be able to criticize his uncle without fear of being overheard.

They stood and followed a walk that led away from the Hag's temple. "But people need to worship, don't they? If they haven't got someone to call on, someone bigger who helps them with their troubles, what can they hope for? All creatures need hope— two-leggers or beast-People."

"My uncle says if they need to worship someone, they can worship him." Kaddar's shoulders drooped. "He says that he can change or ruin their lives more quickly than gods bother to."

The hair on the back of her neck stood up. "But that's fair *crazy*."

"You noticed."

For a long time they walked in silence, Daine mulling over what she'd learned. They reached the gardens that supplied the kitchens with common herbs, part of the working areas behind the palace.

"We have a choice from here," Kaddar said. "We can turn south and visit things like the wood shops, forges, stables, kennels, and so on. If we turn north, we'll come to the training yards used by the nobles and bodyguards. The warhorses are stabled out that way. My friends should still be there, practicing their battle and hunting skills."

She had made him take her to the chapels, knowing he didn't really want to go. "Why don't we see the training yards?" Shielding her eyes to look up at him, she was rewarded by his grin.

As he led her down the small roads that marked this area into neat squares, she asked, "Why were you so upset by those soldiers before?" The worry and concern that had marked him behind the Hag's temple returned to his face, and she almost wished she'd kept quiet.

"It's a breach in custom," he explained, nodding to the group of hostlers who bowed to him as they led horses past. "Traditionally, the army is forbidden to come closer than a mile to the palace. The men said the orders came from my uncle, who commanded regular small patrols through the palace and gardens, starting last night." He shook his head.

"Is that such a bad thing?" she wanted to know. "At home we have the King's Own, the Guard, and the Queen's Riders all quartered at the palace."

"Tortall's armies have never had a habit of rebelling against its rulers—ours do. Evidently my uncle—" He looked at Kitten. "No one's listening?" The dragon shook her head. "Thank you. My uncle doesn't think he needs to be wary of the army. He looks more at certain nobles who have protested the state of things in the empire, and who live here. He should worry about the army. Too many officers come from conquered lands and have no reason to love any of us."

At the archery butts they found a handful of males their own age, practicing with short, double-curved bows. They were laughing, well-groomed young men, their skin ranging from tan to brown to black. All were dressed simply in brown, knee-length tunics and leather sandals. Their rank and wealth showed only in their jewelry—earrings, nose rings or nose buttons—and in the high quality of their weapons.

When Daine stayed with the Queen's Riders, she took a daily turn shooting with them, or with the guardsmen, pages, and squires. Now her hands fairly itched to try that short, well-made bow, but she was too shy to ask. Instead she watched, leaning on the fence that separated yard from street, as the youths joked and pummeled Kaddar. They didn't appear to be in awe of the heir, but treated him as an equal. For a moment she saw Kaddar relax, becoming as carefree as any of them. The sight of his wide grin and dancing eyes told Daine how much on guard the prince acted with her.

As she waited, Zek climbed onto the fence to

observe. Kitten wriggled under the bottom rail and sat up to watch. It was the flash of the dragon's blue-gold scales that drew the attention of the young men. Kaddar, recalled to his duties, introduced Daine to everyone. The foreign names and titles flew in and out of her ears. She hoped no one expected her to remember all of this information, but nodded and smiled cautiously. She did *not* like the way they looked her over, bold eyes lingering on her face, her chest, and everything from the waist down.

Of course, she thought, red-cheeked from embarrassment and irritation. They don't usually see women with no veils, and in breeches.

"Daine is from *Tortall*," Kaddar said warningly, noticing the same thing that Daine had. "She came with the peace delegation to care for my uncles' birds."

"I have birds, sweetling," teased one youth. "Would you care for them, if I asked you nicely?" He barely flinched when Kaddar jammed an elbow into his ribs.

"Tortall—that's where they have a *female* as King's Champion," remarked another.

"Maybe Tortallan men are easily beaten," said one. "No *Carthaki* men are bested by a woman."

Daine inspected her fingernails. Anger was a warm, comforting fizz under her cheekbones and along her spine, driving off the gloom she had felt since her visit to the chapels. "And are you willing to bet on that?" she asked gently.

"Bet that we could beat your Lioness?" asked someone.

"Oh, no—she's busy. I can't bother her to teach a lesson to *boys*. *I'll* beat you. At archery."

They laughed, even Kaddar, and her blush spread. Kitten was muttering to herself, not at all happy with the way this talk was going.

"Sorry, Daine," said Kaddar, "but we have only men's bows. You couldn't draw one."

Her blue-gray eyes glittered up at him. "Oh?" She let herself into the yard. "You'd be surprised what I can do," she told the grinning young men. "Have you longbows?"

The young nobles laughed, or groaned. One of them teased, "Oh, I'm scared."

"Careful, Kaddar, she might be one of those Queen's Riders, the ones that let *females* join!"

"Or so they say. *I've* never seen one of these Rider maidens, have you?"

Daine's smile was sweeter than ever. "I work for the Rider Horsemistress. Trust me—there are females in the Riders, and they *work* for a living." To Kaddar she said, patiently, "A bow?"

The prince took her into a shed at the side of the yard. "They will be too strong for you," he remarked as she checked the unstrung longbows placed in wooden racks on the wall. Much as she wanted to try the recurved bow they used, she felt she ought to stick to the weapon she knew best.

"I'll judge what's too strong for me, thank you." Running her fingers down two bow staves, she shook her head. The next felt better, but when she lifted it down she could tell that the balance was off.

"We assumed those tales of women fighting among the Riders were only tales. No woman has ever asked to enter *our* armies."

"With you so open and welcoming of the idea,

I'm not surprised." She found one that might suit her and examined it carefully, warming the stave in her hands as she checked grain and texture. "This will do. Have you strings?"

He stalked to a cabinet, reminding her of an offended cat, and opened a drawer to reveal coils of bowstring, each in oiled paper. She picked one out.

"Women aren't up to the discipline of military life."

Looking over quivers full of arrows, she chose a handful. "You must tell Lady Alanna that sometime. I'd do it from a distance."

"I hope you lose," he muttered as she went outside.

In the yard she backed up to the fence, since her bow had greater range than theirs. The targets were eighteen inches across, with two rings and a bull's-eye — a difficult shot even for a good archer. The Carthakis watched as she stuck her arrows point-first into the ground, keeping two. These Kitten held as Daine looped the string around the foot of the bow and stood that end between her feet.

"She'll never bend that," she heard someone mutter.

If only she had her *own* bow, the one that even the Lioness had trouble bending! Holding the stave in one hand, the free end of her string in the other, she easily slid the loop over the top end of the bow. When she had taken her stance, left side toward the target, Kitten handed over the first arrow. Daine put it to the string, careful to keep the arrow pointed at the ground.

"Stand back, or I'll hurt you," she warned her

observers, then added, "Tortall and the Queen's Riders!" She swung the bow up, and loosed. Bow down, second arrow from Kitten, to the string, up and loose. The target was in her mind, not her eyes; she didn't have to take the time to aim that these males did. Now, pulling the arrows one by one from the ground, she fired until they were gone. Done, sweat gleaming on her forehead, she told the Carthakis, "You may check my aim."

At first nobody moved. Finally one of them went to look. Their judge carefully examined the arrows, by eye and by touch, where they were clustered in the center target. At last he called, "We must cut them loose from the bull's-eye. They are too deeply embedded to be removed by hand."

The young nobles crowded around her. She was incredible, they told her; could all the Tortallan women shoot like that? When she mentioned she'd like to try the recurved bow, six of them were offered at once.

SIX

CARTHAKI MAGECRAFT

Finally Daine and Kaddar returned to the palace, the prince carrying the dragon, Daine cradling Zek. They entered by the marble water stairs that led from the river to the guest quarters.

On her arrival that first day, the girl had been too busy keeping Zek warm to notice the statues on either side of the stairs. She stopped now to look them over. The crowned images were both Ozorne: one simply dressed, with birds on his shoulders and a pile of scrolls and books at his feet; the other draped in robes, a jeweled scepter in one hand, a crystal orb that sparked with gold-and-green fire in the other.

"In case you'd forgotten whose house this is." Kaddar's dry remark was made quietly, for her ears alone—the ambassador from Tusaine and his staff had come out to take the air. "You could say my uncle has two faces." He smiled politely as the others approached.

The ambassador shook his head. "It did not go as well today," he remarked with a sigh. "Problems arose over fishing rights. One could have wished for a more flexible attitude from all parties. If only the strait between your lands were not so narrow—"

The sky was bare of even the tiniest cloud. None of them expected a loud crack of thunder to interrupt the ambassador as it ripped through the air, drawing shrieks from Kitten and Zek. Lightning flashed down from above. Splitting in two above the stairs, it struck each of the imperial statues with a roar. When Daine's vision cleared of spots, all that remained of Ozorne and his two faces were globules of molten gold and charred, shattered marble.

No one moved for a long moment. Then, without speaking, they all rushed inside.

Returning to her room to calm down, bathe, and change for supper, she discovered something was missing. Where was the king vulture? The desk where he'd settled was empty, but its top shimmered. Rising on tiptoe to look at its surface, Kitten squawked in outrage.

Daine looked. There was a message scratched into the varnished wood, in writing that glowed.

Dearie, I came to fix your room, but some mortal took care of it first. Very nice work on the vulture. I'm taking him with me, so don't worry about him. We'll talk soon, never you worry.

Burned into the wood in silver was the print of a rat's paw.

"She is getting on my nerves," Daine told Zek and Kitten. "The things I am going to tell her—"

The writing vanished. Only the paw print remained. Furious, the girl shed her clothes, muttering about gods who hung around where they weren't invited or wanted.

That night's banquet was held aboard a large boat kept for the emperor's use. Once his guests took places at tables in the stern, the emperor—seated in lonely state on a deck raised above them—nodded to a nearby slave. The man lifted a silver pipe-whistle to his lips and blew a wavering string of notes. In the bow and in the stern, three men and a veiled woman, in the scarlet master-of-sorcery robe from the imperial university, clapped their hands and bowed their heads. The vessel shuddered, and began to move north on the river, slowly at first, then gaining speed. Soon they were moving faster than oars or sails could drive them, while other craft drew closer to the banks to get out of their way.

What a waste of magic, Daine thought to Zek. We could have stayed at the palace.

"Would you like to visit the university tomorrow?" asked Kaddar, offering her a bowl of olives. "Master Lindhall will be here, and he's said he wants you to see his workroom."

"I'd like that. Kaddar, what did your uncle say when you told him about the lightning that—"

She stopped, puzzled. The prince was shaking his head vigorously. "Don't talk about it," he ordered, lips barely moving.

"Why? It happened, didn't it? And he can't have a listening spell on us, or Kit would've said something." The dragon, sampling pumpkin slices stewed in cumin, and sea urchins in bay sauce, shook her head. "So why can't we talk about it?" Daine asked reasonably.

The prince took a deep breath, as if he were about to yell, then let it out slowly. Still hardly moving his lips, he said, "Among the servants, he has spies who read lips."

She digested that for a moment, and accepted the olive that Zek offered. "Are there *many* things you aren't allowed to talk about?"

Kaddar propped his chin on his hands. "You have no idea."

They had just finished their main course, stuffed goose, when Numair came over to their table. "May I join you?" he asked, and sat down. He leaned forward, smiling at the prince. "We haven't really had a chance to chat. I understand you're studying with my friend Lindhall Reed."

The prince nodded. Daine peeled an orange for Zek while Kitten munched on a goose bone.

"What course of studies, may I ask?"

"The relation of men, animals, and plants to one another, with a matching course in law. Next spring, if things permit, I hope to go south with Master Lindhall and a group from the university to look into the causes of the drought. We're hoping — well, the masters are; I'll just be there to carry things — we hope to find some way to end it. Five years is a long time."

"I see. Commendable. With regard to your

position as his heir, has your uncle arranged a marriage for you?"

Daine looked sharply at her teacher. What was he doing, asking such a personal question?

Kaddar passed his goose bones to Kitten. "He is negotiating with the king of Galla for the hand of one of his daughters. There is also a princess in the Copper Isles who my uncle feels is a possibility."

"I see. But you are involved with girls, are you not? Students at the university, young noblewomen. Are they aware you are not permitted to marry to please yourself?"

Daine, cheeks flaming, kicked Numair under the table.

Kaddar stiffened. "No gentleman deceives a woman in that manner, sir."

"Indeed not. Stop kicking me, Daine. You understand, she is very important to a number of powerful nobles and mages in Tortall." Numair's voice was quiet, almost friendly; his eyes were hard. "Their majesties. Lady Alanna and her husband, the baron of Pirate's Swoop. Me. All of us would take it amiss if we thought for one moment she was being trifled with, particularly by a young man who wasn't free to do the right thing by her."

"Numair," Daine growled. "Can I speak to you *privately* for a moment?"

"No. Stepping on my foot won't work, either. Do I make myself clear, Prince Kaddar?"

The younger man sat up straight, eyes glinting. "I understand you well, Master Salmalín."

"Good." Numair stood. It seemed to take him forever to rise. When he was up, he looked taller than ever, and faintly shadowy around the edges. "Lindhall tells me you also have an excellent memory. I hope so."

Daine covered her face with her hands as he returned to his own table and Varice. "I'm going to *kill* him," she whispered, shamed almost to tears.

Kaddar drained his cup of pomegranate juice. "Nonsense. He was just looking out for you."

"I can look after myself," Daine retorted.

Kaddar smiled. "You are lucky to have someone who cares so much about you. He knows we're spending—"

Drums began to hammer, on their boat and in the distance. Ozorne rose and walked to the bow, his guests following him. Moving under the power supplied by the master wizards, they had reached the imperial harbor in Thak's Gate in little more than an hour, a voyage that normally took three hours. A lighthouse on the far side of the lock admitting vessels to the commercial harbor shone its beacon overhead. Even with its beam it was hard to tell what lay past the lock, but Daine could just make out a forest of masts.

A horn call sounded from the harbormaster's tower on the breakwater. Sparks of magical Gifts flared from a hundred sources just beyond the lock. Fiery ivy sprang from those sources to climb masts and twine around yardarms. More and more such "vines" sprouted, until Daine realized that each belonged to a single ship, docked or anchored in the commercial harbor.

Another horn call: a shout went up from the assembled ships. The vines grew brighter, larger, until they burned like trees around the shadowy masts. Now the entire harbor was visible, as colored lights bounced off shield rims, armor, and spear points. They were looking not at civilian shipping vessels, but at war galleys with two or three banks of oars, fully manned.

The whistle on the emperor's barge trilled again. From among the guests, Master Chioké and three other mages, who'd been pointed out to Daine as the most powerful at the imperial university, stepped up to join the red-robed mages. Chioké and those wizards who had been with the guests lifted their arms to point upward. Magical fire stabbed into the cloudless night sky. The mages who had brought them downriver leaned over the rails, allowing their power to fall into the water.

Timbers creaked; wooden joints popped. Fire ran from one red-robe's hands to the next, until the hull lay in a disk of light. Chioké and the three mages in civilian dress cried a single word; the streams of light from their hands broadened. Slowly, its timbers groaning, the boat rose into the air.

Kitten shrieked. "No, Kit, stop," Daine whispered. "Be quiet, understand?" The thought of what might happen if any mage lost his or her concentration made her queasy.

The dragon shifted from paw to paw, chattering angrily as she buried her face in Daine's skirts.

Kaddar knelt beside them, petting Kitten's slender neck. "I can't say that I blame her," he growled softly. "I hate it when he does things like this. Why can't he put such power to use against the drought, instead of staging idle dis —"

"Hush," Daine said gently. "It isn't safe to talk, remember?"

The boat continued to rise. Sweat gleamed on the faces of the mages who controlled its motion.

At last the whistle shrieked again. The rising boat stopped, nearly eighty feet above the imperial harbor. The lighthouse beacon went out. From the harbormaster's tower came another, different horn call, one that was picked up by horns in the ships below. Kitten, Daine, and Kaddar returned to the rail. Zek, seeing where they were, squeaked and tore Daine's hair from its knot so that he could hide, trembling, in her curls. She didn't have the heart to scold.

More horns bellowed. New fires sparked, past the white finger that was the lighthouse tower. Like those in the harbor, these new flames became vines growing up and along some dark trellis. They flared, magic piercing the night, to reveal hundreds of vessels lying at anchor past the harbor.

There was a roar or shout of some kind. Torches were set to globes that burst into flame. They were balls of liquid fire, lit as they rested in the slings of catapults aboard the infamous Carthaki war barges. At one catapult per barge, Daine calculated, there were twenty outside the harbor, forming solid ranks between the breakwater and the naval vessels further out.

"Is he *mad*?" Kaddar whispered, appalled. "This isn't just the northern fleet—he's brought the western one up as well! Did he do it to—to *brag*—"

A hand gripped his arm. "Shut up," Varice said fiercely. "What's the matter with you? Do you want to disappear like his *last* heir?"

"But—"

Daine elbowed him—hard. "She's right—shut up!" Kitten closed her jaws lightly on the prince's leg. "If I tell her, she'll bite," Daine said coldly. "And you haven't been bit till a dragon does it."

Kaddar's hands clenched, but he shut his mouth and gritted his teeth; they could see his jaw muscles twitch. The emperor's boat hung in the air for a few more moments, then descended slowly. Except for sailors passing on orders, no one aboard said a word. Only when they were safely in the River Zekoi again did Kitten release the prince's leg.

The red-robed mages who had brought them downriver were replaced by four new, fresh masters. They clapped in unison and were bowing their heads when a ringing sound, like a gong being struck, shattered the air. It was followed by another, and another, and another. It sounded, Daine realized, like a horse's walk.

The air around the harbormaster's tower was glowing. From the emperor's frown, this was not part of his planned entertainment.

The clanging drew nearer. Around the tower's side and down the shortest breakwater, enclosed in a loose ball of light, appeared a golden rider on a golden horse. The clanging sound came from the animal's hooves as they struck the boulders. Together rider and mount were twice, nearly three times larger than normal. Both slumped, as if stricken with weariness or grief, the horse's muzzle barely a foot off the ground. The sword and shield that the man held drooped from his hands.

"Goddess bless," whispered Kaddar. All around them hands made the Sign against evil.

Do two-leggers grow so big? asked Zek, awed.

"No," Daine whispered. "That's not a two-legger. Zek was asking," she explained when Kaddar and Varice looked at them.

"It's a statue," Varice replied softly. "Of—of Zernou, the first emperor. It stands in Market Square, in Carthak City, before the Temple of Mithros."

"I don't think it's standing there anymore," Alanna commented from the shadows nearby.

Horse and rider reached the lock between the imperial boat and the harbor, and stopped. The horse reared, pawing the air with his forelegs. The rider cried out a word in a voice like a giant gong. Again he cried out. The third time, he shouted words in a strange, guttural language. He pointed to their vessel with his sword. Instantly magical defenses went up, forming walls of light between those onboard and the statue, but no attack came.

The horse gathered itself and leaped, clearing the lock, to land on the seawall on the far side with a ringing crash. Horse and rider galloped down the wall, striking sparks from the granite boulders. Just before they reached the lighthouse, the glowing figures leaped off onto the ocean's surface, and raced across it, dodging the naval vessels and heading north. Daine watched in silence as the glow that surrounded them faded, and was gone.

"What did he say?" Varice asked Kaddar, voice hushed. "It was Old Thak, wasn't it? The first language of the empire?"

"He said 'Woe.'" The prince's voice was quiet and even. "And 'Woe.' Then he said, 'Woe to the empire—we are forsaken. The gods are angry!'"

❉ ❉ ❉

In her dream, she glided down a green river in a flat-bottomed barge, a silly, overdecorated affair painted yellow and white. A dainty yellow awning kept off the sun overhead. A rat offered her a white straw tray filled with a choice of small tarts. Two more rats slowly waved huge fans made of black feathers. Looking around, the girl saw vultures perched on the forward rail.

"Don't worry, child. I may not even need you." The Graveyard Hag reclined in the straw-and-white striped cushions next to Daine, choosing tidbits from the tray held for her by yet another rat. These appeared to be made of worms, beetles, fungi, and moss.

Daine shuddered. The food being offered to *her* seemed normal enough, but she decided not to take a chance. "No, thank you," she told the rat serving her. "I'm not at all hungry." He waddled away, awkward on his hind legs.

"It's quite possible Ozorne will heed the three warnings." The Hag chewed noisily, her mouth open. "Still, here you are, the perfect vessel, should I need one. I wanted to give you the power, just in case. Give you a little time to practice, to get used to it."

"Won't someone else do? I'm supposed to behave myself here. And don't you already know if he'll listen to your warnings? You're a god, after all."

The Hag crackled, spraying food on the cushions. "You *are* a funny thing! No, a vessel for a god's power can't be just anyone."

"Is it because my da really is a god, like the Banjiku said?"

"No, or we'd have even fewer vessels than we

do now. Most mortal women die giving birth to a god's child, for your information. No, for a vessel we need a mortal with imagination, a strong will, and determination. And anger—plenty of it."

"I'm not angry."

"Nonsense, dear. Think of your mother's death. Think of how you were treated in that awful village you came from."

Daine looked down at her hands. The goddess's words had awakened memories of those times, as fresh as when she'd lived through them. For a moment she actually knelt beside Ma's body, feeling how cold she was. Memory flickered: she was shivering, naked, running, the village hunters close behind, calling her name.

As if she'd spoken, the Hag said, "Well, there you are." Briskly she wiped her fingers on the cushions. "And no, I can't tell if he'll attend to the warnings or not. We can see ahead a bit, but not far, and not when the events concerned will create so much change. Ozorne's choice will determine the path that history takes thereafter, which means it's like trying to see through mud. You mortals have to make your own choices. We poor gods only get to come in and straighten up *after* you choose."

Daine raised skeptical brows. The goddess's self-pity was laid on a bit too thick. "I'd no idea what a struggle it is for you."

"Oh, you don't appreciate me. Just because you're a good vessel doesn't mean I'll stand for your sauce! Back to bed with you!" The Hag flapped a hand.

Daine sat bolt upright in bed. She was in her

room in the imperial palace. Kitten and Zek were grumbling at her. "Just a dream," she whispered, and sank back onto her pillows.

Entering the common room for breakfast, she saw only Alanna. "I got rid of the servants," the Lioness said tiredly as she put food on a plate. "I hope you don't mind. I can't deal with slaves, not today."

"Where's Numair?" Daine asked, sitting down. "And Master Harailt?"

In their rooms, reading." Alanna handed the plate to Daine. "The Carthakis have allowed us to see the spells that open gates into the Divine Realms, but we aren't allowed to copy them, and we can't take them with us. Harailt and Numair are memorizing as much of them as they can."

Daine buttered a roll. "Where's the rest? Duke Gareth, and his son, and Lord Martin?"

"Talks won't start today until noon," explained the Champion with a yawn. "If they have any sense, they'll sleep in. Same with the clerks."

"You're not sleeping in," Daine pointed out.

"More 'rest' like I got last night and you'll find me atop some tower, baying at the moon."

"Bad dreams?"

Alanna flicked her fingers at the room's corners. Purple fire raced to encircle them, shutting out eavesdroppers. "Bad thinking," the Lioness said grimly, peeling an orange with callused fingers. "Bad sights."

"What's the matter?"

"Prince Kaddar is right. Carthak's northern fleet is small—about thirty vessels. They don't have many troop ships or war barges—they aren't necessary. This shore of the Inland Sea is all theirs: none of the lands on our side have a navy worth sweating over. They have the war barges and transports for men and horse on the western coast, against Scanran raids, or trouble with the Copper Isles, or to keep their southern holdings in line. They *need* those ships there, unless—"

"Unless he's got something for all of them to do," Daine said. "But—he's going to sign a treaty with us! *No*body brings in the navy during peace talks, do they?"

"If we were actually having peace talks, no; but we bogged down yesterday."

She remembered the Tusaine ambassador's remarks. "Fishing rights?"

"That, and something else. We were told Ozorne wants Kaddar to marry Kalasin in the spring and bring her here to live. No marriage agreement means no treaty, in spite of the fact that he never mentioned a wedding when he and the king arranged these talks."

Daine's jaw dropped. "But she's only *ten*. Queen Thayet won't hear of a marriage being set up till she's thirteen or fourteen!"

"I think the emperor knows that, Daine." The woman looked tired, and older than she had when they landed. "Look. Perhaps I'm being an alarmist, but—he showed us that fleet for a reason, and he's pressing this marriage for a reason. Be *extra* careful, understand? Watch your step. We may have to leave in a hurry. Our permits to be here are good only so long as he says they are."

***

She explained everything to Zek and Kitten as she fed them and got ready to go. On their way to meet Kaddar in the guest courtyard, she peered into Numair's room, hoping for a word with him. Although the door was open, black fire sparkled in the entrance. She could just see him through it, stretched out on the bed with a book in front of his nose. Zek touched the fire and squeaked, yanking his paw back.

Did that hurt? Daine asked.

No. It was only strange. I don't think he wants to talk to anyone, though.

No, probably not, she agreed.

They walked on, emerging into the morning sun in a yard where the guests who rode came and went. Awaiting them was Kaddar, holding the reins of a pair of horses.

They raced to the ferry landing, then crossed the broad river to Carthak City. Zek burrowed into Daine's shirt once they boarded the ferry so that he wouldn't have to look at the river that had nearly killed him. Kitten, sitting up in Daine's saddlebag, observed with interest every sight that met her eyes.

At the top of the far bank the capital stretched before them, avenues beckoning. To their left stood a walled enclosure: the famed imperial university. Humans, afoot or mounted, passed through the gates in a stream.

Once inside, they followed a paved avenue lined by handsome buildings set on groomed lawns. Around her Daine saw every human color in the world, from the blue-black of southern tribespeople to the pale skins of the far north. Most wore overrobes of the same loose cut as those worn by the mages, in a variety of colors. White robes, explained Kaddar, plain or with colored trim, meant a novice in any program of study. Wide bands of color at cuffs and hem meant the wearer was a journeyman in his course of study. Solid-colored robes indicated mastery; trim on a sold-colored robe meant advanced mastery. Daine simply enjoyed the human scenery as they rode down the avenue.

"That's it," Kaddar said, pointing to the large five-tiered building that straddled the avenue. Tall, graceful columns painted a deep blue were arranged across the front of the ground floor, their bases and capitals gilded and bright in the sun. "Lindhall's study and workrooms are there."

Hostlers took Kaddar's mare, Westwind, and Daine's gelding. Something about them was strange, Daine realized, and about the gardeners who trimmed the grass and bushes along the avenue. Stretching her legs, she puzzled out what it was: all of them had hair. "Kaddar, aren't there any slaves here?"

"None inside the university complex. The academics won't allow it. Too many northerners teach here, and they aren't comfortable with slaves."

"I can't imagine why," Daine muttered.

"What is that supposed to mean? Are *you* uncomfortable with slavery?"

"Yes."

"It's the first time you've mentioned it."

The girl shrugged. "Ma always taught me that when you're visiting someone else's house, you shouldn't be carping about the way they clean. Besides, we're supposed to be on our best behavior here. The peace between us is more important—that's what Duke Gareth said." Thinking of those warships the night before, Daine shivered. To a girl whose family had been murdered by raiders, those ships were a bloody promise. She would do anything to prevent its unfolding.

Kaddar picked up Kitten and led the way to doors behind the blue pillars. "And what *do* you think of slavery? Don't worry—I won't repeat it." To Kitten he said, "And no one's listening, right?" The dragon nodded vigorously.

"It makes me think of cages," replied Daine. "And cages make me feel like I can't breathe."

Me, too, said Zek, peering up at her. They put us in a cage. Then they took my family away.

"I know," she whispered, stroking his fur. "He reminded me that he was a captive," she explained to the prince

He looked at them. "I thought it must be wonderful, to be linked to animals the way you are, but it isn't always, is it? I have a bad enough time just knowing human sadness, let alone the sorrows of every other living creature." He shifted Kitten's weight to his hip, so that he could carry her one-armed. "You aren't anything like what I expected."

He led her into a huge, high-ceilinged room where plants grew and fountains played. Daine stopped, awed by the great mosaics that lined the walls. Kaddar followed her, still carrying the dragon, as she went to inspect each one. Mosaics were a Carthaki specialty, but these were splendid even by their standards. Each panel, ten feet by ten feet, depicted a craft or branch of learning. One showed Carthak's famous dyes: a woman dipped cloth into a vat to turn it a rainbow of colors. One panel was dedicated to mages: a red-robed man was halfway transformed from human to horse, a yellow-robed woman had plants growing from outstretched palms, and behind them a black-robed figure, back to the viewer, opened a fiery portal in a nighttime sky. Other panels were dedicated to astronomy and engineering, as well as to glassmaking, weaving, and metalworking. The picture Daine liked the least was of a soldier in the scarlet tunic and gold armor of the Red Legion, standing with one foot on the back of a fallen black man who reached vainly for a spear. To his left, a brown woman in green brocade lifted her hands, pleading; to his right, a pale woman in the tall headdress and tiered gown of Ekallatum pushed forward two naked children, a boy and a girl, in chains.

"Our glorious heritage." Kaddar's voice was very soft; his lips barely moved. "The splendid empire. We loot our conquests until they can no longer feed themselves. Then we take the money from what food and goods they buy to pay for wars to acquire more conquests."

She stared up at him, astonished.

He noticed, and smiled crookedly. "It's true. What's the matter?"

"You're not exactly what *I* expected, either," she said frankly.

"And what did you expect?"

She brushed Zek's mane with her fingers as she considered her reply. "Someone who enjoyed being imperial more. What did you expect of me?"

He grinned and tweaked her nose. "Someone who ate with her fingers."

"There are you!" Lindhall approached, hands out in welcome, open robe flapping behind him. "I am late—forgive me. I just found a reference to ichneumenons, and I was trying to locate its source. Come! I think perhaps the *Analects of Utuhegal the Blasphemer*, or perhaps it was Thorald Moonaxe. . . ."

Kaddar rolled his eyes at Daine as they followed their host down a long corridor.

"I do *not* eat with my fingers," she whispered, trying not to smile.

"The improvement in the emperor's birds is astonishing," Lindhall told Daine over one shoulder. "It's impossible to tell if they were ever ill. He is very pleased with your work. Don't be surprised if he invites you to remain, and even offers you a bribe to do so."

"There's nothing he has that I want," Daine said. "I was just glad to help the birds."

"Which is as it should be," the mage said with approval. "Is she heavy?" he asked, looking at the prince and Kitten. "Could I hold her?"

"Kit?" Daine asked, and the dragon nodded. Kaddar gave her to Lindhall, who looked startled. "She hasn't the weight I would expect of a creature of her mass."

"Dragons are hollow-boned, like birds," the girl explained. "Numair found a scroll that told all about dragons from when they lived in the mortal realms."

"*The Draconian Codex*," Lindhall and Kaddar said together, and smiled at each other.

Making several turns down long corridors, they finally reached their destination, a door with a brass nameplate bearing the words: *Master Lindhall Reed—Plants, Animal Behavior and Habits.*

"Let me in, dolt," Lindhall said, and the door opened.

"That's how he talks to the key spell," explained Kaddar.

"I almost feel as if there is a sprite at work, not a spell." Lindhall placed Kitten on the floor and dumped his robe next to her. "A small, not very clever, *spiteful* one." The robe glided through the air to drape itself over a hook on the wall. That spell Daine had seen before, in Numair's tower.

"What about your assistant?" she inquired, greeting a very large turtle who seemed to have full run of the room. He was pleasant enough to Daine, but tried his best to take a bite of Kitten, who screeched at him. Zek, mistrustful of anything that tried to bite, climbed to the top of Daine's head and clung there.

"Out on fieldwork for the day." Lindhall glared at the still-open door. "Close up," he said crossly. "I don't want any visitors until further notice." Meekly the door obeyed. To the turtle he added, "And that will be enough out of you, Master Sunstone." Picking up the great reptile, who was pursuing Kitten's tail, he carried him across the room to a door beside a cluttered desk. He opened it and put the big reptile inside. Daine, watching, noticed something in there that looked uncomfortably like a human form on a bier, covered with a dark cloth.

Lindhall shut the door before she could get a better look. "What do you think?" he asked, waving a hand to include their surroundings.

Daine put the odd shape out of her mind and looked around. Along the walls were small kingdoms in huge glass tanks. Some were landscapes with plants, streams and enough room for small animals to live comfortably. One tank was set up like a pond, with underwater greenery and rocks to feed and shelter the fish and frogs who lived there.

"I inherited the pond from my master. The rest I made, with help. That is the advantage of a university: someone is always there to help create things, just to see if it can be done. Mages helped glassmakers with the tanks, or we never could have made them so large and so clear. I try to keep the environments as much like the animals' true homes as possible." Lindhall watched as she examined a tank that housed a trio of large green lizards, whose comblike crests ran the length of their spines. "They are iguanas, from the Copper Isles. Are they happy? Do they need anything? I think I would know if they were pining, but I can't ask them, and I don't wish to be cruel."

Daine held up a hand, laughing. "Master Lindhall, if you'll wait a moment, I'll ask!" Well, sun-brothers? she inquired silently. Are you happy in there?

They rushed to the glass. Lindhall reached in and lifted them out, to Zek's dismay.

"They like you," Daine said, listening to the iguanas. "Their only complaint is that it gets close in the tank, but since you let them out all the time, they don't really mind. No, the turtle isn't here right now," she told the lizards, who had asked. As Kitten and the iguanas sniffed each other, Daine walked around, talking to the inhabitants of the other tanks. They had only good to say of Lindhall. Most didn't even know they were confined.

Kitten's voice called her away from these small kingdoms. The dragon stood before an empty corner, expressing indignation as only she could, with a series of bone-piercing whistles. Before Daine could warn whoever was using the invisibility spell, the air shimmered, and Numair appeared.

SEVEN

WAKING DREAMS

❧

"You *had* to inform everyone," the mage scolded the dragon, scowling. Kitten nibbled on his breeches. He sighed and scratched the top of her head.

"But—I saw you, in your room," Daine protested, feeling decidedly odd.

"It was a simulacrum. I'm expressly forbidden to leave the palace."

"What if one of their mages came around, looking for you? What if the emperor spies on you?"

"I embodied it with sufficient amounts of my Gift to deceive anybody. Should someone try to disturb the copy, it will enclose the room completely, so no one will enter until I am back inside."

"And if you're caught?" she demanded. "He'd

love to catch you breaking the rules!"

"Daine, we had to talk." The voice, surprisingly, was Kaddar's. "There's no other way we can do it without being spied on."

Daine faced him and Lindhall. They watched her, not her teacher. "You knew he'd be here this morning. That's why you brought me."

"I also wanted you to see *my* friends." The kindness in Lindhall's voice broke through her anger. She knew him well enough by now to realize that he was telling the truth. "You are more than welcome here in your own right, my dear."

She smiled at him reluctantly, and nodded. To Numair she said, "You *could* have trusted me."

He took her hands in his. "I *do* trust you, magelet. I simply didn't wish to discuss it under Ozorne's roof. You aren't particularly adept at concealing your state of mind. You would have been visibly apprehensive if I had left with you and His Highness, whether I was invisible or not."

Since there was no answer she could make to that, she scowled. "How *did* you get here?"

"Hawk shape. And now, we've little time and much to discuss. Would you mind looking at the aviary for a while? Or would you rather be privy to our discussions?"

"I'll go look at birds," she said hastily. "I'm that tired of secrets. Kit? Stay or go?"

Kitten, who loved secrets, shook her head and sat. The iguanas promptly began to climb on her.

Lindhall opened another door, different from the room with the turtle. Daine entered a large, sunny area with a ceiling that was half glass panes, and closed the door behind her. Under the glass and behind a silken barrier net was an aviary. It was different from Ozorne's: the plants were northern, not tropical. On the trees the leaves had turned color and were falling. Something in the room produced a faint chill, like the kind she'd feel at home at this time of year. The air was drier, and the birds who inhabited the aviary were northerners: lapwings, turtledoves, crested larks, nightingales, song thrushes, and green and gold finches.

"Here's a man who wants to go home," she said to herself, looking at the birds. "Of all the pretty southern birds he could have, he picks you. I like his taste."

The birds flocked to the netting to peer at her and talk. She chatted with them for some time, listening to them gossip about their neighbors and Lindhall. Like the inhabitants of the glass kingdoms next door, these birds had nothing but good to say of the mage.

Once each bird had been greeted, she looked at the counter on the far side of the room. Writing materials were scattered over its length, and a number of animal skeletons stood on it, posed as they would have been in life. She also found a large slab of limestone. Embedded in it was an incomplete skeleton, that of a small animal with only three extremely long, birdlike toes to a leg, and a lizard's bony tail. Its skull was odd compared to those of the birds she knew, but its end formed a beak. Most interesting, in the chipped-away stone around it, she saw outlines of what looked like feathered wings. Missing were the lower ribs on the right, part of the spine, the right femur, and the end of the tail. A label on the front of the shallow box that contained the limestone read, Lizard-bird, found in the Jalban Quarry, Zallara.

"Have you ever seen a bird like this, Zek?" she asked.

No, replied the marmoset. Never.

After the Hall of Bones, she wasn't about to touch the complete skeletons. On the other hand, surely there was nothing wrong with touching a collection of bones embedded in rock, particularly if parts of the entire skeleton were missing. Gingerly, she touched a thin claw with her finger.

The flash burned into her eyes. Blinking to clear her vision, Daine heard the last thing she wanted to hear in the world: the sound of crumbling rock. First to come free was the skull, followed by the heronlike neck. Next came the overlong arm bones, spine, and bits of ribcage. Pieces moved as if connected, even when they weren't. Outlying chunks of bone jumped from the rock and gathered around the main skeleton as the hipbones separated from their tomb.

Look! said Zek, squeaking in excitement. If there's any missing, the bones leave room for it!

"Wonderful," she whispered. She didn't share his enthusiasm: it made *her* queasy to look at those absent — or invisible — chunks.

The legs yanked themselves free. The skeleton tried to stand and was brought up short, its tail still embedded in limestone. It looked back over its rump to see what the holdup was. The beak opened in a soundless cry that revealed small teeth. It switched its hips, freeing its tail. At liberty, the lizard-bird extended its arms, then its legs, having a good stretch after a long nap.

Daine sat on a nearby stool, hard. Zek, who couldn't understand why she was not pleased, jumped from her shoulder to the countertop, skidding until he turned and brought himself around. The skeleton was about the size of a crow. It turned to peer at Zek, crouching to get a better look.

"With eyes that aren't there," Daine said, and giggled helplessly. Both the skeleton and Zek looked at her reproachfully. "Sorry."

"Mithros bless, I didn't know you had the magical assemblage spell!" cried Lindhall. Numair and Kaddar, behind him, only stared.

As if I weren't having enough fun yet, thought Daine.

"It doesn't seem to matter if pieces are missing." Lindhall walked to the counter for a closer look at the creature. "But that's why I didn't use the assemblage spell on my own. It doesn't work if the skeleton is incomplete."

If it knew it was incomplete, the lizard-bird didn't act it. Looking around, it stretched, wagged its arms clumsily, then leaped off the counter. All four humans lunged to catch it, but the skeleton had other ideas. It flew up, bony arms flapping awkwardly, as if it still wore the feathers that had left their imprints in its rock tomb.

"But there aren't any birds with claws in their arms!" Daine protested as the skeleton swooped and turned around the light-globe overhead. "And its bones are solid, not hollow like a bird's. Bats have sort-of fingers, but those are genuine clawed toes, not like a bat's wing."

"It was no bat. It is a link, between the

dinosaurs in the Hall of Bones and animals—birds—alive now," Lindhall explained without taking his eyes from the flier. "The seers who look back in time have seen lizard-birds in the same era as the largest snake-necked dinosaurs and the lesser tyrant lizards. They have followed the lizard-bird's development, and it is true—it comes from the land walkers."

"Instead of scales, feathers," said Numair, as interested as Lindhall. "Also a bird's wishbone and a bird's gripping foot. But it has abdominal ribs, as reptiles do, and a flexible tail."

The skeleton, tired of exercising invisible wings, settled on Lindhall's shoulder. Kaddar leaned in to inspect the empty spaces in the bones, and nearly got pecked. "Stop that," Lindhall ordered, stroking the creature's beak. "He was only looking."

"This isn't the assemblage spell," the prince said, looking at Daine. "I've never seen anything like this in my life. What did you do to it?"

Kitten, who had followed the men, squeaked a reproach at Kaddar's tone. The iguanas came in from the other room, prepared to defend Daine.

"I can't—I'm not—," Daine stammered.

She looked at Numair, who was rubbing one temple. "I think you must explain," he told her.

"These rooms are warded," Kaddar said. "That's how I could talk with Master Numair safely."

"What's in place here is unlike normal warding spells," added Lindhall, leaning against the counter. The lizard-bird on his shoulder ran his beak through the mage's fine, gray-gold hair, grooming him. "The emperor must never suspect these rooms *are* warded, or he would come to discover what I have that's worth concealment. If he or his servant mages try to eavesdrop in these rooms, they will hear only dull, innocent conversations and noises made by my animals."

Daine whistled. After two years with Numair, she had an idea how complex a spell-weave like that would be. "It's a new thing that's happened," she told Lindhall and Kaddar. "I'm not sure of the details. . . . Numair, what should I say?"

"All that you told me yesterday," was the quiet reply.

She obeyed. When she finished, no one said anything. Waiting for *one* of them to speak, Daine went to talk to the aviary birds. They wanted reassurance that the bone thing was not going to get into their home. Daine soothed them until they returned to their normal pursuits.

The first to speak was Lindhall. "You mean it isn't permanent?" The skeleton, bony tail hooked around the mage's neck, was gnawing his shirt buttons. "He'll stop being alive?"

Daine nodded. "I'm sorry, but it does seem to run out, after a time." She wanted to add that she wasn't sure if the vulture *had* run down, since the old woman had taken him, but thought the better of it at the last minute. She didn't want to start coughing again.

"You should try this in the Hall of Bones," the older man remarked, turning the skeleton's head from a necklace he wore under his shirt. "Stop that. If you bite it, you'll hurt yourself. Although I suppose it would be a bit inconvenient if any of the dinosaurs were to walk away."

Kaddar made a face at Daine, who giggled.

"*Inconvenient* puts it mildly," the prince drawled. "But Daine's right to keep this secret. I hate to think what my uncle would do with someone who has such power. Can you imagine? An army of dead creatures that can't be hurt by normal means?"

Daine thought of the great fused lizards, with their plates and spikes of bone, and shivered. One of them would do serious harm in a small village.

"It would be precisely to his taste," agreed Numair. "He might decide such power is worth a war in Tortall, perhaps even all the Eastern Lands."

"Well, while he's with us, I am going to call this one Bonedancer," Lindhall declared, stroking the lizard-bird's skull. "There's one thing I find troublesome about all this, however. Numair is right—wild magic does not function this way, as far as we can determine. What *is* the provenance of this power? Even the Black God is unable to give a semblance of life to the dead."

"Mynoss—?" suggested Kaddar. "No. He judges only."

"In *The Ekallatum Book of Tombs* it's said the Queen of Chaos once raised an army of the dead," murmured Numair.

"But the *Scrolls of Qawe Icemage* refute it," Lindhall replied. "According to him, the Queen of Chaos assembled dead wood and stones to be her army. No, the only god, I believe, who can resurrect that which was once flesh and is now dead is the Graveyard Hag."

"That's right," Kaddar said. "Remember? There are legends of bonedancers—the resurrected dead—from the fall of the Ikhiyan dynasty, and the end of the Omanat priest-kings—" He stopped, realizing what he was telling them, and the men looked at each other.

Daine's throat locked as if a bony hand gripped it. —*Don't even think of it, dearie*—a voice advised inside her head. —*It doesn't suit me that these handsome friends of yours should know I'm about. My, they're a tall set, aren't they? Not a one of them under six feet. I like these big fellows. Make a girl feel sheltered and fragile, that's what I always say.*—

You're as fragile as *granite*, thought the furious Daine.

—*Of course,*— was the amused reply. —*I'm a goddess after all. But it's nice to feel as if I might be fragile, old and rickety as I am. Now, remember, I'm keeping an ear on you, so don't try to warn them. If you force me to silence you fast, I might hurt you.*—

The hand on her throat squeezed, and Daine gasped, fighting for air. When her knees buckled, Numair caught her and helped her to a seat. "Are you all right?" he asked, dark eyes worried. "Bringing things to life tires you, doesn't it?"

She nodded. Kaddar went into the other room and returned with a pitcher and a cup, which he filled and handed to her. Daine sipped. It was water, freshened with a leaf of mint.

"We have to be careful talking about the Graveyard Hag," he said, gently teasing. "Yesterday she had a coughing fit in the Hag's temple. It didn't let up until we were outside."

Lindhall frowned, troubled. "Should you have visited her temple?"

"We visited them *all*," said Kaddar.

"It's my fault," Daine said, voice hoarse. "I wanted to look at them."

"Uncle can't fault me for doing it when he told me to take her wherever she wanted."

"No, of course not." Lindhall still looked uneasy. Clearly shaking it off, he said, "Numair, I think you must be getting back—it's almost noon. And what will you young people do? I could have lunch brought to us and then show you around a bit."

Daine smiled at the fair-haired man. "I'd like that, if it's all right with Kaddar. I can get to know *your* friends better."

Lindhall smiled as the lizard-bird preened feathers that were long gone. Numair took a deep breath and began to shape-change. Only when he was completely a hawk, oversized and black, did Lindhall open a door so that he could fly into a garden, and away.

That night, Varice shifted the banquet to a series of broad, shallow terraces overlooking an ornamental lake. Daine and the prince were dinner partners once more, seated at the end of the main group. Harailt was on Daine's other side. When the opening course was served, he amused himself by slipping tidbits to Kitten as he filled the two younger people in on the uneasy progress of the talks.

The emperor hadn't even made an appearance at the talks that day. Duke Etiakret, head of the Carthaki negotiators, walked out after Duke Gareth said King Jonathan and Queen Thayet would not agree to buy silk, dyes, and glass from no one but Carthak. Etiakret returned, only to say that Carthak refused to surrender one of its lords, a pirate who often raided Tortall, to northern justice.

When Harailt turned to the woman seated on his other side, Daine told Kaddar, "It doesn't look at all good, does it?"

"Do you see *any* happy faces around here?" he asked, indicating to the servers that they would have the catfish.

Daine shook her head. "Nary a one." She leaned back and reshaped her ears, knowing the growing shadows would hide the change from most. Scraps of talk came to her and faded as she twitched them to and fro.

"—am *not* going to let those things ruin this party, Numair. His Imperial Highness was simply in a mood. Etiakret will come to your people tomorrow, all smiles and conciliation—just you watch. Try the dormice, won't you? They're rolled in honey and poppy seeds—"

Daine winced—in her view dormice were food for owls, cats, and snakes—and listened elsewhere.

"—the result of a misunderstanding on my part, my dear Lord Martin. The emperor has taken me sternly to task and, I assure you, the progress of the talks in the morning will be far different—"

"—to honor her for her service to our treasured pets, Duke Gareth. Surely your rulers will not ask a penniless child to turn down a title and property of her own."

Daine made a face. She wanted no lands or title from the Emperor Mage! With a sigh she returned her ears to their normal shape and concentrated on the meal and her companions. As the sky darkened, they nibbled fried pockets of noodles and pork in a sweet sauce and talked about Kaddar's mother and sisters. Kitten, thinking herself unobserved, gobbled boar's tail with hot sauce, then had to leap for the water pitcher.

"Does she ever get sick from eating human food?" Kaddar watched as the dragon managed to dump half the water down her throat and half all over herself.

Daine smiled. "She never gets sick from *anything*. Once she ate a box of myrrh. She was only three months old. I thought every little accident she had would harm her for life."

"She didn't get sick?"

"She burped smoke for a week, that's all."

"I should have a stomach like hers. Especially these days." Kaddar's eyes flicked to where Ozorne sat, fanning himself idly.

"Come back with us," she said impulsively. "Make a *real* life, one with no cages in it."

His smile was both sad and bitter. "I cannot. He's got my family, my friends, even my horse. Do you think he would stop at hurting them to bring me home?" He patted her hand. "No. Once he claims something, he never, *ever* lets go. It's a miracle your Master Salmalín has managed to remain free and unharmed all this time."

Daine, knowing that Numair had worked as a street magician and nearly starved during his first years in Tortall, shook her head. Not daring to use his Gift out of fear that Ozorne would learn of it and hunt him down, changing his appearance and name, moving often before he made friends who brought him to the king's attention—to her that said he'd paid a high price for his miracle of survival.

Dishes came and went until the meal was over at last. By then the light-globes were burning, and musicians tuned their instruments at the far end of the terrace. Slaves arrived pushing a large metal cart slowly down the line of tables. It bore an immense cake, the pinnacle of a pastry cook's art, shaped like the imperial palace down to each bay, ell, and tower. Looking at it, Daine now saw that the palace was built like a rising sun, a large half circle with wings like short and long rays.

"The cooks made each piece and all the spun sugar, cream decorations, and so on," explained Kaddar, "but it's Varice who designs the cake and puts it together and supervises the decorating. Without her magic they couldn't do anything so fancy."

The guests applauded; Daine, reluctantly, clapped as well. Varice looked proud of herself as she offered the pastry knife to the emperor. Ozorne smiled and indicated that she should do the cutting.

As the blonde turned to the cake, Daine realized that something was wrong with Kitten. The little dragon was clawing at her muzzle and rocking back and forth. Bending close, Daine could hear her squeak, as if she were trying to talk with her jaws glued shut.

"Kit, what's the matter?" She bent down to grab the dragon's forepaws. "You're—"

Varice's shriek raised echoes on the lake. A slave filling Gareth the Younger's glass dropped his pitcher; it shattered on the flagstones. Daine jerked upright.

Rats—mostly browns, with a smattering of black ones—poured out of a hole in the front of the cake in a stream, their numbers far greater than even this cake would hold. They tried to climb Varice's skirts as the blonde continued to scream. Alanna was on her feet, groping for a sword she didn't wear; the mages were helpless, unable to throw fire at the animals without hurting Varice.

"Stop!" Daine cried, running out from behind her table. The rats turned to stare at her. "I said, *stop!*" Opening herself up, she let her power flood out until it swamped them. In their minds she read the knowledge that they were passing through a magical gate from their riverbank homes into the center of the big confection. She also saw clearly the image of the Graveyard Hag in their thoughts, pointing them to the gate with her gnarled walking stick.

"Imperial Majesty!" someone cried, shaking Daine's concentration. The moment she faltered, the rats broke free. Six of them launched at her face; she slammed them with her power, killing three instantly. Two fled; one fastened his teeth in her sleeve. Coldly Daine shook him off.

The man who'd broken her concentration was still yelling. "Majesty, even you can't continue to ignore the portents! You must—"

Ozorne pointed; emerald fire lashed to wrap around the speaker, a Carthaki nobleman. Emerald flames leaped from his skin. He had time for one agonized shriek before the fire ate him up.

Daine took a breath and renewed her magical grip on the rats, yanking them back from tables and guests. They fought hard. She dug her nails into her palms, hunting for something to make her *furious*. She found it when she saw the ruin that had come to the cake Varice had worked so hard to create. Gathering up the anger she felt on the part of Varice, she turned it on the rats.

We don't have to obey you, snarled a brown. We don't owe you anything!

We serve a powerful mistress, added someone else. Next to *her*, you are only a shadow!

She bore down, producing shrieks of rage and pain from them. "Back into that cake, buckos," she ordered, eyes glittering. "Back where you came from. Do it *now*, before you *really* vex me."

They struggled wildly, but she had them. When she began to tighten the pressure, she felt their surrender like the buckling of a wall. She called silently, Tell your mistress, if she has a bone to pick with Ozorne, pick it with *him*, not with them that have to obey him!

The rats leaped onto the cart and into the cake, vanishing through the gate. When the last of them had gone, the pastry collapsed.

She looked around. Slaves propped up a fainting Varice. Numair climbed over his table. Giving his wakeflower vial to Harailt and pointing to Varice, he came over to Daine. "Are you all right?" He cupped her cheek in one large hand, eyes worried. "One of them bit you—"

She held up her arm to show him the rip in her sleeve and smiled. "Didn't even nick the skin. It was only *rats*, Numair."

He looked at the chaos around them. Slaves who had fled the rodents stayed in the shadows, afraid to come out. Duke Gareth and Duke Etiakret were debating hotly in whispers, as Gareth the Younger looked on. Harailt was pulling the wakeflower from under Varice's nose as she coughed and gasped. Alanna talked softly into Kaddar's ear; she had to stand on tiptoe to do it, and Kaddar had to stoop a little.

"We need to get out of here before the sky starts raining blood or something equally pleasant," Numair remarked. "Where's Ozorne?"

The emperor had left.

The banquet was over. Varice, hysterical after she roused from her faint, was only able to cling to Numair and cry. All the guests, Carthaki and foreign alike, talked of the ominous signs they had seen and heard of in tense, lowered voices. No one seemed to care if the emperor spied on them or not.

Daine and Kaddar watched, quickly getting bored. "It's not as if we can *do* anything about all this," complained the girl, cradling a dozing Zek. "I get the feeling the only ones who can do something are your uncle and his ministers."

"Would you like to go for a walk, then?" Kaddar asked. "Is there anything you'd like to do?"

Daine looked around. On the far side of the lake, behind the willows on its shore, she could sense the menagerie. "Can we go look at the animals again?"

"Let me ask." The prince went to talk briefly with Alanna, who came back with him.

"I don't blame you for wanting to go someplace else," the Lioness said with a glare at Varice. "Just don't be gone too late. Tomorrow is another day—provided it comes, of course."

Daine stared at the Champion. "Do you know something we don't?"

Alanna shook her head. "Only that I didn't reach my station by ignoring the gods. If his imperial majesty doesn't consult them—soon—he will wish he had. Now scat, before *I* start crying."

They scatted, passing a squad of guardsmen on their way around the lake. Kaddar slowed and stared at them after they passed, his mouth tight. Then he shook his head, and they walked on. On reaching the menagerie, he left her at the closed, locked gate. When he returned, he bore a huge key ring. Sorting through the keys, he read their tags by the mage-light he cast over their heads.

"What kind of Gift do you have?" Daine asked. "Nobody ever said what you can do."

"Very little." He chose a key and fitted it in the lock. "Call light, move things a short way, call fire." The gate swung open. "What I do best is grow things. Trees, flowers, vegetables. I like to garden. The plants Lindhall has for his creatures—I grew those." He closed the gate behind them.

"That's wonderful," Daine replied, opening herself to the captive animals. "A shame you're stuck being a prince when you can do something important. Do those keys open the cages and enclosures? I want to go inside."

Startled, he yelped, "You want to—" Remembering where they were, he finished in a rough whisper, "—what? Go *in*? Out of the question. Absolutely out—"

"Don't be missish, Kaddar," she replied flatly. "If you don't let me in proper, I'll ask Kitten to do it, and maybe she'll melt the locks off."

Kaddar looked at the first enclosure, the lions'. "You swear you won't be harmed?"

"Goddess strike me if I lie," she said, holding up her right hand.

Shaking his head, Kaddar went to a door set into the wall next to the lions' pit, looking for the right key.

Zek watched, fascinated. *These keys things—do they always open cages and doors?*

"One of them is just called a key," replied Daine. Kaddar glanced at her. "Zek's asking," she explained. To the marmoset she added, "They open what doors and cages they're made to open. Two-leggers make locks to keep doors shut unless you have the right key. It keeps folk from stealing what's ours. It also helps us keep prisoners."

Then a key is magic, Zek said, gray-green eyes locked on Daine's face. *If I'd had keys, I could have freed my little ones and my mate.*

Next time, I will have a key.

Daine cuddled him, "No one's ever going to cage you again, Zek; I promise."

Kaddar unlocked the door. Open, it led to a small, dark stairwell that wound downward.

"Lights?" asked the girl.

"Just snap your fingers."

She made a face at him. "I can't snap my fingers, Your Highness."

"You *can't*? Really? But it's easy. You just—"

"I know what you just. I've been trying to for years."

He grinned, teeth flashing against his dark

skin. "You don't know how much better that makes me feel. You can outshoot me and talk with animals, but you can't do this." Raising a hand, he snapped his fingers, and small light-globes embedded in the wall flickered on.

"No need to rub it in," grumbled Daine. "Kit, are you coming?"

The dragon went in, but Kaddar hesitated. "Maybe Zek would rather stay with me."

I would, Zek told Daine, nostrils flaring as the scent of big cat rolled up the narrow stair.

Daine handed him to the prince. "Will I need keys down there?" she asked.

"No. The inner doors are held with bolts. They aren't locked."

May I see his keys? asked Zek. When Daine translated, the prince smiled and held the ring up for the marmoset to examine.

Daine followed Kitten down the stairs and opened the door that took them into the lions' pit. The cats were awake. Moving to look at Daine, they caught a whiff of Kitten's alien scent and snarled. "It's all right," Daine assured them, bathing the big animals in reassurance. "She's a friend. I'd think, downwind of those immortals, that you'd be more open-minded."

There was a laugh from above. She looked up and saw Kaddar leaning on the rail. "Is that what upset them?"

She smiled crookedly. "You'd think they never smelled a dragon before," she joked, holding her hands out for the lions to smell.

Entering their minds, she could feel they missed open ranges, even the ones who were bred in captivity, who learned of their true, wild life from the others. That had bothered her from the first, the sadness of their days even in confinement as pleasant as this. She could not turn them loose. Even if she could, they would be hunted down. Now, at least, she could do something for them. Lindhall had given her the idea when he showed her the small worlds he'd fashioned for his friends.

She asked the cats' permission first; they gave it. Starting with those born wild, she used their memories to build a waking dream. From different parts of their minds she drew scents, images, sounds, until she felt as if she'd been transported to a hot, distant land. She gave the dreams shape with the chill of winter rains, air perfumed with dry grass, zebra dung, fresh blood, the grunts and lowing of herds of fat prey. Carefully she sowed the dream in each lion, rooting it firmly in their minds. Now, when they chose, all they had to do was shut their eyes and remember. The dream would awaken; they would be home and free.

With Kitten she climbed back up the stair and went to the chimpanzee enclosure. Kaddar moved away from her as she passed, and looked at her with awe as he unlocked the chimps' prison. One by one, she visited all of the menagerie captives. Dream planting wasn't physically hard, but it was time-consuming. Kitten grew bored and joined Kaddar and Zek. The prince, to his credit, never complained about how long this took.

At last she reached the hyena enclosure. All three inhabitants sat at the bottom of the glasslike wall, dark eyes up and watching, rounded ears pricked forward.

"Perhaps you should pass by these," Kaddar suggested.

She stared at him. "Goddess bless—why?"

"They're not like other animals, Daine. They're cowards. If an animal fights them, they run away. They steal kills from lions, cheetahs. They even devour their young."

She scratched her head. For some reason, what he said irritated her. "Steal kills, is it? Doesn't Carthak do the same? Carthak has eaten all her young—Siraj, Ekallatum, Amar, Apal, Zallara, Shusin—even Yamut, all the way to the foot of the Roof of the World." He stiffened up, offended. "Forgive me for speaking so plain, but you *do* make them sound like this country of yours. I'm sorry to be rude when you've been kind to me, but animals, at least, do *every*thing for a good reason—to eat. To survive."

His smile would have gone unnoticed if she hadn't given herself cat eyes to see into the shadows around them. It was sour, but it was a smile. "You just reminded me that hyenas are sacred to our patron goddess. You know—the Graveyard Hag."

"How delightful for them," she replied, also sour. "Will you let me in there or not?"

He shrugged and opened the door that would admit her to the stair down. Once she emerged into their pit, the hyenas surrounded her, sniffing eagerly.

So you came back after all, remarked their leader, the female. I am Teeu. Meet my boys—Aranh is the one with the nicked ear. Iry has more spots than he can use.

Daine smiled, running her hands over powerful shoulders, exploring the muscles under the hyenas' rough and wiry fur. "I'm honored to meet you, all of you."

Too bad you weren't here before, Teeu said, touching Daine's closed eyes with her cold nose. This close, the reek of musk and dead meat made it hard for the girl to breathe. The hungry one was here.

This time he wasn't just hungry; he was scared. It's the best we ever smelled him.

"What hungry one?" she asked, curious.

The hungry one, said Teeu, sniffing Daine from top to toe. The one who wants to eat the world. He hates us, but he can't stay away. And tonight he was *sooo* afraid.

"How do you know?"

We smell it, Iry's voice murmured. We can smell him quite well when he stands up there.

May I? Daine asked Teeu. The female let her into her mind, to experience the world as they did. Kaddar was partly right when he spoke of hyena nature. Teeu had killed her twin not long after they were born; it was hyena custom. In some ways they thought like a wolf pack, but their noses were ten times better than even a wolf's. They mapped their landscape with scent as a bat wold map it with sound. She breathed with Teeu, and learned. The wind brought a bouquet of odor to the nose, one the hyena sorted through for her. She smelled Kaddar: lavender from his clothes, his own unique personal smell, each food he'd consumed that night. Kitten's scent was completely alien, even to one who lived on the other side of the wall from the immortals' menagerie. Teeu savored it, making sure it would never be forgotten, before she turned to Zek. His odor was musky, touched with hints of the fruit he loved, and mixed with the fear he felt as the hyenas' smell reached *him*.

What about the hungry one? she asked Teeu.

The hyena's memory for scent was as vivid as Daine's for sights. Their "hungry one" smelled of expensive cloth, soaps and hair oils, amber and cinnamon, spicy food and wine. The girl was startled to recognize it, though her memory of that particular odor was far less strong than Teeu's.

Leaving the hyena's mind, she comforted Zek briefly. When he was calm she called up to the prince, "Kaddar? Why is your uncle afraid of the hyenas?"

The prince leaned over the wall to look down at her. "Who told you that?"

Daine rested a hand on Aranh's sloping shoulder. "*They* did. They smell it on him. Kaddar, I swear these creatures can smell *anything*."

Kaddar fingered his eardrop. "Kitten, is there a listening spell on us?" The dragon whistled. The sound produced flares from Kaddar's gems—nothing else. "Thank you. Whenever you wish, you may live with me." Lowering his voice, he told Daine, "When Uncle took the throne, a prophecy was made that hyenas would lead his doom to him. If Chioké hadn't reminded him that hyenas are sacred to the Graveyard Hag, he would have killed every one in the empire. Instead, he keeps these. We have a saying about things like that: 'buying off the grave diggers.'" He lifted his head. "What was that?"

She gave her ears bat shape and listened. "There are humans in the immortals' menagerie."

"No one can go there without my uncle's permission." Kaddar examined the keys. "I should check."

"Can't we leave it be?"

"No. Do you know the magic that can be done with griffin's blood or spidren wool? If you want to wait, fine."

She looked at her new friends. "Do you want the waking dream, the one I gave the others?"

Teeu yipped her amusement. We would rather have what is here, she replied. The smells in this place are much more interesting than the ones at home.

She left them, racing up the stairs to the main walk. Kaddar was quietly trying to fit keys into the special menagerie's lock. When she joined him, he was scowling.

"Splendid," he muttered. "The guards have a way in, at the back of the immortals' enclosure, but I don't want to go past them. I'd hoped I'd find a normal lock, one for the cleaning slaves, but there isn't one. This lock is magical and my Gift won't open it. I don't know if the underground tunnels come out this far, either."

She heard voices on the far side of the gate. "Are you sure this is needful?"

"A drop of saliva from a flesh-eating unicorn in a man's food will kill him after three days of intense pain. It's undetectable as a poison unless you know *exactly* what to look for."

Daine sighed. "I suppose that means yes. Kitten? Don't melt it; just open it."

The dragon sniffed the keyhole. Backing up a few steps, she gave a demanding whistle, and the gate swung open. Kaddar strode past Daine. Zek, on his shoulder, leaped into the girl's arms, and she and Kitten followed.

EIGHT

ΤΗΕ ΒΑDGER
RETURNS

⟲⟨⟨⟨⟩⟩⟩⟳

Humans were in the courtyard between the
cages. Some were the Banjiku she'd met, as well as
other tiny black men and women who could only be
their kin. The remaining humans were slaves. They
were placing offerings—fruit, flowers, incense—
before the immortals' cages. Apparently they'd heard
nothing outside the gate: they froze in shock when
Kaddar reached them.

No one spoke. At last the Stormwing queen
unfurled great steel wings, the metal flashing in the
light of torches set around the courtyard. "So, girl who
slew Zhaneh Bitterclaws." Her voice was dry and
stern. "Do you come to taunt my consort and me?"
The humans went to their knees, bowing to Kaddar

until their foreheads touched stone flags.

"Does *every* one of you know what I look like?" Daine asked the Stormwing.

"Your face is in our minds," was the icy reply. "It is rare that we are bested by one so small, and unGifted." The queen turned dark eyes on the prince. "Have you come to see what you will inherit, mortal? Do you think to master *us*? You mean nothing. These others at least know they are slaves and give me fear because they know nothing else."

Her mate shifted on his perch, sidling to and fro, never taking his eyes from Daine and Kaddar. The female was Barzha Razorwing, Daine remembered, and he was named Hebakh.

"I'm not that different from these slaves," Kaddar said politely. "Perhaps all I know is fear. It seems that way, often enough."

"A pretty reply." The queen spat on the floor of her cage. "That is what I think of it."

"Stormwings," Daine muttered. "Anything they do, they have to be disgusting first."

"How else may we act, mortal?" demanded Hebakh, burning eyes fixed on Daine. "Our nature is what it is, don't you see? Our very immortality makes us immune to change."

"Mortal? No, no!" The protest came from Tano, the Banjiku who had done most of the talking when Daine first met him and his people. "She is a god, or the daughter of a god whose name she does not know. She is no mortal."

"Nonsense," scoffed Barzha.

"Forgive, forgive," said Tano, "but how can Banjiku be wrong about god things? Our tribe was birthed by Lushagui, sister to Kidunka, the world snake, the all-wise. To us it is given to bind men to beast-People, to know gods, and to be slaves."

They must thank their gods every day for that last, Daine thought to Zek, who nodded.

"Nonsense," Barzha repeated. "Look at her. She is a scrawny, underfed, unattractive spawn of mortal get, a killer of Stormwings."

Hebakh bated, then settle down. "There's evidence of the Banjiku gifts, my dear. I recall hearing about it from Lushagui. Girl. You know Rikash Moonsword?" He sidled across the cage to a perch near the bars, where he had a better view of her. "You told him we are here."

"Yes, sir," Daine replied.

"Why? Why tell Rikash anything?" demanded Hebakh. "You hate Stormwings."

Suddenly the griffin gave a shuddering, screaming roar, unfurling her wings as far as the confines of her cage would permit. She took a breath, then roared again, and again.

"We must go," said a slave urgently. "The guards will come any moment to silence her."

"Follow us," Tano instructed Daine and Kaddar, pointing to an open trapdoor. "There are tunnels for slaves to work here. We will guide you away, and no one will be the wiser."

"So the tunnels *do* come out this far," Kaddar muttered.

Daine hesitated, wanting to help the griffin. Reaching with her magic to ask the great creature to be quiet, she felt what was in her mind. The griffin was half crazy from imprisonment. Soothing her would take precious time. She could already hear raised voices behind the door at the rear of the courtyard, the guards' entrance that Kaddar had mentioned.

"Daine, come on!" hissed Kaddar.

Daine, Kitten, and the prince raced to the opening and down the ladder that led from it. Last came Tano, who drew the door shut and threw the bolt. A gnarled finger to his lips, he grabbed a lantern on the floor. Already the others were gone.

They followed their guide down a long, winding corridor for nearly sixty feet, where it branched in three different directions. Each one was marked with pictures in softly glowing paint: a bucket on one, a trio of brooms on another, and a horse's head on the third. That was the one chosen by their guide.

"What were you doing?" Kaddar demanded softly. "You know you aren't supposed to be in that area unless you work there, and even then only during the day."

The old Banjiku replied, "We worship captive gods."

"*Worship—*" sputtered the prince.

Tano stopped and looked up at the tall young man. "Worship," he said firmly. "Someday they will no longer be caged, young master. When they are free, will not their anger be terrible? Better to make offerings now, so the great ones will remember not all men are jailers."

Daine shivered. His words had sounded much like a prophecy.

"They aren't gods," argued Kaddar. Now they passed other stairs out of the tunnel, each marked with a picture. "They can be killed. That means they're not gods."

"No more is your master a god, Nobility," Tano said cheerfully, "but he wants offerings from all. When Black God claims us, who will be punished for giving worship and power to a false god? The prince? Or Banjiku? Now." He stopped by a ladder marked by an image of a flower and a fountain "Go up here and you will be in garden of guests, where lady stays." He bowed to Daine.

"I'm not a lady," she said, offering her hand. "Just Daine. Thank you, Tano."

He took her hand in his callused ones. "We are friends of the People together."

Kaddar had gone ahead and was holding the trapdoor open. "There's no one about. Come on."

Impulsively, she leaned down and kissed the little man on the cheek, then followed the prince.

They emerged between two hedges. The guest quarters shimmered whitely nearby. Once Kaddar shut the trapdoor behind them, it looked like part of the gravel walk. There was a small birdbath next to it; Daine suspected it was there so that the gardeners might find the door again. "Are there tunnels just under the gardens?" she asked. "There are tunnels everywhere under the palace," he replied. "Mostly used by slaves, but others find them handy, too." They fell silent, enjoying the cool evening. Kaddar moved first, stretching his arms. "We're in trouble, Daine. All Carthak is. See that?" He pointed at the sky.

Daine looked up. Stars spilled everywhere overhead. The moon was a sliver; another night, or two, and it would be full dark. The dark moon, for the working of dark magics, she thought, and shivered. "See what? Stars?"

"You *shouldn't* see them. This time of year, the skies *should* be thick with cloud. Maybe an opening or two, but not clear skies, night after night. We've had very little rain. In the south, people starve while my uncle readies for another war, so he can waste taxes, food, slaves, men. . . ." He looked at her and smiled bitterly. "You are too gods-blest easy to talk to, Veralidaine. You watch me with those big eyes, just listening, and the words drop off my wagging tongue." He shook his head and offered an arm. "I'd better escort you to your room. It's getting late."

She rested a palm on his arm and looked away as he led her inside. She wished he hadn't found her easy to talk to. There was nothing she could do to help a Carthaki human friend. He wasn't a mongoose or giraffe. She couldn't give the emperor's heir any waking dreams.

In her dream, she stood with Kitten and the Graveyard Hag at a crossroads in the middle of a barren land, and argued. An audience of rats and hyenas looked on. The Graveyard Hag wanted her to go left, into a fenced-in graveyard, where the tombstones leaned at strange angles and human bones poked through the earth. Daine wanted to go right, where she could see dinosaur skeletons embedded in the ground. Kitten, chattering furiously, wanted Daine to go back the way she had come. She slashed at the old woman's legs with a forepaw.

"Enough, dragon," the Graveyard Hag said. "I can't stop your coming here, but I don't need to put up with your impertinence, either. You aren't *near* old enough to do battle with me." She smacked Kitten on the muzzle with her gnarled stick, and the dragon's jaws snapped shut. She pawed at her mouth, but it remained closed.

"You stop doing that to her, and stop pushing me around," Daine told the goddess flatly. "I'm not one of yours, and I'm getting tired of your playing with me and my friends."

The Graveyard Hag grinned, showing all five teeth. "You're a sassy one, dearie," she said with approval. "Well, I always did like a girl who could stand up for herself But you're being naughty all the same. Come into my little garden here and play."

Hands on hips, Daine shook her head. "By the time you bury two-leggers, they're glad to rest," she retorted. "I don't *want* to play with them. They've earned the right to be let alone. Look at the way you've left them, all higgledy-piggledy like that. I should think you'd have the decency to straighten up around here." Part of her mind knew all this was a dream, but what on earth were they talking about, anyway? It made no sense.

A gnarled hand that had been empty suddenly boasted a silver dice cup. The Hag rattled it, her one good eye twinkling cheerfully at Daine. "Toss you for it."

"No. You cheat. C'mon, Kit." They marched toward the dinosaur bones. At first the going was hard. It took all Daine's might to lift her legs, and she could tell that Kitten was having equal trouble. The girl clutched the heavy silver claw around her throat. It dug into her palm, drawing blood, and suddenly she was moving forward along the barren dirt road.

Then she slowed, frowning. Things were changing, as they did in dreams. The dirt under her bare toes felt like cold marble, polished smooth. The blackened hills and barren trees of the orange-lit world around her were fading, becoming shadows that hinted at great shapes within.

Daine opened her eyes.

She was not in her guest bedroom, with its luxuriant bedclothes and sweet-smelling wood. Though she still wore her nightgown, cold stone under her bare feet was much too real to be a dream, and the draft that flowed against her back made her shiver. Kitten was dragging on the hem of her nightgown, chattering softly with anger and fear.

"Kit?" Daine asked, kneeling to cuddle the dragon. "I'm sorry—did I sleepwalk?" She'd never done so before, but things had been too strange during this journey for her to be much surprised. She changed her eyes to those of a cat, thinking she'd wandered out into the common room, or even the hall.

They were in the Hall of Bones.

"What in the name of the Great Goddess—" she breathed. "How did we get in, without the spell to open the lock? Kit—did you open it?" The dragon shook her head.

Crazy as it seemed, Daine had a very good idea of how they'd gotten here. "When I get hold of her, I will snatch what hair she's got left," she growled. "That's it for her toying with *me*!"

Turning to leave the hall, she stumbled and went down. Throwing out her hands to catch herself, she struck the thing that had tripped her, the stand for the mountain-runner nest. One hand plunged in among the eggs.

There was a blinding flash, one that etched in

lightning both the baby dinosaur standing by the nest and the eggs. She heard a distressed shriek from Kitten, but lacked the strength to tell her dragon that she was fine, just a little tired. She fainted before her body crumpled.

She and Kitten walked a trail that led up a densely forested hill. Suddenly the girl felt better than she had for days. Surrounding her was a northern woods, the air scented with pine, leaves turning color. The day was fading, but even so, everything she looked at seemed extra clear. An owl called; in the distance a wolf sang the first song of the night. All around she heard small woodland creatures prepare to go to bed, or to start their night's foraging.

The peace around them seemed to cow the dragon. Staring at everything, she walked so close that Daine nearly tripped over her several times.

Ahead was a thatched cottage, its white plaster walls gleaming as the night drew down. Light poured from the open door and windows. On the threshold, a man with antlers rooted in his curly hair argued with a badger. She heard them clearly, though she was only halfway up the hill.

"—ask you to keep an eye on her, keep her safe, and you allow my child to be used in *that*!"

"Flatten your fur, Weiryn," replied the badger. "What makes you think I had any choice?"

"The Great Ones can find another instrument! Why didn't you tell them so?"

"I did tell them, you horn-headed idiot. They didn't listen. *She* didn't listen. If you have a complaint, *you* take it up with the Graveyard Hag."

A woman appeared in the doorway behind the

horned man, drying her hands on a cloth. She was graceful and solidly built, firelight from indoors gleaming on her pinned-up golden hair. "Weiryn, does the badger want to sup with us? We—" Looking past the man's shoulder, she caught her breath; one hand went to her cheek. Man and badger turned to see what had gotten her attention.

Weiryn pointed at Daine, but it was to the badger he spoke. "There! *You* said she would be fine, and here she is. You know what that means! You *never* should have left her there—"

"If you were so interested in fathering, you shouldn't have put her in my care. She's old enough to get into her own tangles, whether you like it or not." The badger sighed. "I'll take them back. Talk to the great ones if you want, but I think it's too late. Can't you feel things moving forward?" He trundled down the path toward Daine and Kitten. "This place isn't for you. Turn around—"

"Badger, that's my ma," she protested. "And— my da?"

"Yes, yes; you should listen when the Banjiku tell you things. Turn around."

She obeyed, and fell into a mass of rolling gray clouds.

When she opened her eyes, she was flat on her back.

The badger stood on her chest, claws digging into her shoulders.

—*Idiot kit!*— he snarled. —*You drained your life force for this. You're supposed to use a spark, just a spark, to wake them up!*—

She blinked dazedly at him. "How was I to know that, pray? You didn't tell me anything. You just breathed on me and left."

—*Nonsense. Of course I told you.*— Daine shook her head. —*No?*— The badger climbed off her. —*Then I lost my temper, at being used to place this on you. I should have taken time to explain. It was a grievous mistake, and a disservice to you.*—

Kitten, much vexed, chattered at the badger, punctuating what she had to say with earsplitting whistles.

Daine groaned and covered her ears, while the animal god turned on the immortal.

—*When I wish for your opinions, dragonling, I will ask for them. Silence!*—

Kitten subsided, muttering under her breath.

Daine sat up. "Kitten was there with me," she said, frowning.

—*Of course,*— the badger said —*Dragons go where they will, even the young ones.*— He snorted rudely. —*Pesky, interfering creatures.*—

Kitten made an equally rude noise in reply.

Daine heard a rapid clicking, as if something bony ran on the marble tiles. Instantly she checked the mountain-runner nest. Not only was the standing skeleton gone, but the eggs had hatched.

—*That is why it killed you,*— said the badger, peering at the nest. —*You woke them all. What were you thinking of? The energy to spark this waking magic has to come from wild magic. Waking the whole nest drained you. You'd better find a way to draw the spark from other sources. I can't bring you back from the Divine Realms whenever you make a mistake and die.*—

"Die? But—I thought—humans go to the Black God's realms when they die."

—*Humans do. You will have a choice, the Black God's kingdom or the home of your father, when the time comes. You must be careful not— What do you lot want?* —

His question confused Daine, until she noticed the mountain-runner skeletons to her left, the ones from the nest. Seven of them were only a foot tall. The last was the eighteen-inch skeleton. All watched the badger, the tilt of their small skulls giving them an odd look of attentiveness.

"Oh, no," she whispered, and covered her face with her hands. "However do I explain *this*? Badger, I can't be going about waking up dead creatures. I'm no god!"

—*No, but the Graveyard Hag granted you this power to further her own ends,* — he retorted. —*I am sorry, my kit. I was not given a choice.* —

"She can push you around?"

—*In Carthak, which is her own, she can do whatever she pleases. Here she is one of the great gods. In Tortall you would be*— he snarled. —*We would be safe from her. She is only a minor goddess anywhere but the empire. Here, Bright Mithros, the Threefold Goddess, all but the Black God must bow to her, and she is the Black God's daughter. In Carthaki matters he listens to her.* —

"Lovely," Daine grumbled. "The boss god of all Carthak wants to get me in hot water. Next time I get the notion to travel, I'll remember this and stay home." She sighed and looked at the mountain-runner skeletons. One, braver or more foolish than the rest, had crept forward, and reached out to touch the badger's coat.

—Don't you dare— snarled the badger. The mountain-runner leaped back and tripped on its bony tail. Kitten rushed over to place herself between the downed lizard and the badger, scolding loudly, the color in her scales turning pink.

"Kit, hush! He didn't mean to frighten the little one. Someone will hear; *please* be quiet."

The badger sighed. *—It is time for me to go, and for you to return to your room.—* To Kitten, he said, *—If you do not behave, I will tell your family that Daine is spoiling you, and that they had better take you from her care if they do not wish you to be ruined for life.—*

Kitten shut up with a last cheep.

Daine hid a smile. Looking at the mountain-runners, she said, "But what about them? I can't hide these. And I've no idea of when they'll go back to sleep. The lizard-bird I woke at Master Lindhall's was still up and about when we left."

The badger scratched an ear. *—Most of those you wake will sleep when the Graveyard Hag's need, whatever it is, ends. Only a few will care to stay, when their kind and their world are gone. As for these—* He eyed them. They had crept around Kitten and were stroking his fur with gentle forepaws. *—They will go with me. It is the least I can do. I made a mistake, not helping you to understand what you can now cause.—*

"Badger—do *all* gods make mistakes?"

He glared at her. *—Rarely. I have not made one in ten centuries, so perhaps I was due. Even the greatest gods err, now and again. When they do, the results are catastrophic.—* He looked at the dinosaur skeletons looming in the shadows. *—Their world ended through a god's mistake.—*

"Horse Lords," whispered the girl, eyes wide.

The badger looked at the mountain-runners.

—Climb on. And no pulling my fur.—

The mountain-runners lost no time in obeying. Clustered on the god's broad back, they reminded Daine of nothing so much as children on a boating holiday. "Badger? Does it hurt them to die again? Or if a mage blasted them, say?"

—How could it hurt flesh that is not there? This awakening you give them is not true life. When they sleep again, they will return to the otherworld that serves the spirits of the People. Now, go back to bed,— he advised. *—And tell the Banjiku that Lushagui never meant for them to be slaves.—*

Silvery light bloomed. It winked out, and Daine and Kitten were alone.

As they sneaked back to Daine's room, the girl began to yawn. Her body ached as though she had been pummeled. Gently moving Zek from the center of the bed to the side, she got in next to him. Kitten gave a small croak, and the lamps went out. Daine's last thought was of moving her feet to make room for the dragon, and then she slept.

The odd night she'd had didn't cause her to sleep late, but as she cleaned her face and teeth, dressed, and brushed her hair, she felt as if a griffin had landed on her. Kitten roused as she buttoned her shirt, and uttered a forlorn cheep.

"No, don't," the girl said, voice gravelly. "One of us ought to rest."

Kitten nodded agreement and went back to sleep. Zek, curled up on Daine's pillow, sat up. You vanished, he said. Kitten got angry and vanished, too. Why didn't you take me?

Daine smiled. "I didn't know I was going anywhere, Zek, or I would have taken you. Remember, I promised you'd be safe from now on. I won't leave you behind. Now, go back to sleep." Ever agreeable, the marmoset obeyed.

Closing her eyes, Daine reached with her magic for the emperor's birds: she wanted to check their progress. The moment she found them, she knew something was wrong. Each appeared in her magical vision as a tiny ball of light. On a handful, shadows dimmed their fire. Some of the birds were falling sick in the same way as they had before.

Leaving a note in the common room, she trotted along the shortcut to the aviary, frowning. In conversation with Lindhall the previous day she had learned he would never change the birds' feed without an excellent reason. He'd also said that the emperor was too good with birds to meddle with their diet when they'd been sick, and she believed him. Then why were they ill again, and how long would it be until the disease spread to the entire flock?

When she reached the door in the glass wall, she saw emerald fire around its edges. Gingerly she touched the knob. If the magic was to foil intruders, it failed: she felt nothing. She went in and closed the door quietly. When she turned away from it, an oval patch of emerald fire hung in the air before her. It rippled; the face of the Emperor Mage appeared. He was bare of all makeup save for the black paint around his eyes, with only a few gilded braids in his casual hairstyle.

"Veralidaine, good morning," he said. "I thought it might be you. Will you come to my table? I'm by the door into the palace."

She scuffled a shoe against the ground, not wanting to say why she was there until she had a better idea of what was wrong. "Could I look at the birds first, please, Your Imperial Majesty? They need me to check them over a bit, now they've had a couple days free of the sickness." To excuse herself the half-lie, she crossed her fingers behind her back, where he couldn't see.

"Far be it for me to come between you and your charges." His smile was sweet, if a bit melancholy. "You will come to see me, though? Once you have spoken with them?"

She didn't want to, but there was no graceful way to refuse. "Yessir."

"Very good." The image faded; the fiery oval collapsed on itself and vanished.

Parrot finches came to lead her up the curved stairs to a pair of stricken birds, red-crested cardinals. They clung side by side to a branch well away from the sun, blinking. She saw no signs of trembling, and their eyes were bright, but she could feel the illness starting to work in their bodies. She gathered the male into her hands.

What have you been into? she asked silently so that the emperor wouldn't hear. What have you been eating or drinking to make you sick again?

The bird looked at her dully. He couldn't remember. He was fine the day before, visiting all his favorite places. And he wasn't sick, precisely. Just a bit off his feed.

She opened her mind to his. The illness showed as black threads running along the bird's nerves, growing toward his spine and brain. Once they reached those, he would know he was sick. She bore down with healing fire, burning out every thready trace.

When he was well, she opened her eyes to find he'd marked her arms and feet with thick white droppings. She frowned. The night she'd first come to the aviary, her mind was too full of the things she had seen and the work she was doing for the birds' dung to register as anything more than the reason for the loss of a pretty outfit. Now she scooped up a bit and rubbed it in her fingers. It was heavy, almost pastelike. What it should have been was compact, wet, dark, with perhaps a few undigested seed hulls mixed in.

The female red-crested cardinal had the same kind of droppings.

Daine spread her power through the aviary, calling the other three whose new illness she had detected: a green-and-gold tanager, an orange-bellied leafbird, and one of the royal bluebirds, with its impossibly blue wings and tail feathers. All three nested close to the glass wall. All three of them emptied themselves of heavy white droppings as she healed them. She held them away to spare her clothes more damage.

With them taken care of, she summoned the red-crested cardinals back to her. All five of her patients clustered on branches around her at the topmost level of the stair, looking at her curiously. Where do you nest? she asked the cardinals.

The male flew to the tree where he lived, and back. Like the others, he nested by the glass.

Some kind of magic gone awry in the windows? she wondered. Getting her handkerchief, she scrubbed her hands with it as she thought. Glass splinters falling into the nest or the food? she wondered, but that wasn't right. If splinters had caused the damage, the birds' dung would be bloody and black, not white. White paste—why did she think there was something important about white paste?

A picture came to life in her memory, of Numair making paints, using—

Lead compounds, she thought, eyes lighting up. They're getting *lead*! That's what's coming out of their bodies when I heal them! Tell me what you eat here, she ordered.

Red-faced parrot finches had come to watch everything she'd done, fascinated. Now they chorused, Seeds.

What *kind* of seeds? she asked. What do they look like? Show me.

All the birds came, to shower her with images of seeds.

Enough! she ordered when they began to repeat themselves. Only seeds, or is there other food?

Fruit, said the tanagers. Figs, grapes, fluffy leaves with plenty of wet in them.

Daine smiled, recognizing the image of lettuce in their minds. What else?

Sometimes green food, said a parrot finch, perching on Daine's shoulder. It's good. It's different. His red face twisted up to hers. *They* had green food, he said, meaning Daine's patients.

So what is it? she asked. What kind of plant?

Not a plant, exactly, the helpful parrot finch said. He gave up trying to see her face from her shoulder and perched on her hand.

Not a plant. Green *seed*? she asked.

No, said the parrot finch. It is green food. Over here.

He fluttered up into the air, and darted at the glass. She was about to warn him not to hit it when he stopped, clinging to a vinelike tendril. It was a decoration on one of the metal strips that held the glass panes there. He pecked at the green enamel surface.

"Goddess bless," she whispered. She reshaped her eyes and face to give herself a hawk's vision, and focused on the metal strips near the parrot finch. With so much extra visual power, she noticed a glossy surface on the enamel that was clear, a layer that had to be lacquer of some kind. Cracks ran through it like fractures in ice, and tiny bits had flaked off, revealing the less-shiny green enamel underneath. Everywhere she looked, the clear surface was pitted. In a number of locations, the damage to the clear lacquer was even greater, and there were pocks in the green material itself. She would know the distinctive marks of beaks and claws anywhere.

Is that what you've been eating? she asked her patients, remembering to do it silently.

It's good, replied the green-and-gold tanager, cocking his head at her. It tastes different. I'm always thirsty after the green food, but I still like it. The others chorused agreement.

Daine put her hands on her hips. Salt in the enamel, she thought with disgust. Only they're eating lead along with it.

She called all the birds to her, even those begging tidbits from Ozorne. Now listen to me, she told them when they were quiet. The green food is *killing* you. It's poison. You have to promise me you'll never, *ever* touch it again. As she spoke, she pressed down, reinforcing her words with magic so that they would avoid the stuff forever.

I still have to tell the emperor to have the coatings changed, she thought as she trotted gleefully down the stairs. Or new strips put in, or something.

"I found out what made them sick!" she said when she found him. He was seated in the area with the marble bench, a seed-filled bowl at his side. A table and two chairs had been placed there, and breakfast was already laid out. "The enamel on the metal things that hold up that glass? They're eating it for the salt and taking in lead. If you change the paint, or cover it with something that won't crack or break, they won't get sick again. I've talked to your birds"—they were coming back to him now, perching on his shoulders and on nearby branches as he offered them food from the bowl—"and *they* won't go near it anymore, I made fair sure of that! But you'll have to fix it before any chicks hatch, because doubtless I won't be here to make them leave it be."

He smiled up at her, holding seed-filled palms steady as birds perched and ate. "You have done me a tremendous service, Veralidaine. Will you do me another and take breakfast with me?"

She looked at the table, set with filled crystal goblets, delicate porcelain and silver, then looked down at herself and blushed. "Your Imperial Majesty, I'm a mess. It would hardly be fitting—"

With a gentle movement he dislodged the birds and moved the bowl away so that they could sit on the rim and stuff themselves. He closed a hand and opened it, to reveal a ball of green fire. "We require a washbasin and those things necessary for the cleansing of hands. Also a robe—blue, or lilac, blue-gray—suitable for a young lady who stands as high as our chin." He closed his hand, and the fire was gone. Looking up at Daine, he smiled wistfully. "Please accept. I dislike meals taken alone, and it seems—of late—I am not the most sought-out of companions."

What could she say to that? "Thank you, Your Imperial Majesty."

Three slaves came through an arch partly shielded by greenery. One carried a gold basin that steamed faintly; another soap, a washcloth, and a neatly folded towel on a tray; and a third something lilac and very fine draped over his arm.

"Our rooms open into this aviary," explained Ozorne. She noticed that he'd switched instantly to the imperial *we* on the arrival of others. "Our birds will not come there—it is too bright and noisy for them—but we enjoy the sound of the aviary fountains at night."

The slave with the basin knelt on one knee before Daine, holding it above his head like an offering. She stepped back, confused.

"Go on," the emperor said. "Wash."

She was supposed to clean her grimy hands this way? With a human washstand?

The slave with the tray set it on one of the chairs. She and her companion proceeded to delicately unbutton Daine's cuffs and roll her sleeves above the elbow. The girl gritted her teeth and did as she was expected to, wetting her hands and scrubbing them. With the best intentions in the world, she couldn't avoid splashing the boy underneath the basin. When she was finished, the slaves dried her hands and helped her into the lilac robe. She winced as it closed around her dung-streaked clothing. The garment, a finely made thing with silver braid and tiny pearls worked around hem, collar, and cuffs, would never be the same.

Once she was covered, the slaves served the food as Daine and the emperor each took a chair. When they were done, Ozorne dismissed them. "I find mutes make the best slaves," he remarked, curling one hand around a crystal goblet. Daine had one just like it before her, filled with something that was the bright red of fresh blood. "They do not chatter. Shall we have a toast, then?"

Daine stared at him, hands tucked into her lap. "A toast, Your Imperial Majesty?"

He raised his goblet. "To birds," he said gravely.

Relief filled her: she had feared he'd want to toast Carthak, or the ruin of Tortall. Don't be silly, she scolded herself as she raised her goblet. He wouldn't try to make me do something bad like that, not when I just helped him.

She sipped the red liquid. It was pomegranate juice, a bit thick and oversweet. She would have preferred to water it down, but the emperor drank all of his straight down. Good manners dictated that she do the same. When the goblet was empty, she drank from another, filled with cold water, to rinse the heaviness out of her mouth.

"What do you think of the progress being made in the peace talks?" he asked, delicately cutting a bite of ham. "Have you been kept abreast of what transpires here?"

She fiddled with the napkin she'd put on her lap. "I know it's not going very well."

"No. It was too much to hope for, really, with so much else taking place—all these dark omens. Do you know why the gods are angry?"

The girl shook her head. It was much too hot in here. Sweat was trickling down her temples, and it was a little hard to follow what he was saying. It also didn't seem like the time to mention that she had some idea of the source of the gods' displeasure.

"I let a threat to Carthak exist. A powerful criminal, sheltered by my enemy, Jonathan of Tortall. The gods do not love a ruler who permits a threat to survive. It was made clear to me, the night of the naval review. Zernou himself pointed out my error, and suddenly I understood."

She took a deep breath. It was an effort to draw air in. "He pointed to you," she whispered.

Ozorne's smile was amused and pitying. "Not to me, Veralidaine. To the criminal. To Arram Draper—your teacher, Numair Salmalín. I knew that I was moved to allow his return for a good reason. My hand was guided by the gods themselves." Rising, he came to her side of the table and lifted one of her arms, placing his fingertips over her pulse. She tried to yank away, but all she could think of was Numair.

"You cannot fight dreamrose," Ozorne remarked. "It's a cousin of wakeflower, and very strong. A spear dipped in it will drop a charging elephant. Frankly, I am amazed you are still awake."

"You—can't hurt us." She fought hard to say it. "Ambassadors. Sacred—"

"I will hurt no one, my dear." He placed her

arm in her lap again and brought his chair close, sitting where he could watch her face. "You will run away and vanish into the kingdom. I will be furious. For all I know, you are among criminals in the underground, urging them to rebel against me. Your friends will be forced to leave immediately, under guard. Even Tortall's allies will be able to see that these talks failed due to *you*, not to me. I will have my Tortallan war, and no one will stop me.

"Better, I know that he loves you—the traitor Salmalín. That I could see when he came here seeking you, and the night Zernou pointed him out to me—the night the traitor warned my heir not to trifle with you. Since we will go to war in any case, Salmalín will return for you, and I will have him." There was nothing in his voice, or eyes, but kind interest. "This will turn out for the best. I *like* you, Veralidaine. The way you have with my darlings—" He shook his head admiringly. "You will have a title—countess, perhaps? Even duchess. You will have your own estates, your own slaves, whatever you wish. You will even have the dragon, too. It will be necessary to keep her under the sleep until you are well settled here, but once you are, she will be content as long as *you* are content. I will not risk waking her until I am certain she will not turn on me."

Sleep was wrapping around her like a cloud-filled blanket. "Numair . . ."

Ozorne stood. "He dies, my dear. The gods demand a blood sacrifice, and so do I."

NINE

DAINE LOSES HER TEMPER

ᏬᏬᎬᎪᏫ

She had the oddest dream. She was Zek, and
the world was *huge*. Kitten, who to Daine was the size
of a medium-tall dog, looked like a three-horn to the
marmoset. He watched the dragon sleepily from the
bed as she walked to and fro on the floor, talking to
herself. He could tell she was worried, but not about
what.

Then a section of the wall that was farthest
from him swung open without a sound. Zek/Daine
leaped from the bed, and hid underneath. Kitten
whirled, turning orange with fright, as the Emperor
Mage came in, a solid black crystal in his hand. He
lobbed it gently at the dragon. It shattered on the floor
without a sound, filling the air with smoke. When Zek

could see Kitten once more, she was frozen in place, unmoving.

Ozorne knelt in front of her and drew a hank of thin, black cord from the pouch at his belt. Swiftly he unrolled it and bound Kitten's muzzle and paws, tying the two ends together when he was done. When he let go of the cord, it shone green, then vanished completely. Kitten's eyes closed, and she collapsed into the emperor's arms.

Ozorne pointed to the door; green fire left his finger, spreading to cover the opening. He then waved to someone in the hole in the wall. Slaves came, gathering up Daine's things. "Be certain you take *all* of her belongings," he instructed quietly. "Not a single hairpin must remain."

Zek, wits made sharp by exposure to Daine, looked around. There was no place under the bed to hide if they looked there, and there was magic on the main door. He didn't know what lay beyond the opening in the wall, but in any event the emperor was between him and it. He peered at the corner near the windows. A cloth hanging was on the wall. Above it, near the ceiling, he saw a rectangular opening: an air vent.

The emperor's face appeared under the foot of the bed. "There you are." Fire collected at his hand, and lashed forward.

The time to think was past. The marmoset raced from under the bed, scrambled up the hanging. Emerald fire lashed the cloth below. It burst into flame. Zek jumped into the vent and found himself in a long, dark tunnel not much bigger than he was. Turning, he saw that the tunnel ended nearby in an opening with a fine screen over it: no escape that way.

"Where are you, little rat?" he heard Ozorne say. Zek fled down the long end of the tunnel, into the palace depths.

Daine continued to dream after that, funny images that had little in common with the dreams she was used to. She wondered if she ought to complain to whoever was in charge of these things, but Gainel, the Master of Dream, was not one of the easily found gods. With no one to protest to, she paid attention once more to the dreams.

Guards formed a square around the Tortallans, marching them to a waiting ferry. Alanna walked grim-faced behind the covey of clerks, eyes watching everywhere. Duke Gareth, Lord Martin, and Gareth the Younger kept their heads together, whispering urgently. Harailt gripped one of Numair's arms, talking fast as he half trotted beside the much taller man. Daine wondered at the look on Numair's face. His nostrils and lips were white-rimmed; his eyes blazed. His unfastened robe spread behind him like black wings.

The scene changed. She was in the immortals' menagerie, watching as Ozorne himself gently placed the sleeping Kitten on a giant cushion inside a cage. Next to it, flesh-eating unicorns looked on with eyes that blazed hate.

The next dream was an entire play set in a cramped shipboard cabin. It glowed in the corners with sparkling fire, shielding against eavesdroppers. Harailt, Gareth the Younger, and the clerks were absent. Lord Martin and Duke Gareth were side by side on one of the bunks, watching Numair on the other. Lindhall was also present, Bonedancer the lizard-bird on his shoulder; he looked deeply worried. In her dream, Daine was mildly surprised to see that Bone was still awake. She noticed, fascinated, that his empty eye sockets followed each speaker.

"Impossible," Lord Martin said curtly. "Our duty is to return home and warn the king."

"She's one of *ours*," retorted Alanna. The Champion leaned against the wall, fisted hands thrust deep into her breeches pockets. "That letter's a forgery—it must be. He's keeping her somewhere, and using it as a pretext to end the talks and declare war."

Duke Gareth looked at her, eyes sad. "We cannot prove that, my child. Neither can we help Daine; we *must* warn the country. As it is, Tortall will stand alone against him. By announcing it before the foreign ambassadors, he made certain they believed his proof that Daine conspires against him. As far as our allies are concerned, *we* caused the talks to fail."

"You can warn Tortall, then, and the king," Numair said quietly. "I won't leave without her."

"We never should have brought that child," snapped Lord Martin. "I knew it would be trouble!" Standing, he approached the door. "Let me pass," he ordered. A hole appeared in the magic; he opened the door and left. Once he was gone, the fire sealed the room tightly again.

"Arram, there is more at stake than any girl, even this one." Lindhall's absentminded air was gone. "The information passed to you—contacts, new routes for the slave underground, conspirators' names—it *must* go north, *now*, before the borders are closed by war. We may have to get the prince out in a hurry if the emperor begins to suspect him, and the only way to do it safely is to have all prepared on your end."

Numair shook his head. "I don't care. Someone else can take the information to the king."

The Champion whirled and slammed both fists into the wall. "I *hate* not doing something!" she cried. "I *hate* it! I want to go back there and—"

The lizard-bird leaped from his perch on Lindhall, flapping clumsily across the room to land on Alanna's shoulder. He ran his beak through her hair, trying to comfort her. "Go away, you old Bone," she whispered, but her heart wasn't in it.

"You cannot, my dear," Duke Gareth said, his voice filled with pity. "We are going to war. Your place is at home with the king and his armies."

Alanna's eyes brimmed with tears; she turned away from the men.

"Numair, if you choose to remain, I cannot stop you—you are too great a mage," the duke said. "Please think, then. The emperor is mad, but not stupid. He *knows* you wouldn't leave Daine here. My concern is that he has planned for just that eventuality."

Numair and Lindhall exchanged looks. "I'm aware of the danger, Your Grace," Numair said quietly. "I have taken precautions. They may be enough. Ozorne has trouble believing in his heart that anyone else has more of the Gift than he does, even when his mind knows there are more powerful mages. I can use that to fool him. As for the knowledge of the prince's conspiracy—"

"Give it to me," Alanna said curtly. "It's the least I can do." She handed Bonedancer to Lindhall.

Numair looked at the duke, who sighed and nodded. Getting up, the tall mage went over to Alanna and placed his fingers on her temples. Black fire sparkled where they touched.

Daine would have liked to view more, but the dream was pulling her away, and her head ached.

The dream headache turned into a real one as she awoke. Putting up a hand to shield her eyes from a light-globe overhead, Daine found that she was stiff in places she hadn't known could get stiff. Arms and legs alike were slow to respond as she sat up and put her feet on the floor.

Here was a strange thing—she sat on the floor. The bed on which she lay was only a thick pad covered with a blanket. A stack of clean, fresh clothing lay next to the pad.

As her eyes got used to the light, she realized that she was someplace totally unfamiliar. The room was a box; its white plaster walls, floor, and ceiling were bare of any ornament. Three skins of liquid and a napkin bundle rested beside the pile of clothes. The skins contained water, the napkin stale rolls and grapes. A wooden bucket sat in the corner, she assumed for use as a privy.

Fear chilled her. The door had no handle or knob. Running her fingers along the frame as high as she could reach, then down to the floor, she sought a lock or latch without success. She stripped off the clothes soiled in the aviary and put on the clean garments. It didn't escape her attention that they were her own things. She ate the rolls and fruit greedily and could have eaten more. How long had she been asleep? How long would it be until someone let her out?

Did anyone mean *ever* to let her out?

She searched the room, seeking locks, vents, or anything else. Only plaster met her fingers. A year earlier Numair, telling her of his captivity before he'd escaped to Tortall, had said there were rooms under the palace that canceled magic, used from within them or from without. If she was in such a room, Numair, Alanna, and Harailt might seek her with their Gift and never find her. And what about her dreams? Had they been true? Were her friends still in Carthak?

By then she was trembling. She was caged.

"I want out," she whispered. The room was stuffy. She tried to fill her lungs, without success. With no vents, she might run out of air. The walls drew closer. In a moment she would stretch out both arms and be able to touch them— "No!" she screamed, slamming into the door. "No! No!"

The pain cleared the last traces of drug from her mind, and she could hear her friends outside. Her prison might cancel the Gift, but not wild magic. The People screamed with her, throughout the palace and in the city, over the river. Daine roared her fury. Animals turned on the two-leggers. Dogs set on master, cats the nearest passerby. Birds drove nearby farmers out of their fields. Daine was in all of them, shrieking defiance of cage builders.

In the palace, dogs and cats leaped for the mage Chioké. He threw up his hands: orange fire lashed, crisping their bodies. Daine shrieked as their agony shot through her.

"Stop!" she cried to the others. "No, don't! Stop! They'll hurt you, they'll kill you!"

A hunter shot his horse with a crossbow; a soldier speared his camel; Ozorne flamed a charging pet monkey. The rest of the People calmed down and hid from sight. Daine collapsed to the mattress and wept. She had gotten her friends killed, and she was still trapped.

She heard a thump somewhere near, and a click. Taking a deep breath, she shaped herself. Bones shifted. Skin and senses changed swiftly; claws sprouted from paws the size of plates. Daine the bear plodded over to a corner behind the door. Rearing up on her hindquarters, she waited.

The door opened. A cheetah entered the chamber, with Zek on his back. The marmoset clutched silvery metal in his paws. He looked at the bear, and showed her his prize.

Keys, Zek said proudly.

Zek and his new friend, Chirp, the Banjiku performers' male cheetah, led Daine through the web of branching tunnels under the palace, avoiding humans. At last they came to a round chamber deep underground, where odd-looking signs and runes had been painted on the walls. Tano, Chirp's trainer, waited there with fruit and water for Daine.

"It is safe to speak here and to be here," he told the girl as she ate. He pointed to the signs on the walls. "This is protected place. Slave magic protects here from owner-mages. Tell me what you need, and we will find."

She swallowed a mouthful of grapes. "My friends—are they here?"

He shook his head. "Two days ago emperor say you run off to get slaves to rebel. His warriors take your friends to boat and guard it until they leave. The armies prepare for war. Their great drums pound all night." He shook his head. "Sleep very bad."

She thought over what all of that meant. The armies wouldn't march; her animal friends would see to that. "I need to talk to Prince Kaddar. Will you trust him if you bring him down here? Or you could blind-fold him, if you aren't sure. But I trust him, if that means anything."

Tano nodded. "You will leave this place, go home?"

"I have to do one or two things, but then I'm going." Now that she was awake, her dreams felt *solid*, more like visions than dreams. If that was so, then Numair was here, somewhere. "Tano—I have a mes-sage for you, from the first badger. The male badger god. He said to tell the Banjiku that Lushagui *never* meant for you to be slaves."

The black man frowned. "Never?" Daine shook her head. Tano thought this over, pulling thoughtfully on his lower lip. "We must talk about this, the Banjiku. Talk comes later. I go for prince now—you wait."

As he trotted away, Chirp curled up next to Daine, while the girl petted Zek. "How did you find the keys?" she asked. "Where were they? How did you know they'd be the right ones?"

I found the emperor when he went to feed his birds, Zek replied, nibbling a fig. Then he went to his room. In his wall, there was a way down to the cage where he put you. He went down twice to look at you. Afterward he put the keys near his bed. I took them and asked Chirp to bring me to you a different way than through his room. All the People knew how to find you once you woke up. Smugly he added, but I am the only one of the People who knows about *keys*.

"You are the wisest, cleverest creature I've ever met," she whispered, cuddling him. "You saved my life *and* my wits. Did you see where he took Kitten? I dreamed he enchanted her."

Zek shook his head. He did not visit her, the marmoset explained.

Daine leaned back against the wall. "He wouldn't hurt her. I'm not at all sure he can. So he's put her somewhere—perhaps in the menagerie with the other immortals. I dreamed that's what he did, anyway. We'll look and see."

Still cuddling Zek, she dozed off until Chirp nudged her awake. Kaddar and Tano were coming. When the prince saw her, he stopped, dark face turning ashen. "Daine? Tano didn't say—"

She glared up at him. "You know what your uncle did to me?"

"We have to get her out of here," Kaddar informed Tano. "Once he finds her gone, he'll tear the palace apart."

"I'll go happily, once I get Kitten back," she said. "Tell me something, if you please. Do you know anything about a drug called dreamrose?"

"It produces sleep," he replied promptly. "And true dreams."

She nodded. "All right, then. I think—I'm fair certain—Numair's still in Carthak. Once I find Kit, will you smuggle me to the university? I can't leave this place without him. He—" The look on the prince's face brought her up short. "Something's wrong."

"Daine—"

She rose. "*What?*"

Kaddar put a clumsy hand on her shoulder. "Please, try to remain calm."

"*Your uncle* tricked me, drugged me, put me in a locked room with no air and stale food, and then he made my friends leave without me. He also kidnapped my dragon, and I want her. And he's using this as an excuse to start a war with Tortall. I won't be calm for *weeks*, so you'd best tell me!"

"They caught him. Master Numair. He gave them the slip in Thak's Gate, but they found his hiding place at the university. And my uncle wouldn't risk his escape. Not a second time. He was executed, a day ago."

For a moment she listened but heard only an ominous thudding in her ears. Then she said flatly, "You're lying."

He squeezed her shoulder. "Not about something like this."

"Then Ozorne lied to you."

"*I saw it.* He made me watch, along with everyone else at the university. Daine, I'm sorry. Numair Salmalín is dead, and we *have* to get you out of Carthak."

Coolness trickled into her mind until her skull was filled with it. Her world seemed extra sharp and extra real. Part of her, someplace deep inside, wailed; *that* seemed unreal, as if she watched a crying baby from a very great distance.

Kaddar was shaking her. "Daine! Can you hear me?"

She gently pushed his hands away. "Stop that. I'm thinking."

His eyes and Tano's held the same worried, frightened look. "You weren't answering. You looked frozen —"

She put a finger to her lips, and he shut up. A thought was coming in the distance. She waited, patiently, skin rippling in brief shivers, until it reached her: Ozorne had to pay.

The gods had taken too long to say whatever it was they'd planned to say here. With all those omens and portents they had sent, the sole effect had been her kidnapping and her friend's execution. Plainly she would have to take care of this herself. If any gods tried to stop her, they would regret it.

"What time of the day is it?" Her voice sounded distant, but reasonable. Something about her, though, must not be right. She saw that Chirp backed away to press against Tano's legs, fur on end. Both men began to sweat.

"Mid-afternoon," replied the Banjiku, eyes bright with concern.

"Where is Emperor Ozorne, Your Highness?"

"Across the river, reviewing the Army of the North. They march in two days to the staging point in Thak's Gate."

She had no interest in armies at this moment. "Will he return today?"

"Yes. He has to meet with some officials —"

"When?"

Kaddar wiped his forehead on his arm. "After sunset."

"Tano, could you pass word to all the slaves by

dusk, if you had to?" The black man nodded. Daine looked at Kaddar. "Does anyone that you care about live in the palace?"

He wet his lips with his tongue. "Yes. But—"

"Tell the slaves and your friends to be ready by nightfall. When things break loose, they must leave the palace. I don't care where they go, so long as they do." She sat down again and let Zek climb into her lap.

"You can't just—"

Something in her face made him step back. "Please don't say what I must and mustn't do, Highness." It was amazing, how cold she felt. "Hurry, now. Dark comes early here, I've found. Tano—the emperor's birds."

The little man bowed deeply, hands crossed over his breast. "One of the tunnels opens inside the glass birdhouse, Great One."

"If I tell them to go with you and your folk and not be frightened, will you carry them to a safe place? They won't try to escape you."

Tano nodded. "We will take them away, gladly."

Daine nodded. "Thank you. Before dark, please!"

Tano bowed again, and drew the prince away. Chirp followed them into the tunnels.

Dry-eyed, the girl stared at the ceiling. "You don't have to stay, Zek. It may be scary."

I will stay, replied the marmoset. Scary with you is better than scary without you.

Daine tickled his stomach gently, then closed her eyes. "I didn't get to say good-bye or anything." She swallowed hard. Her friend, her teacher—he had shown her the use of her wild magic, looked after her when her first trial with it backfired, taught her the science that enabled her to learn more about the People than she had ever dreamed of knowing.

Gathering up her power, she spoke first to Ozone's birds. It was quick work to persuade them to go with the black men and women who had already begun to emerge from an opening in the aviary floor. Once all of them had gone back into the tunnels with the Banjiku, she cast her wild magic to the far side of the River Zekoi, and summoned every small creature that crawled, walked, or flew to the camp of the Army of the North. Let Ozorne see how far his soldiers could march with gnawed rope and leather, bad food, foul water, and useless weapons. Anyone who tried to use ballista or catapult would be in for an unpleasant surprise, as would the wagon drivers. Mule skinners and horsemasters wouldn't go very far without their charges.

She had done it before, calling on her friends to harass the enemy in a siege or to keep soldiers too busy to go to anyone's aid. Never before had she done it on this scale, but it wasn't that hard to summon thousands instead of hundreds or tens. It was almost a relief.

If Ozorne's gods weren't prepared to instruct him on polite behavior, she would have to do so.

The mingled voices of her friends above the ground told her at last that dark had come. Guided by a helpful cat, using cat's eyes to see in the dark, she found her way through the underground tunnels, until they had reached a trapdoor that opened into the Hall of Bones. "Thank you," she told the cat as she tucked

Zek into her shirt. "And now, you'd best get out. It's going to be very busy here for a while."

The cat rubbed affectionately against her shins and raced off into the darkness.

"Ready?" Daine asked Zek. She could see his wide eyes and feel him tremble slightly.

No, he told her. Go ahead anyway.

She climbed the ladder to raise the trapdoor half an inch. The room above was dark and empty. Climbing out, she looked around.

She was in a niche between the mountain-runner nest and the hall where the smaller skeletons were kept. These wouldn't do. Turning, she entered the hall of the larger dinosaurs, and went to the three-horn that faced the main door. It seemed right to begin with him. Rubbing her hands, she touched the skeleton's long nose horn. White fire blazed. The dinosaur tossed its head, as if to shake off sleep.

"Now, that's the wrong way to go about it," said a cracked voice. "You'll kill yourself again, and you won't rouse nearly enough of them."

Daine faced the Graveyard Hag. "*You,*" she hissed coldly. "Am I angry enough now? Isn't this what you wanted?"

"No," was the frank reply. "I *wanted* you to wake the human dead. Give 'em a start to see corpses dancing in their streets. It'd be just like the old days. Well before *your* time, of course."

Daine rested a hand on the three-horn's neck frill. It had moved up beside her and stood firmly braced, as if telling the goddess that she would have to go through it to get to Daine. "And when the dead lie back down, the mortals will forget. A couple weeks, a month, and it'll seem like a bad dream. I want to give them a lesson that will keep them busy awhile."

"What might that be, dearie?"

"Palaces are important," replied the girl. "Rulers keep their gold and gems and art in palaces. The tax rolls and imperial records are here somewhere. If I rip this palace apart, it'll take them *years* to clean up. They'll have something besides going to war with their neighbors to do. And if I kill *him*, a new emperor might not be so bad. Guaranteed, they'd go back to proper worship of the gods—I imagine that would make all of you happy."

The goddess frowned. "It's not what I would do."

"What *you* would've done you should've done *years* ago!" Daine cried, voice breaking. "If you hadn't let it go, and let it go, things might not have come to this state! But you didn't, and you left it to me, so now we'll do it like *I* want to! Add your own flourishes if you wish, but either help me or get out of my way!"

The Hag sighed. "You don't understand."

"I don't *want* to understand!"

"We can't just *do* whatever we feel like," the goddess said. "There are rules, even for us. We can only work on something like this through a mortal vessel, for one thing. Do you know how *few* mortals can be used as a god's vessel without dying on us? And I was reluctant to act, I confess. That nice boy Ozorne wooed me like a maiden—flowers on my altar every day, precious oils, public feasts in my honor—oh, it was grand! So, maybe I wasn't strict with him, and now he's too big for his breeches. It hurt when he stopped leaving flowers, you know. I was the last god still defending him in Mithros's court." She sighed and shook her head. "These men say they care for me, and I fall for it every time. Too good-hearted—that's me."

"My heart bleeds buttermilk," Daine snapped.

The Graveyard Hag shook her stick at the girl. "If I didn't need you—"

"But you do. You said it yourself—vessels are hard to come by. So, can we get on with it, please? I need strength enough to wake up *all* these big ones."

"Strength." The Hag rubbed her chin. "There's always the rats. You'll have to offer them something, though. Even *I* can't make them help for nothing. There's—"

"Rules, yes, you told me."

The Hag tapped her on the head with her stick. "Don't be impudent, Weiryn's daughter! And think up something nice to offer my rats!"

The tap made her ears ring and her eyes burn. She rubbed both; when she looked around again, the Graveyard Hag was gone.

Zek poked his head out of her shirt. Are you all right? he asked. Your bones are humming.

"I'm not surprised," she murmured, patting the three-horn's neck frill when he nudged her. "Zek, what can I offer rats?"

Food, he replied immediately. Rats are *always* hungry. I could do with a bite myself.

She dug in her pocket for raisins left from the meal Tano had given her in the tunnels. As the marmoset nibbled them, she thought hard and fast. On the edges of her awareness, she could feel rats approaching, hundreds of them. Where could she get enough food to bribe them all?

She was in a palace. Most of the provisions for Varice's fancy dinners were already here. Of course, the food stores were guarded by an army of rat catchers.

Smiling grimly, she called to the hundreds of cats and dogs who worked the palace and grounds.

As she conferred with them, rats streamed into the Hall of Bones through every hole, vent, and crack. Once the dogs and cats agreed to her request, she looked around. The great dinosaur skeletons now bore passengers: rats, black ones and brown, large and small; well-fed, glossy ones and scrawny river rats decorated with scars.

A brown female with one missing eye stood at Daine's feet. Herself told us you want to make a deal, she said. Something to trade for our wild magic, so you can wake these old bone piles.

The three-horn apparently heard this. It looked down and nudged the rat with its nose horn.

The rat bared yellow incisors. You don't scare me, dead beast! she snarled. There's enough of us here to do for you!

Daine patted the skeleton's neck frill. "It's all right. They're on our side — I think."

We don't side with anybody that ain't a rat, the female snapped. From the darkness all around them came chittering agreement from the others. Pipe down! ordered the rat chieftain. So what's the deal, then, two-legger?

"I plan to leave this palace a wreck: plenty of supplies buried under stone and in rooms the men can't reach," replied Daine. "So, *if* you give me what I need, the dogs and cats agree not to hunt anywhere in the palace or on the grounds for a year and a day. I can't get rid of the human mages, but the dogs and cats will go—if you help me. That's the deal."

The rats conferred, their whispers loud in the echoing hall. Finally the one-eyed female—who looked like the Graveyard Hag herself—squealed, We have a bargain!

The rats moved into the second hall, where the smaller dinosaurs were kept. Once they were settled, Daine got to work, drawing on the power they gave her as, one by one, she woke the great skeletons. Down the row of horn-faced reptiles she went, rousing each of their kindred: the bull, spiked, close-horned, one-horned, thick-nosed, and well-horned dinosaurs. None were shorter than a man's height at the shoulder, and some were half again as tall. Each came to life at a white-fired touch, and stretched lazily. They seemed to know she had business with them, for while they flexed limbs, tails, and bodies, they stayed in place, waiting.

Next she went to the armored lizards, with their back and head spikes and their bone-tail clubs. Mixed in among them were their cousins, armored lizards, who had traded the tail club for heavy side spikes. Most of the armored lizards were as tall as the horn-faces. They, too, woke readily at her call, working kinks out of muscle and cartilage that were no longer there.

After them she went to the plated lizards, remembering their macelike tails. Next she woke the snake-necks. While they weren't armored as the others were, their bulk and long tails would make fast work of obstacles.

At last she reached the tyrant lizard and his kin, the meat eaters. Originally she'd thought they would be little help, since their arms were so weak-looking, but she had reconsidered. Something about those great skulls, with their forward-pointed eyes and saw-edged teeth, told her they would make excellent hunters. Their cousins the wounding lizards had stronger arms, with large claws.

Once they and the eight mammoths were awake, she went to the front of the hall. Now she heard booming sounds at the doors; evidently some-one had raised an alarm, and humans were trying to come in. Even if they had a mage to speak the opening spell, it would still take them awhile to enter. The bull three-horn leaned against the inward-opening doors, holding them shut.

"Friends," the girl said, voice echoing, "the master of this palace killed my friend, stole a dragon, and tried to cage me. He is a thief and a murderer. He needs a lesson. You can't be hurt as my mortal friends can. *You* are ancient and powerful. Will you help me get revenge? I would like to rip this palace apart, stone by stone. I want to topple the columns, break the walls, crush the fountains. Will you do it?"

From tyrant lizards to horn-faces, the skulls of her allies pointed to the ceiling as one. She couldn't hear their roar of agreement, but she felt it in the quiver of the ground under her feet.

A four-toothed elephant wrapped his trunk around her waist, and placed her gently on the back of a shaggy mammoth, out of harm's way. "Thank you," she told him. To the others she said, "I'd druther not kill any two-leggers, but I know if you're attacked, you'll fight back. Just, please, look where you step, and don't hurt anyone who's smart enough to run."

The bull three-horn backed away from the doors. Both leaves slammed open, to reveal a very young mage and a squad of men from the Red Legion. The Hall of Bones was still unlit: the mage clapped to waken the light-globes. When they blazed into life, they revealed nearly seventy long-dead creatures who had left their pedestals and were walking toward the intruders.

The mage screamed and ran. The guardsmen followed, dropping their spears.

Outside the Hall of Bones, Daine's army split into three groups. One, led by the great three-horn she had awakened first, turned in the direction of the wing in which the palace records were kept. The second group, led by the chief tyrant lizard, began in the great hall where they now stood, smashing pottery, windows, and benches; ramming the walls; and toppling fountains. A plated lizard discovered the anchor chain of an immense light-globe chandelier and began to tug it from its mooring.

The third group, which included Daine, her mammoth, the bull three-horn who had blocked the door into the Hall of Bones, and others, was ready to go. "Zek," she asked the marmoset, "could you find the way back to the emperor's chambers?"

He clambered down the front of her shirt and along the mammoth's back until he perched in solitary grandeur on the creature's head. That way, he said, pointing left.

Daine tapped the mammoth with her left foot, and he obediently moved forward. The tiny animal on his skull lurched and almost fell, then grabbed tufts of the mammoth's fur to use as reins.

Two snake-necks, each over eighty feet long, wound their tails through the door handles to the Hall of Bones, and began to walk away. They didn't stop, even when their tails were stretched as far as possible. In the end, it was the doors that gave way, snapping out of the frame and leaving it in splinters. The snake-necks then followed Daine, freeing their tails from the wreckage.

Behind them a ringing crash signaled the end of the plated lizard's attention to the chandelier.

Zek's next turn brought them into a long gallery lined with niches. In each stood a gold statue of a Carthaki emperor, decorated with gems and designed to show the monarch with those things that symbolized his reign. The dinosaurs got to work, pulling statues down and trampling them flat. One plated lizard made the windows his sole task, smashing each and every one with his spiky tail. A four-toothed elephant ripped doors off hinges with his trunk. People spilled from the rooms that opened into the statuary hall, stared at the dinosaurs, and fled.

Near the end of the gallery, a side door leading to the nobles' wing crashed open. Five people rushed in. Two of the women were veiled; a female slave carried a baby. When the women saw Daine's friends, they began to scream. The old man and the boy put themselves between their womenfolk and the threat, though their hands trembled as they gripped their weapons.

"Stop that noise," Daine ordered. "No one's hurting you." The only one to listen was the slave, who tried to calm the shrieking infant. "Get out of here," the girl went on. "My friends won't hurt you if you don't attack them and don't get under their feet. Now move!" The humans ran.

Daine looked at Zek. "Do we go the way they did?"

Zek shook his head. Straight, he said, pointing to the doors at the end of the hall.

In the distance they heard the crash of falling stone. Behind them the thick-nosed horn-faced dinosaur leaned on the marble wall. When an armored lizard joined him, the blocks of stone began to give way.

Zek led them through a tree garden, which they left as it was. The next turn brought them into one of the palace's many bathhouses, this one set aside for nobles. It seemed that those inside had not heard the distant sounds of mayhem. They were taken completely by surprise and fled without recovering their clothes. Tyrant lizards ripped up sections of the tile floor, laying bare a forest of gleaming pipes. A mammoth and a four-toothed elephant seized these, yanking them from their moorings and showering everything with hot and cold water. Armored lizards walked through rooms where clothing, robes, and towels were kept, catching them on their side spikes and dragging them along. Mud baths were overset, rubbing tables torn apart, steam rooms dismantled.

Their next turn led them through storerooms. Snake-necks destroyed countless jars of raisins, olives, dates, fresh fruits, and vegetables, wielding their tails like whips. Tyrant lizards tore their sharp teeth through pounds of dried and salted meat. Daine noticed cooly that the food vanished once it had entered their mouths. The others preferred the grain stored in great burlap sacks.

The last storeroom held drinkables in bottles, jars, and barrels. They had gone to work when the other mammoth in their group lifted a screaming female from a hiding place behind the casks. Pale blue fires danced around her body as she fought the trunk around her waist, without success. The mammoth brought her to Daine and set her gently on the floor.

Daine stared down at Varice Kingsford, fingers knotting in her mammoth's long fur. "Tell me why I shouldn't have you ripped to pieces?" she demanded. "Were you at his killing? Were you serving pretty food and fancy wine?"

Varice got herself under control, and shook her head.

"Did you betray him to the emperor?"

"I don't expect you to believe me, but no. Maybe I would have, if he'd come to me. You don't know what it's like, to be in the service of a man like Ozorne. But I didn't betray Arram."

Zek looked at Daine from his seat on the mammoth's head. Why are you angry? he asked. She has been sad. She isn't wearing the smelly stuff she likes, or the pretty colors on her face and hands.

He was right. The woman was pale, her eyes red with long weeping. She wore no makeup at all. Her blonde hair, uncurled and unarranged, hung lank and straight down her back. Even her dress was plain, a loose-fitting gown of dove-gray cotton. Her mage's robe was nowhere to be seen.

Varice met Daine's eyes. "You must think I'm

useless and silly. Maybe I am. I just like things pretty. Is that so bad, to want people to enjoy themselves? Only, when you have the Gift, you can't just go to parties and keep house. They expect you to study, and to *do* something in life. Arram—he always wanted me to learn more spells and be famous. I don't want to be famous! What I do is useful. And I *like* using my Gift for cooking and baking. Great power hasn't brought the mages I know happiness or peace of mind."

Daine stared down at the blonde. Varice sounded like Ma, whose greatest pleasure had lain in dancing and working in the garden or kitchen. Quietly she said, "You needn't explain yourself to me."

Varice blotted her eyes on her sleeve. "I begged," she said, voice hoarse. "Sometimes it works. I said, what's the point of killing Arram? Other monarchs would fear Carthak more, if he showed mercy to his betrayer. But it didn't help. He made me watch when they killed— I'll never forget that as long as I live."

"Varice," Daine said. The cold inside her prevented tears, but she felt bad for the older woman. "We have no quarrel with you. The gods are unhappy with Ozorne, and I'm helping them, but you don't have to be involved. Get out of here. Shelter at the university, if you can get across the river, or the estates outside the palace grounds. You won't be safe here."

Varice nodded and gathered up her skirts. Daine's army parted to let her pass, then set about destroying the room. The horn-faced lizards, testing the walls, found they were wood, not stone. They began to smash them, wall after wall, working back through the storage rooms. When Daine moved on, some armored lizards and a mammoth stayed, as did the bull three-horn, to handle the stone walls. The echo of crashing stone followed Daine out.

TEN

STEEL FEATHER

They came to a long passage where the ceiling was supported by columns studded with semi-precious stones. At the end waited a squad of determined-looking soldiers. Half bore small, double-curved bows; the rest long-bladed pikes.

She held up a hand; her army stopped. "I wish you no harm," she called. "But I want the emperor. Give him to me or get out of my way, but choose."

"We will defend our emperor to the death!" cried one.

"That's fair foolish. My friends are a bit hard to kill. They've been dead already."

One of them fired. His hands shook so much that the arrow flew wide.

"Witch!" a man screamed. "Sorceress!"

Did they think names *mattered* anymore? "For the last time, *get out of my way.*"

They did not move. She waved: the spiked three-horn came up and lowered his head, the spines on his neck frill like rays of the sun. Five armored lizards stumped into place behind him. A wedge formed, the skeletons headed for the guards. Arrows flew. Those that struck their targets shattered; the rest could as well have been rain. The pikemen lunged, to find their weapons gripped in bony jaws and wrenched from their grasp.

Those still on their feet ran. Three lay on the floor after being knocked down. The armored lizards nudged them out of the way.

Impatient, the spiked three-horn rammed the door. It shattered. Orange fire billowed out of the room; the skeletal creature exploded into a million fragments.

The armored lizards opened their jaws in what Daine knew was a silent roar, and charged. Orange fire ripped the side off a double-armored lizard and broke the right-side spines on its neighbor. The remaining skeletons kept going. Daine covered her eyes against a bright flare of magic beyond the door, then urged her mammoth forward. Inside the doorway, Chioké lay crushed. He was pinned there by a thirty-three-foot-long armored forest lizard whose skull and front half were melting. Daine slid down and went to the dinosaur, trying not to cry as it fought to look at her.

"Go back to sleep," she said, patting the undamaged spine. "You've done a wondrous thing here, and I thank you. Go back to sleep."

The dinosaur relaxed, letting what remained of his head drift to the floor. For a moment copper fire shone brightly in the girl's eyes, running along her friend's bones. In it she saw the forest lizard as he must have looked in life, skin a gleaming chestnut brown, all his spines and plates whole. He was trotting away from her, bound for a lush forest that shone in the distance. When her vision cleared, even his skeleton was gone.

Checking the pair who had been half destroyed outside the door, she saw that they, too, had vanished.

A snake-neck grabbed her by the waistband and lifted her onto the mammoth's back. Please be careful about getting down! scolded Zek. Even if we fight the ones with magic, you are safer up here!

The mammoth waited for the last of the skeletons to enter Ozorne's rooms, then followed. Two snake-necks, finding that they would never get their large bones through the door, began to lean against the walls, trying to force them.

"Emperor Ozorne!" shouted Daine. No one answered. The girl looked at her warriors. "I think you'd best go to work."

They ripped the elaborate suite of rooms to shreds. They tore open chests and closets, broke whatever could be broken: furnishings, tiles, glass, pottery. The secret exit through which Zek had seen Ozorne go to visit a captive girl was laid bare. Daine urged her mammoth through the different chambers until they passed through Ozorne's bedroom and entered the aviary.

Here were the benches, and the table where

he'd fed her dreamrose. A book lay open on it, and a decanter of wine had shattered on the floor. Someone had been here recently, and had left in a hurry. Looking around she saw that the panes of the rear wall were shattered, as though a giant fist had punched through the glass and its green metal fittings. Soot streaked the panes on the outside; the odor of scorched bone hung in the air. More than ever, she was glad she had arranged for the birds to be taken away before any of this began.

Her mammoth followed the tyrant lizard through the broken wall and into the gardens. Here lay some of the warriors from another part of her army: a four-toothed elephant, two plated lizards, and a snake-neck. Their remains were blackened and twisted by magical fire.

"Thank you," she whispered to all of them.

Copper fire bloomed; scorched bones rose and became whole bodies. The dinosaurs headed toward a distant forest, to vanish as the copper light faded.

"Curse it," she muttered, looking at the burned area where they had lain. "Curse it, curse it—" She pounded the mammoth's back in fury. Where had Ozorne gone, if indeed he was the one who had done this? He could be anywhere, up to any kind of mischief!

A small, winged shape with long, leathery ears dropped to flutter before her nose, squeaking a wel-come. This was a large, mouse-eared bat, on his night's hunt for insects. He was glad to see her, he said. All kinds of strange things were going on tonight. Was there anything he and his colony of the People could do?

Zek eyed him suspiciously. Can they be of any use? he asked.

"One way to find out," she replied with a grim smile.

Cradling the bat against her shirt, she called the others, both mouse-eared bats and common pipistrelles. The ones close by came to Daine herself, gripping her clothes or lighting on the mammoth's wide back. Those bats within the range of her magic but not close enough to reach her in person found roosts and waited to hear what she had to say.

As Zek peered curiously at these new guests, Daine built for them an image of Ozorne as he would "look" to bats, his face and form drawn with sound, not light. She gave them everything, from the tinny echo of beads in his hair to the clear whispers that would return from his gems. "Can you hear him?" she asked. "Is he anywhere near you?"

Wait, they told her in a single voice, and took to the air.

As the rest of her third of the skeleton army caught up, Ozorne's chambers now so much rubble, she wondered what to do if the bats were unsuccessful. They could find him outdoors, even if he were invisible: no cloaking spell was invulnerable to sound. If he were indoors, or wore another shape, that was a different matter. They would recognize the form, not the wearer.

If he couldn't defeat the dinosaurs, would he run? It was hard to imagine the Emperor Mage running from a girl and her army of dead animals. Still, blasts like the one that had finished the dinosaurs outside the aviary had to be costly in terms of his magical strength.

Reports began to come back from her spies.

Bats were fast in the air, and they built sound pictures quickly. Within minutes Daine knew that not only was the emperor nowhere in the gardens, towers, or outlying buildings, but that parts of the complex were in flames.

"Pull back, then, all of you," she said, wanting to cry. "It's no good you getting cooked."

Maybe we can help, a voice said from behind her.

Daine turned, and gasped. The hyenas were out.

"How—what—?" she stammered.

Teeu, the boss female, came forward to sniff Daine's mammoth. The Mistress let us out, she said. Old One-Eye. She is a goddess of two-leggers, but she helps us, too, now and then.

Light reflected from metal in the air. Rikash landed on a balcony nearby. "I believe she felt you would require assistance," drawled the green-eyed Stormwing. "You might want to know, a company of dinosaur skeletons opened the menagerie cages and dumped trees into the pits so the animals could climb out."

"Kitten?" she asked Rikash. "My dragon? I dreamed she was in the immortals' menagerie."

"You dreamed truly. She is there under a sleep spell," he replied. "Your friends tried to break into that collection, but failed. The spells on the gate and cages are keyed to Ozorne. They won't give way until he dies."

We are going to find this Ozorne, Teeu said cheerfully. The Mistress reminded us: we have a score to settle. She said you might want to come, too.

Daine thought fast. A hyena's sense of smell was keener than any other living creature she'd ever met. She was willing to bet Ozorne wouldn't think to change the unique scent given off by his body, no matter *what* shape he took. Better still, Teeu and her "boys," Iry and Aranh, were creatures Ozorne had reason to fear. What better hunters could a girl bent on vengeance ask for?

"Lift me down, please?" she asked the mammoth, who complied. On the ground once more, she looked at Teeu. "I want to shape-shift and become one of you. Then we can hunt the emperor together, if you're willing."

Teeu gave a strange-sounding yip—a hyena laugh. Get on with it, the hyena urged. The night is young, and Ozorne has a head start.

Daine looked up at Rikash. "It just occurred to me—what in the name of all the Horse Lords are you doing here?"

The Stormwing ruffled his feathers. "I was paying my respects to my *true* sovereign, Queen Barzha, and her consort."

"Rikash—" she said warningly, not believing him.

"Well, as it happens, I'd heard that tonight would be an interesting night for Carthak."

"You mean the Graveyard Hag told you."

"Perhaps." The Stormwing's eyes glittered as he smiled. "There's a chance the emperor might feel the need to use the gift that I gave him. I wanted to be here to see the fun."

"If he has any sense, he's run off."

"Ah, but a man with sense never would have

ignored so many warnings. I doubt he has fled."

"He killed Numair," Daine said hoarsely.

"I know." The immortal rocked to and fro, cleared his throat, and said, "I am sorry."

"Me, too," she whispered. She rubbed her sleeve over her eyes and turned to her skeleton army. "Will you go on tearing things up? I don't know if you can follow where I'm about to go, and I really want to leave this place a ruin."

All of them nodded. Zek clambered down from the mammoth's back. She patted each skeleton and elephant as they passed her, wishing them a good hunt and giving them her thanks. When they had gone, she asked Rikash, "Would you look after Zek and see he comes to no harm?"

He frowned, but nodded. "If he does not object, I will place him in the dragon's cage." He jumped to the ground, using outspread wings to slow his fall.

It will be good to see Kitten, Zek said. Even if she's asleep.

"I'd hate for anything to happen to Zek," Daine said quietly, meeting Rikash's eyes with hers. "Mithros knows why, but I trust you." She kissed the top of the marmoset's head, then held him out to the Stormwing. Zek climbed over Rikash's shoulder, where steel grew out of flesh, and hid under the Stormwing's long hair, grasping handfuls of it.

He smells *terrible*, the marmoset confided to Daine.

"Good hunting," Rikash said, and took flight. Before he and Zek had gone from sight, Daine began the painstaking business of entering hyena form. She drew her memories of Teeu's mind around her, letting her body shift. Her jaw spread and lengthened to become a muzzle. Her teeth broadened, widened, sharpened. At last she sat on the stone of the court-yard, a spotted hyena.

We can pick up the scent inside, she told her companions. *His rooms are through that hole in the glass.*

Teeu grinned, showing bone-crushing teeth. *By all means, let us get a whiff of his lair.* Daine and the males grinned back.

The dinosaurs still at work inside paid no attention to the four hyenas sniffing the emperor's bedclothes and garments. The reek of Ozorne's many perfumes made Daine feel queasy; smells that had been almost too much for her as a human were far more powerful to a hyena's nose.

I don't see why he soaks himself in all this, Iry complained. *It's disgusting.*

Don't whine, ordered Teeu. *You should be grateful he left such a clear trail for us.*

As they followed the scent through shattered glass to the outside once more, Daine found changes in it. Bitter tones, more powerful even than the per-fumes, lingered around his steps. Outdoors, where smells of burned ground and scorched bone filled her nose, she could still find those bitter traces. The hye-nas snuffled the earth, their nostrils taking informa-tion from the odors there. Daine growled, her rage surfacing at last as a hunter's eagerness to find her prey.

Got it? Aranh asked.

She realized she would know Ozorne's scent

for the rest of her life, perhaps even in human form. Got it, she replied.

Then let's go, Teeu said.

The hyenas picked up the trail along the outside wall of this wing of the palace. Teeu led the way, Daine at her side. The males spread out behind them, chattering in yips and whines.

What are those bad smells in his spoor? Daine asked the female. The ones that came into his odor as he left his rooms?

Teeu bared her teeth in a laugh. Fear, she replied gleefully. Your friends chased him from his lair and into the dark, on foot. Those are fear scents in your nose. If he were a wildebeest with that smell, you'd know it was beaten and you were about to make a nice kill.

They stopped at a fresh battlefield. A dead human in armor lay against the wall. He'd dragged himself away from the mammoth that had crushed his lower body. The mammoth itself was a pile of embers that burned copper and vanished when Daine pawed at it, whining. Two more skeletons nearby had been crisped by magical fire. They vanished like the mammoth's remains when she touched them with her paw. A red-robed mage lay moaning in the bushes where he'd been thrown.

Come on, Iry called to Daine. The trail will get cold!

They found two more sites where the Emperor Mage had been forced to defend himself. There were so many bodies at the second—seven in all—that Daine thought of the sacrifices demanded at the funerals of ancient kings, whose households were put to death so that the king might have attendants in the afterlife. Carefully she thanked each of the fallen dinosaurs and elephants that had died a second time for her, and watched as their remains vanished from sight before moving on.

Next the trail brought them around a corner and into the light. At the end of a short mall ahead, the palace was ablaze. Between the hyenas and the fire stood a squad of armed guards. One of them yelped, seeing the beasts, and brought up a loaded crossbow.

Aranh leaped, strong legs propelling him across the distance between them, and tore the weapon from the guard's hand. Bats swarmed out of the dark, blinding the other men with their wings before they could shoot the attacking hyena. Snarling, Aranh crushed the bow stave, making the weapon unusable. The rest of the guards dropped their weapons and fled.

The hyenas moved on.

The night air carried a thousand messages. Daine ignored the unimportant ones and concentrated on the odor of her prey. The emperor's scent changed as they followed, as if it were a living thing that grew under her eyes. In his rooms it had been one of a very well tended man, tinged with almond rubbing oil, aloe lotion, orris-scented shampoo, perfumed makeup, the acrid smell of gilding powder and gold, lavender from his clothes, and the personal scent of a man who ate and drank richly. In the aviary, anger and then fear had been added to the mix. Outside he'd acquired a touch of charred hair and bone. Now the smell of burned things was much thicker. So was the fear.

Thunder rolled overhead. Flagstones gave way

to gravel as the hyenas followed a path between tall hedges. The smell of recent burning drifted into their faces. Three dinosaur skeletons must have come at Ozorne from the far end of the path: their blackened remains lay in a heap there. The emperor had fled though an opening in the hedge. Stopping to thank those fallen allies, Daine trembled. He'd escaped her army again. A growl rumbled in her throat, and her mane stood up.

He's weakening, remarked Teeu as the heaped skeletons shimmered and vanished. All the bones of the others were black through and through. These had white in them, and they still held together instead of breaking apart.

Good, snarled Daine. The less magic he has, the better!

The hyenas yipped agreement and picked up the emperor's trail, laced now with blood and sweat. His thin shoes had given out on the gravel, leaving footprints etched in blood. Their path twisted around a fountain, followed the curve of the artificial lake, and headed straight down a path shaded by willows. Here the great three-horn, the first dinosaur she had awakened, and a huge snake-neck must have been waiting for him.

The snake-neck was the first they'd seen who bore few marks of burning. Instead tiny cracks had riddled its bones. Some had disintegrated completely, leaving small powdery heaps. When Daine nudged its skull, the skeleton shaped itself, becoming a living dinosaur. The snake-neck waited patiently while the girl turned to the three-horn. Ozorne had tried to burn him without success, then melted him, the way Chioké had melted the bull three-horn. The great skeleton had gone down fighting: blood painted the tip of a long, sharp brow horn. Daine sniffed it: the blood was Ozorne's.

He's running out of fire, Iry told the others with savage glee. *Look at this one—barely charred!*

Sadly, Daine licked the three-horn's beak. It gave under her tongue as flesh might.

Why are you unhappy? Teeu wanted to know. *Does it hurt them to die?*

No, Daine replied softly as copper fire raced over the half-melted skeleton, calling the owner back to the true shape of its living days. *The badger said it didn't, anyway. It just hurts me.*

The great three-horn stood, his beaded hide a deep, golden bronze, his face, with its horns, restored. Through him Daine could see the trees dimly. *Good-bye,* she said, though she knew he couldn't hear. *I'll miss you.*

The three-horn bowed his head, touching her gently with his nose horn, then followed the snake-neck down a road to a distant jungle. The vision faded as they left the hyenas, until only the garden trees were left.

Rage and sorrow built in Daine's heart until she thought it might burst. *I want Ozorne!* she snarled at her companions. *I want to rip him up like he's ripped me up!*

Then hunt, cried the hyenas, eerie voice echoing in the dark. *Smell, and find!*

Daine set off, nose to the ground, the others behind her. Ozorne's scent was nearly fresh and thick with the sourness of exhaustion. Drops of sweat had fallen with his blood, the red liquid dripping heavily now that the three-horn had marked him.

The trail turned beside a wall and passed through the shattered gates of the menagerie. Inside the mortal animals' enclosure, no animals were left. The cages were open, the fences pulled down, and trees reached from the pits to the ground level. The gate of the immortals' menagerie stood open and whole: someone who knew the spells had unlocked it.

He's here! she cried, and leaped.

Kaddar stood before the griffin's cage, hand upraised. At the hyenas' snarl, he whirled, and the shape he wore evaporated. It was Ozorne.

The moment he spotted her and the others, the reek of fear almost wiped out his other smells. He was disheveled, sweat-soaked, bleeding, soot-streaked. He wore only a light green robe and costly, shredded slippers. The fabric over his chest was torn: beneath lay a long, open wound that still bled sluggishly.

He's trying to escape on the griffin, I bet, Daine told her companions. He can think again!

She sprang and hit the emperor's magical shield headfirst, making it flare briefly. She howled, barely noticing the pain of a bruised head and neck as she dropped. Far more important than pain was the fact that the magical shield had weakened a hair when she struck it.

Teeu and Aranh leaped and hit the barrier, sparking twin flares in it. They fell, snarling in fury. Daine, watching, saw that the flares weren't as bright as when she'd hit. Iry attacked from Ozorne's left. This time the emperor's shield only flickered from the impact. It still held firm, but he was losing strength.

The caged immortals watched silently.

Emerald fire gathered, slowly, around Ozorne's hands; he swayed as it grew. There was a white-hot edge to its glow, the kind that left a streaky imprint on eyes that watched it too long. The hyenas circled to the man's left and right, yipping with excitement. Daine stayed in front of him, teeth bared, mane erect.

One more blow should do it! she told the others. One more and he's *ours*.

"No!" cried a human voice behind her. Sparkling fire leaped through the air to form a bubble around the emperor.

Daine snarled without looking away from her quarry. How *dare* two-leggers cheat her of what she had won? She threw herself against the new fire barrier, and received a nasty shock on her delicate nose.

"You'll have to choose, Uncle." This voice was different from the one that had cried "No." "Abdication and imprisonment—or the hyenas. You must give in. Your Gift is almost used up. We can see you're taking it from your own life force now."

Ozorne's fire had evaporated. He swayed, his skin gone cheesy white under streaked facial paint. "Abdi—? Never!" His voice was hoarse with effort.

"Then it must be the hyenas, Uncle, just as the Graveyard Hag promised."

"Give him to the animals!" cried the female Stormwing, Barzha. "They have worked hard for his flesh—let them have it! Let them feast, so *we* can sup on his fear!"

The emperor stared at the female immortal in open terror. Daine, Teeu, Aranh, and Iry cried their triumph in a series of hollow yips that made Ozorne shudder. Daine stalked up to the sparkling barrier, intent on the man inside. You're *mine*, she thought, and bared white, bone-crushing teeth. For Numair, you're *mine*.

Ozorne's eyes brightened feverishly. "Promises, is it? Well, I have a promise in reserve!" he grabbed the hair on the back of his head, fumbling among its strands.

A rattle of steel made Daine glance to the side. Barzha and Hebakh were at the bars of their cage, staring at the Emperor Mage with grim concentration. Above them, on the roof of their prison, Rikash had also come to watch.

"See!" Ozorne cried. Daine's head whipped around. The emperor held a metal feather—the one Rikash had given him, pulled from a braided strand of hair. "I have *this* promise!"

She snarled in fury and threw herself at the barrier as Ozorne drove the feather through his arm.

Something exploded in a burst of light. Daine, falling through a vanishing barrier, slammed into metal that cut. She rolled away and struggled to her feet. A Stormwing with Ozorne's face and hair stood where he had just been. Steel feathers and talons gleamed as if newly minted. The gash on his chest was now a clean, broad scar.

Chimes filled the air. One after another the cages disappeared, releasing the inhabitants. The griffin and hurroks wasted no time: they fled into the night sky, filling Daine's ears with the sound of flapping wings. Magic of a deep-gray shade, almost like fog, washed and wrapped itself around the killer unicorns, spidrens, and killer centaurs, holding them where they were, as the more peaceful centaurs fled. Kitten, in a cage at the far end of the courtyard, sat up with an inquiring cheep; Zek clambered up her back to perch on her shoulder. The Coldfangs looked around, tongues sliding out to taste the breeze.

Barzha and Hebakh stretched their wings in a slow, ominous movement, exercising each feather. "Humans, stay out of this," commanded the queen. "Now he is in *our* form; he must answer to Stormwing justice!"

Ozorne gaped in horror. "No! I am the Emperor Mage, lord of Carthak—"

"No immortal may hold a mortal throne," Hebakh said, rocking to and fro. "Wake up, *Emperor Mage*! Do you understand *now* the trap that was laid for you?"

"No immortal may rule over humans or use human magic." Rikash had drifted gently to earth, wings outstretched, when the Stormwing cage vanished under him. Now he stood behind his queen and her consort, razor-sharp teeth bared in a nasty grin. "Go ahead—try it."

Ozorne croaked a word. Something boomed, and he went flying end over end, as if blown by a powerful wind. He smashed into the menagerie's rear wall and lay stunned.

"You forgot our earliest lessons, Ozorne," said a voice behind Daine. It struck a chord in her memory, but if her life had depended on it she couldn't have looked away from the drama taking place before her nose. "Once you take immortal shape, you can never change back."

"We are free!" cried Barzha in triumph. "First I take payment from that motherless worm Jokhun and then I will tend to *you*, Ozorne!" She took to the air, Hebakh behind her.

Ozorne screamed and struggled to stand up on his awkward new claws. "I have magic! I—I have Stormwing magic!"

"Of course you do, sweetheart," Rikash said pleasantly. "Do you know how to use it?"

A scarlet bolt edged with gold struck from overhead to blow a hole in front of Ozorne. For a moment he stood there, panting, mouth working as he tried to speak. Sweat rolled off him.

"You'll get the hang of it in a few days or so," Rikash told him with false sympathy. "If you live that long, of course. There is a reason the former King Jokhun didn't want to fight Barzha Razorwing on her terms."

A second bolt struck the flagstones behind the new Stormwing, spraying him with sharp fragments. Ozorne cursed blackly, then leaped, pumping his wings clumsily. For a moment he dropped. At last he began to rise, bit by slow bit. Everyone watched as he climbed into the darkness overhead.

Rikash sighed. "I must go after him. I wouldn't like him to lose interest, not after it took so much work to get him into the proper claws. Barzha will want him eventually, after all." He looked at the hyenas. "Is one of you Daine?"

The girl trotted to the edge of the dais that had once been a Stormwing cage.

Rikash waddled over to look down at her. "If it counts for anything—though I'm not sure that it does—you have my gratitude. And things aren't as bad as you think. You might look around." He took flight and sped away, calling, "Ozorne, my precious, where are you?"

The hyenas gathered around Daine. What did that mean? asked Teeu. Look around for what?

I don't know, the girl replied, turning to find the human mages behind her. Kaddar was standing by the griffin's empty cage. Lindhall, Bonedancer on his shoulder, was keeping the killer centaurs, spidrens, and killer unicorns penned with his fog-colored magic.

In the gateway stood Numair Salmalín.

Daine gasped and lost her grip on the hyena shape. She turned human instantly—human and unclothed—and sat down hard. "No," she whispered, breathless. "Gods, this is too horrible. Don't do this to me."

The hyenas shifted to form a circle of furry bodies, concealing her, as the man came forward.

"I'm real, sweetling. It truly is me."

"Kaddar and Varice saw them kill you. You're a—a ghost, or a —puppet. A simu-thing."

He lifted a hand: black, sparkling fire grew around it. "Ozorne couldn't attach magic to a simulacrum, remember?" He let the fire die as the hyenas watched, heads cocked in interest.

She swallowed. "Very well, then—you're one of *Numair's* simal —"

"Simulacra. Magelet, remember how we met? I was a shape-shifted hawk. You nursed me until Alanna helped me regain my true form. Last year, in the courtyard of Dunlath castle, I changed Tristan Staghorn into an apple tree with a word of power." He removed his cloak and tossed it toward her. Borne by his magic, it settled onto Daine.

Rising, she wrapped the cloth around her with numb fingers. She didn't *think* a fake would know so much. Gingerly she stepped away from the hyenas and reached for him, then yanked back, terrified that if she touched him, she would know he was dead.

"Kitten?" she cried. "Is it really him?"

The dragon chortled happily and nodded.

Numair waited, one hand extended to her. Steeling herself, she reached again and placed her hand in his. Roughly he pulled her into an enveloping hug, arms encircling and lifting her off her feet. Nose buried in his shirt, she breathed his unique smell, one of spices, soap, and clean clothes. No one would think to copy that, she realized, and began to cry.

He murmured softly to her, arms wonderfully tight. When at last she stopped, he let her go and produced a handkerchief.

Obediently she wiped her eyes and blew her nose. "Where have you been?"

"At the university. Once the emperor's men arrested my simulacrum, I had to play least-in-sight for a day or two."

"But—they knew—Varice and Kaddar were *sure* it was you."

"It was a very good simulacrum, my dear. I worked on it for weeks in secret and had it shipped to Lindhall from Tyra. I didn't quite trust Ozorne's good intentions, I'm afraid."

Memory flared: in Lindhall's office, Lindhall had placed the turtle in another room, and she had seen a shape like a body covered with cloth.

"Why didn't you tell me?"

Numair sighed and smiled ruefully down at her. "I have no idea. I think I forgot."

"Oh." That made more sense than it didn't. "How'd you find out? About—all *this*, then?"

"Kaddar made it across the river. We have enjoyed a most informative evening. Are you aware that the entire west wing and Astronomer's Tower are burning?"

She scuffed a foot on the ground. "I thought they'd killed you. I lost my temper."

Numair's eyes danced. "Magelet, that is the greatest understatement I have heard in my life."

"She had help," said a cracked female voice. "She couldn't have done it without me." The Graveyard Hag had appeared at the back of the immortals' enclosure, cane, eye patch, and all. The badger waddled at her side.

"That's true enough," Daine snapped. She hadn't forgotten her anger with the goddess. "But if you'd done what you're supposed to, none of this would've been necessary."

"And *I* told *you*, we have rules." As she passed the Coldfangs, they slid their tongues out, tasting her cape. "Oh, go away, you," the goddess ordered. Silver light gathered around the Coldfangs, and they were gone. "You, too," she said, pointing at the spidrens, then at the killer centaurs and unicorns with her cane. "I'll talk to you when I get back." Silver fire gathered, and they vanished.

"Interesting company you keep these days," Numair told the badger as Daine stifled a yawn.

—*If I'd had a choice, I would have given up the expe-*

rience, — was the grumbled reply. —*You did very well, kit* — he told Daine.

She smiled at him. "Thank you, Badger. Coming from you, it means a lot."

The Graveyard Hag came over to Daine. "Well, dearie, it's been fun, but you have something of mine, and I want it back."

Numair put a protective arm around Daine's shoulders. "She doesn't have anything of yours, Goddess—does she?"

"Bringing the dead animals back," Daine said, yawning. "That part's hers. You can have it." she said, extending a hand to the goddess. "It makes me nervous."

The Hag wrapped a gnarled hand around Daine's. White light blazed, and vanished. Suddenly the girl's knees felt rubbery. She swayed, and Numair caught her. Kitten, who had managed to leap down from the platform of her former cage with Zek on her back, trotted over, whistling angrily at the goddess while her scales turned pink.

"Oh, stop it," chided the Graveyard Hag. "She's just a bit tired. It's only to be expected."

"Goddess—will you listen to me for a moment?" They had forgotten that Kaddar was also there. When they turned to look at him, he went down on one knee. "Please?"

The Hag grinned cheerfully and leaned on her gnarled stick. "What have you got for me, handsome?"

"Gracious lady, my uncle's palace is a shambles, its treasure burning or scattered or buried. His chief mage is dead, as are many of those mages who supported him. There are people of good will in this realm, people who feared to cross my uncle while he ruled. I know the gods are angry, but—please, will you stay your hand from more destruction? Intercede for us before Mithros's court? Give us a chance to prove our worth. I represent a secret fellowship of nobles, academics, and merchants who genuinely wish things to change here. Carthak is not beyond hope."

Lindhall bowed deeply to Kaddar. "Your Imperial Majesty," he said.

"So he is," remarked Numair, and bowed.

Daine, after a moment's hesitation, copied them, yawning. When she straightened, the Hag fixed the girl with her one good eye. "What do you recommend? Seems to me, since you did the hard work, you ought to have a say."

"Give him the chance," Daine said, fighting yet another yawn. "Prince—*Emperor* Kaddar, I s'pose—he cares about the land and the people. If you gods were only interested in destroying the empire, not saving it, you wouldn't have waited to use me. You'd've gotten on with it."

The Graveyard Hag grinned and looked at the badger. "You were right about her," she said. "Sharp as a Shang blade, she is." Looking up, she said, "Well, my brothers and sisters? What do you think? I say let's give 'em the benefit of a doubt."

For a moment nothing happened. Then a rich wind filled with the scent of growing things filled the air. Overhead, thunder boomed again, a long, rolling crash that seemed to peal forever. When it ended, rain poured down in sheets, drenching everyone.

"Very good," the Graveyard Hag said with approval. Gripping her cane, she stumped over to the new emperor. "Get up," she commanded. "Silly for a ruler to kneel in a cloudburst."

Kaddar obeyed, looking dazed.

"I hope your memory is better than Ozorne's, sonny," she informed him. "I won't be ignored! Not in my own empire! Now, give me your arm. We need to talk."

The young man swallowed and offered his arm to the goddess with a courteous bow. She took it cackling.

"*That's* more like it," she said, leading him toward the gate. "Now, don't worry about the army and the Guard. They were told to stay put or they'd risk the gods' wrath if they came to help your uncle tonight. By dawn they'll be ready to go to work. Oh, wait."

She looked back over her shoulder. "Arram, or Numair—whatever you call yourself—put that girl to bed. She'll sleep for three days, give or take." To Kaddar she said, "Where was I? Now, I like fresh flowers in my temples, and no more cheap pine incense." Her voice faded as they walked off into the gardens.

"Three days?" Numair asked, looking at Daine with concern.

—It was divine power moving through her,— said the badger.

Daine found that talk was too much work just now, as was standing. She sat and smiled up at Numair.

—Sleep is all she needs.—

She smiled agreement, then hugged Kitten and a deeply unhappy, wet Zek.

—Don't worry about the escaped menagerie ani-
mals. —

The badger's voice was the last thing she would
remember as she closed her eyes.

*— We animal gods will see to it that they reach their
proper homes unhurt. It is the least we can do. —*

EPILOGUE

❦

When she opened her eyes, it was raining softly outside her window. A breeze carrying the scent of wet earth came in, to mingle with the scent of sundried cotton sheets. She inhaled, smiling, and a joyful, earsplitting trill sounded from around her feet. When she sat up, Kitten leaped forward to strike her chest, almost knocking her back down. "Easy, Kit, easy," she protested, laughing. "Calm down!" Zek jumped onto the bed and came to curl up on the girl's shoulder.

"So you're awake." Alanna came over to the bed. "How do you feel?"

"Rested." Cuddling dragon and marmoset, Daine frowned. "Weren't you shipped back home?"

"We were called back. You were busy to some purpose here, youngling!"

Daine had the grace to blush and look down. "I lost my temper—"

"And the gods did the rest. At least you're alive and well, after such an experience!"

"Is Carthak still going to war against us?"

Alanna shook her head. "Kaddar's—the emperor's—ministers are signing the treaty with Duke Gareth today. Not that the Army of the North could march in any case. They seem to have run out of supplies that are fit to use." She lifted an eyebrow at Daine, who blushed again.

Alanna filled her in as the girl cleaned her teeth and dressed. She had slept for four days, and they were in guest quarters at the university. At first they had gone to Kaddar's mother's house. That had lasted until the princess learned the full story of the events at the palace. Once the word got out, nothing the new emperor could say would convince her or her servants that Daine, asleep in the women's quarters, would not pull the villa down around her ears.

"That's what they'll think back home, too, isn't it?" asked Daine.

Alanna handed the girl some breeches. "Not necessarily. See, youngster, it's a good thing that all this happened in Carthak. By the time those in Tortall hear the tale, they'll think it's just a tale."

"Really?" Daine asked, clinging to her friend's hand. "They won't shun me, like the servants and the princess and all?"

"Trust me. There will always be *some* who dislike you, but that's life. Over this business?" The

Champion grinned. "People like to *hear* tales of things in distant realms, but they never believe them. There might be strangeness at first, but you'll be surprised how quickly they forget."

Daine rested her head on the woman's shoulder. "Good," she whispered. "I don't like the person I've been here."

Alanna held her. "No one can refuse a god." Her voice was kind. "It's over, and you're the same person you've always been. Once you're home, it will seem like a tale even to you."

The next day, in a break between rains, she and Numair were sitting in a garden, watching Bonedancer, Kitten, and Zek play with brightly colored stones, when Alanna brought Kaddar to them. He smiled hesitantly as the girl and Numair got to their feet.

"May I talk with you briefly?" he asked Daine. "I won't take much of your time."

"Take all you want, Your Imperiousness," she replied with a grin, patting the chair next to hers.

"Here, laddybuck," Alanna told Numair. "You come with me."

The tall mage sighed, but didn't argue. The Champion led him back into the house.

"Sit, please, Daine. I know you haven't been up very long." Kaddar joined her. The new emperor was dressed simply, as he'd been on his tours with her. The only changes she saw were a gold sunburst ring on his left index finger, and an air of purpose. For a moment they watched the animals play.

"What about Lindhall's Bone?" he asked. "The

other dinosaurs you awoke have vanished, but he's still here."

"I don't know," Daine admitted. "It seems to be up to Bone."

Bonedancer looked up at them and nodded, a trick he'd learned from Kitten.

"This is the first time I've seen him away from Lindhall. He must like you." Kaddar looked at his hands. "They'll be going north, too, it seems."

"Numair mentioned it. I'm sorry," she told him. "I know you'll miss Lindhall."

"I offered all I could to get him to stay. Gold, books, a menagerie like your king is building. Head of the university, or just of the School of Magecraft. He says he's borne it here as long as he can. He wants to go north, where he won't see another slave." He laughed shortly. "It seems his only reason for staying this long was to help runaways out of the country!"

"Are you surprised?" Daine asked.

"No, not really — I had my suspicions all along. I just wish he could stay. I trust him. I don't know about some of these other people, particularly the ministers who served my uncle."

"Can't you get rid of them?"

Kaddar shook his head. "The country's already in turmoil. I need to keep a few of the same faces around, at least until I get their measure."

"It doesn't sound like much fun. I wish you luck with it."

"I'll need luck," Kaddar took her hand. "Daine, I found my uncle's papers. He was going to have me arrested and charged with conspiring against him — which means he planned to have me killed. I owe you my life. I know this will sound trite, but I mean it: whatever you want that I can give, even to half of my kingdom, all you need do is ask."

Daine gave him a skeptical look. "Your ministers wouldn't like the half-kingdom part."

He grinned. "Actually, they want to arrest you for crimes against the state."

"*Me?*"

"It will take a year just to figure out how much we lost. We have to do a census now, and draw up new records and tax rolls for every part of the empire." Daine whistled, impressed. He went on, "What amazes me is that creatures dead long before man ever walked the earth fixed on the treasury and the imperial records, where they could do the most damage. We'll never replace it all, and what we do replace will cost a fortune."

She fingered the badger's claw around her neck. "I had help," she reminded him.

"Yes, but haven't you seen how often people look for someone to blame? Not to find a way to keep some bad thing from repeating itself—just to blame."

"Send them to the Graveyard Hag," Daine suggested impishly. "*She'll* set them straight."

Kaddar shuddered. "My blood runs cold at the very thought." He squeezed her hand. "I mean what I say. I want to reward you, so think fast. Your ship sails at dawn. I know you've no family or home of your own, so shall it be gold or jewels? My own wealth was invested here in the city, and there are imperial treasuries all over the empire. We may not have a palace, but neither are we poor. Name your desire."

She stared at the dragon, marmoset, and skeleton. Bone had discovered a puddle to splash in. "I want some humans—slaves—to be freed, with enough in their purses to start a new life. A *good* life, with work they enjoy, the chance to buy apprenticeships for their children, and proper clothes and food and such. If they want to return to Tortall with us, they can."

"All these things for others? Nothing for yourself?"

"No, Kaddar. The Graveyard Hag did most of this, not me. Use whatever you might have given me to help them that suffered in your famine."

He looked her in the eyes for a moment and saw that she meant it. "Name these people, then."

"The Banjiku—all of them, please, and their animals. And the emperor's mutes."

"The *mutes*?" She nodded. "But—they're useful, and since they're mute already—" Daine stared at him. The emperor sighed. "Very well. I have to bustle, if they're to leave tomorrow."

As he tried to get up, Daine held him back. "Kaddar, it's not my place to criticize the way you live, but if I were you, I'd think about your slaves. Animals endure cages if they must, but not two-leggers. If your slaves ever think to break out, it'll make what I did look like mud pies."

He sat down again. "It would beggar the empire if we freed them. No one could pay wages to so many when they pay only for room and board now. My nobles would rise against me. Even my soldiers would rebel, thinking that freed slaves would attack and their homes and families would be in danger."

"I know it'd be hard, but please, think about it. If you whip an animal long enough, it turns on you. If all the world were slave, I don't know if it would be so dangerous, but all they need do is look across the Inland Sea to know life doesn't have to be like this."

To her surprise, he lifted her hand to his lips and kissed it. "I will think about it; I promise."

At dawn, she stood on one of the ships that would convey the now much larger Tortallan party north to Corus, the Tortallan capital. Their small convoy would raise anchor once the Banjiku and their animals boarded Daine's ship. The mutes—those who had chosen to come—were already aboard another vessel. To Daine's surprise, half of them had chosen to stay behind. Talking in sign language to Numair, they had explained that they preferred to stay with the life they knew. Emperor Kaddar would be far kinder than his uncle, they were sure, and Carthak was their home.

"When's the coronation?" she asked Kaddar, who had come to see them off. Numair, standing nearby, picked up Kitten, trying to pretend he wasn't listening.

"Full moon," the young man said. "I wish you could be there."

"I don't," grumbled Numair. Daine kicked him gently.

"You'll write?" asked Kaddar, turning to go. The Banjiku had finished boarding. "You promise?"

"I'll write," she replied. The early fog had burned off at last, giving her a clear view of the palace. While some parts remained as they had been, she saw plenty of cracked and broken walls. The upper reaches were scarred by flame and soot. Of its five towers, only three remained standing.

She also saw one more thing. "Your Imperial Majesty? Kaddar!"

On the dock, he looked up at her. "Yes?"

"About the palace? I wouldn't rebuild over there, if I were you. You're going to have a dreadful problem with pests, and no dogs or cats will stay in it." The captain shouted the order to cast off. She waved cheerfully.

"Pests?" Kaddar glanced across the river. The entire slope between palace and water was covered with rats.

It's ours, now, they thought to Daine.

It's only fitting, she told them, and waved good-bye. Thunder rolled softly overhead as, once more, it began to rain.

Acknowledgments

Once again I would like to express my thanks to those people without whose expert help I would have been hard pressed to get things right:

Mr. Ford Fernandez of Bird Jungle, on Bleecker Street in Manhattan, for advice on how tropical birds get sick;

Mr. James Breheny, the head camel mahout of the Bronx Center for Wildlife Conservation, for his aid in tracking down the ills to which camels are prey (and for the knowledge that there are very few diseases to which camels are prey), even though I had to cut the camel diseases in the final draft(!);

Usborne Publishing Limited of London, England, whose many reference books on classical and medieval times gave me invaluable help in visualizing Carthaki life and society;

Craig Tenney, who introduced me to metal and hard rock;

MTV and the Headbanger's Ball; and

Richard McCaffery Robinson, whose timely advice regarding galleys kept me from venturing into rough waters, and who owes me a freebie or two when his own work gets into the stores.